WALPOLE TOWN LIBRARY

3 4611 00110

S0-ARO-393

BUTTERFLY TATTOO

By Marilinne Cooper

WALPOLE TOWN LIBRARY
48 Main Street P.O. Box 487
Walpole, NH   03608-0487
603-756-9806
walpoletownlibrary.org

Copyright© 2014 by Marilinne Cooper
All rights reserved

This is a work of fiction. Names, characters, places
and incidents are either the product of the author's
imagination or are used fictitiously. Any resemblance to
actual persons, living or dead, business establishments
or events is entirely coincidental.

CHAPTER ONE

EMPORIA, VERMONT – AUGUST 15, 1989

"Suzanne, I'm going to be out of the office for a while and I'm expecting an important sample to be delivered. Would you mind...?" Not waiting for an answer, Nicholas flashed a smile and headed for the door. For a fleeting instant Suzanne could recall the handsome young man he had once been before everything from his jowls to his abdomen had given in to gravity.

Her eyes returned to the computer screen where she was updating the catalog mailing list, entering addresses written on tiny coupons that had been clipped from magazine ads. Sometimes at the end of a day like this she could only lie on the couch with a cold washcloth over her aching eyes. It was a boring job, but at a small mail order company like Newfield's, everybody had to do everything. At least as supervisor she had her own desk and did not have to endure the banal chatter of the telephone order girls across the room. They were half her age but she couldn't remember ever being like them, not even in her early twenties.

Suddenly Nicholas was back, waving a yellow legal pad at her. "I forgot about this letter. It needs to be in the afternoon mail. Thanks. Oh, and make sure Mr. Martin, the man who's dropping off the sample package, gets the envelope in my top desk drawer."

Sighing, Suzanne stood up and went through the door to Nicholas's private office to use his electric typewriter. Nicholas did not like how his correspondence looked when it was printed on the computer printer. And Nicholas got whatever he asked for.

I shouldn't complain, she told herself as she settled in the comfortable, expensively upholstered chair in front of the typing station. Look at all he's done for me. I owe him big time.

When she'd been released from prison nine years before, Nicholas had given her a job when no one else would. He had not pushed her to talk about the years that had passed since they had lived together in the late sixties while he was in college. He had kept her secrets, but there was a price to pay. Suzanne was so grateful for the job and the security of the quiet Vermont town where no one else knew her, she did anything he asked.

At first, she had not minded being his lover again. It was a bona fide affair, clandestine but safe. He invested in an old plantation house on a tiny island in the Caribbean where they would fly off together two or three times a year "to oversee the renovations" of having it made into an inn. By making her his private secretary and supervisor of customer service operations, they were able to conceal the true nature of their friendship from the other employees at Newfield's.

When his wife found out and threatened to divorce him, Nicholas did not argue. He bought out her share of the company (which they had started with her family's money) and then proceeded to drown his sorrows in drugs, alcohol and other women. Suzanne had ended their physical relationship at that point, although they were still close friends. He still took her with him on trips to the Caribbean, but she had her own bungalow now.

In the last few years, as he began to grow bored with Newfield's Woolen Sweaters, he had become increasingly self–abusive. His muscles began to sag as his paunch grew; he spent more time entertaining clients and salesmen than he spent looking at their wares. His reputation at the night spots in the area surrounding the small town of Emporia disintegrated to the point where he was only able to pick up women from out of town who didn't know him.

4

Suzanne stuck by him, although she tried to stay out of his way. She did her best to keep the other office workers from noticing his personal deterioration by fielding his calls, picking up his office, and covering for him when he didn't show up for days at a time. But his behavior was rapidly getting so out–of–hand that there was little she could do about it. Like the story that had circulated through the building about an all–night hot tub party Nicholas had apparently thrown Sunday night; although Suzanne knew for fact it had really happened, she had openly scoffed at the idea as a mere rumor.

Shaking herself, she slipped a blank sheet of paper into the typewriter and began to transcribe Nicholas's scrawl.

The ring of the telephone made her jump. "Yes?"

"There's a guy here to see Mr. Newfield. Says his name is Fred Martin."

"Oh, right, Nicholas said someone was coming to drop off a sample of some sort. Send him in." Suzanne typed the last few lines of the letter rapidly, finishing it as the door opened.

"I'll be right with you, Mr. Martin," she called over her shoulder. "Mr. Newfield was called away quite suddenly, but he asked me to get your samples from you."

As she rose to greet the man who entered, her pleasant facade faded. She watched his eyes dart furtively left and right in a manner that reminded her of someone she had once known long ago. Someone who had looked very much like this dark, stocky man with thick black hair and bushy eyebrows.

"Samples? Yes, the samples." The heavily accented voice had the gravelly sound associated with a lifetime of smoking too many cigarettes.

Weak in the knees, Suzanne felt for the chair behind her and sat down, trying to control her trembling. She told herself it was just the power of suggestion; for the last few weeks she had been thinking about Woody and the old days in Mexico, trying to get up the courage to

5

call him. She was imprinting someone else's face on this stranger who stood in front of her.

He was opening a briefcase now, pulling out a flat, oblong box wrapped in brown paper. Suzanne tried to calm herself; this was just another sweater salesman dropping off something for Nicholas. He happened to be Hispanic, from a Spanish–speaking country. It was just a coincidence.

But as she reached to take the box from him she glanced quickly at his right wrist. And then she knew she was not mistaken. Although it had faded over the years, the tarantula tattoo peeking out from beneath his cuff was unmistakable.

Faking a sudden fit of coughing, she turned away from him. Rico Martinez, aka Frederico Martinez, aka Fred Martin, was only five feet away from her. After years of searching, he had finally caught up with her, but so far he hadn't realized it. How could this be happening?

For the first time Suzanne was thankful that the fiery red hair of her youth had faded to a sandy shade of blonde. Because of the eyestrain of her computer work she had been forced to get glasses a year ago; now she was glad of her horn–rimmed disguise. Rico was probably still searching for a young beauty with a long, wild flaming mane, not a middle–aged woman with glasses, lines in her face, and the remains of last spring's perm still lingering in her frizzy curls.

But what was Rico doing here? He was no sweater salesman, not by any stretch of the imagination.

Suzanne stole a glance over her shoulder at him between coughs. In that familiar macho way, he was impatiently ignoring her, inspecting the sailing trophies which Nicholas had displayed so prominently on the bookshelf.

"Excuse me." Her voice was barely a whisper. "I have a touch of laryngitis." Frantic, she was groping for any possible way to conceal her identity. Changing her voice, keeping her hand over her mouth, not making eye contact – all these things would help. "Let me take that box from you so you can be on your way."

Rico did not appear to be ready to hand it over. "I am so sorry Mr. Newfield is not here in person. Did he leave any – anything for me?"

Suzanne did not answer for a second. She was thinking that she had never heard Rico speak English before. She was sure he hadn't known the language twenty–five years before. "Oh. Yes. There is an envelope here in the desk."

It was a plain white envelope without the Newfield's logo printed on it. Rico did not give her the package until he held the envelope in his hand. As she backed away, putting the length of the room between them, she watched Rico quickly open the envelope and inspect the contents. She supposed it probably contained a check, but she could not help reflecting that this was a rather odd procedure for a vendor. Generally samples were sent free of charge and if they were not of interest, they were returned. She herself had typed the rejection letters dozens of times.

"All there?" she croaked, clutching the package to her chest.

"Yes, thank you. Tell Mr. Newfields I will contact him next week some time to see if he is interested." Tucking the envelope into the inside pocket of his jacket, Rico cocked his head suddenly and his eyes narrowed. She felt his piercing gaze like a burning laser as he stared at her sandy hair and then worked his way down her body, taking in her gray silk shirt and trousers and ending at the huarache sandals on her feet.

The sandals were Mexican; surely he wouldn't make the connection. This conservative middle–aged secretary in front of him could bear no relation to the full–breasted, barefoot senorita from decades earlier with her embroidered blouses and colorful skirts.

Rico shook his head and passed a hand over his eyes. "What is your name, miss?"

Suzanne exhaled the breath she had been holding. "Anne. Anne Laveaux." Close enough to pass for being misunderstood if he mentioned it to Nicholas, but not so close as to be connected with Suzanne Emerson OR Susanna Gonzalez. "Mr. Newfield's secretary. Supervisor of Customer Relations." She tried to intimidate him with her title, willing him to move through the door.

"You remind me of someone, Mrs. Laveaux. But I cannot seem to recall..." He stood in the doorway, still looking at her, his dark eyes making wild calculations.

"Really?" She had to end this interview. "I can't remember the last time somebody used that line on me." Suzanne stepped boldly passed him and opened the door to the outer office. She held it open for him, in a gesture that could not be mistaken. "I'll make sure Mr. Newfield gets this, Mr. Martin. Have a nice day."

Rico took one last scrutinizing look at the bare toes peeking out of her woven sandals before he sauntered away, shaking his head and muttering.

What now? Suzanne sat at Nicholas's desk staring at the package in her lap. It didn't make sense – how could Nicholas possibly know Rico? Unless Rico had truly reformed and really was a sweater salesman. But that exchange with the envelope and the package had seemed more like a drug deal than a –

Suddenly she had to find out what was in the box she was holding. It was definitely not in her job description nor was it her nature to pry, but she had to know. Ripping the brown wrapping paper away, her trembling fingers pried the lid off the white cardboard gift box inside. She pulled back the tissue paper to reveal a pair of colorfully patterned mittens and a matching hat. They had brown cardboard tags pinned to them that said "La Piñata Collection – Hecho en Mexico."

"Unbelievable," she murmured aloud. "He really is above board." She picked up one of the mittens, surprised at the weight of it. It didn't appear to be knit of heavy wool. Slipping it on, her fingers immediately closed around a plastic–wrapped package hidden inside. Pulling the mitten off with her other hand, she turned her fist over to stare at what lay in her palm.

It was a sample all right. Nicholas had forgotten to mention just one minor detail. The sample of white powder in the tightly–taped plastic bag was not for the company, but for him personally. Unless Newfield's was about to start selling cocaine.

Suzanne frowned. It came as no surprise to her that Nicholas might be buying drugs for himself; for the last several months he had been on a binge, desperately trying to escape his feelings of boredom. But the way it was packaged to appear as a catalog product seemed very odd to her. As though maybe Nicholas had other plans in mind, other scams to take the edge off his daily routine. But how did he know Rico? Was it pure coincidence that Nicholas was doing a drug deal with a man from whom Suzanne had been a fugitive for twenty– five years?

She shivered, realizing how close Rico had been to recognizing her. But she also knew it was a short–lived victory. It would come to him soon enough; driving down the road singing some Mexican song or in the sleepless hours of early dawn, it would come to him who "Anne Laveaux" reminded him of, who Anne Laveaux really was.

She had to get away. Fast.

Immediately everything seemed to go wrong. Try as she might, she could not make the hat and mittens appear as they had when she'd opened the box. The paper wrapping lay in shreds on the floor; she would have to throw it away in another trashcan somewhere. Surely Rico and Nicholas would not discuss how the package had been wrapped. If Nicholas found out she had learned his secret and then left town, he'd probably be after her too.

Tears stung her eyes at the realization that her whole life was coming apart. It had been years since she'd made her last hasty departure of this sort; she'd hoped never to move again. Grabbing her purse from her desk, she tried to act nonchalant, as though she were just stepping outside for a moment. She did not turn her computer off or pick up her pencils.

But when she stepped outside and the fresh air hit her face she knew she was not doing this the right way. It was too suspicious to leave everything in midair; Nicholas would come looking for her immediately. She needed to give herself a few days to get away before anyone noticed she was gone.

Taking a deep breath she marched back into the office and headed for the bathroom, slamming the door noisily behind her. She made loud retching and moaning noises and then flushed the toilet a few times. Finally she emerged, clutching her stomach and trying to appear pale.

"Guess I've got a stomach flu," she murmured to the woman who acted as assistant supervisor when one was needed. "I think I'd better pack up and go home. I probably won't be in tomorrow."

The telephone operators turned their restless energy into sympathy for her. They were only too happy to have something new to focus on between calls. One of them help her straighten up her desk and promised to inform Nicholas of her illness.

"Tell him not to call me," she said as she departed for the second time. "I'm going to take the phone off the hook and get some sleep."

The last thing she heard as she left Newfield's was a loud, gleeful whisper. "Do you think she's pregnant? I wonder who the father is."

She cried as she walked around her little house trying to figure out what to pack in her suitcase. She had already decided the best place to go; she would fly out of Boston the next day. Once she was safely away, she could figure out what to do next.

10

Still, she hated leaving her cozy cottage in the woods outside Emporia. Over the years she'd had it renovated to perfection. Walls and floors had been taken out, skylights and French doors had been put in, porches and decks were added on until it was a jewel of a handmade house. The bathroom and kitchen were decorated with ceramic tiles, the hardwood floors had been sanded and refinished. She'd never had a house of her own before; her parents had helped her buy it and had given her free rein to do whatever she wanted to, trusting in her artistic good taste. Although they knew she could not risk visiting them in San Diego, they were happy she had finally settled down safely with a steady job.

Because of her past, Suzanne had never been able to completely let down her guard. Consequently only the handful of people who had been granted a visit to her sunny, private retreat had any idea of how lovingly she had reconstructed it. Sadly, she wondered what would happen to it now. Who would pay the mortgage? What would she tell her parents? They would probably end up selling the house. That thought made her cry so hard she had to sit down for a moment until she got control of herself again.

Across the room, an antique rocker caught her eye. Draped across the back of it was a tattered, embroidered shawl, the last remnant she had of her days in Mexico. Once a brilliant red, it had faded to the color of dusty bricks. But she was sentimentally attached to it; she and Woody had used it as a signal flag when she had lived in Raoul's beach shack. She had been wearing the shawl the day the federales had come...she had worn it as a scarf for the next eighteen months.

Woody. His parents had owned an inn in Vermont. She had tried for years to remember the name of the town. It was his descriptions of Vermont that had brought her here, that had made her think that Vermont would be a good place to drop out of sight. Had it really been twenty–five years since she'd last seen him?

11

She had never been able to locate him. And then, one day at work, a few months earlier, she had picked up another catalog request and squinted at the spidery writing. "Woody Foster," she typed mechanically into the computer. "West Jordan Inn, West Jordan, Vermont..." Her fingers had poised in midair as she stared at the name on the screen. She had taken the rest of the afternoon off and gone home to think about it. In the end she had decided that after all this time, there was no point in trying to reach him. Twenty–five years was a very, very long time. But she had not been able to put him out of her mind.

Now, on a sudden impulse, she reached for the telephone and called information for the number of the West Jordan Inn.

"What harm can it do?" she murmured to herself as she dialed the number. But when a woman answered, she suddenly lost her courage. She felt fifteen rather than forty–five as she spoke.

"Is Woody Foster there?"

"No, he's out at the moment. Can I take a message?"

"Is this – Mrs. Foster?" She was surprised at how hard it was to say those words.

The woman on the other end laughed. "No, it's not. May I ask who's calling?"

Suzanne was suddenly all business. "This is Suzanne Laveaux calling from Newfield's Woolens." She stopped in confusion. Woody wouldn't know her by that last name. "Just tell him Suzanne called. I'll call back later."

After hanging up the phone, she stared blindly at the shawl for several minutes, flooded by memories of that last steamy night in Mexico so many years ago. She could be opening a can of old worms by getting in touch with Woody.

Resolutely, she folded the shawl and laid it carefully in her suitcase. Then with a sudden, angry gesture, she flung it on the floor. If by some chance Rico should catch up with her that tattered piece of peasant handiwork

12

would identify her immediately. The shawl and the tattoo were her only links to that time of her life. Well, she could get rid of the shawl; she would have to live with the damn tattoo.

She lit a match and held the embroidered fabric over it until the match burned down to her fingertips. There was no way she could do it. Instead she picked up a large envelope with the Newfield's logo emblazoned across one edge and jammed the shawl inside. After scrawling Woody's name on it, as well as the address she had committed to memory weeks ago, she slapped on as many stamps as she could find. Then she went quickly outside and stuffed the package into her mailbox, putting the red flag up.

There, she thought with satisfaction. Let it remind him of the promises he made, in the same way it's always haunted me.

If she had thought that physically getting rid of the old scarf would make all her memories go away, she was wrong. Now that she'd begun, she could not stop thinking about that time of her life, and the trip to the Grand Canyon that had started it all. When she turned out the lights that night, the dreams began again.

It had been Suzanne's idea to go to Mexico instead of the Grand Canyon.

"How will they ever know? We'll stop at the Grand Canyon on our way home, take a few pictures, they'll think we spent the whole two weeks there."

Tina and Marie were dubious at first, but over the summer, Suzanne talked them into it. "I mean, come on, guys, this is going to be our last time together before we all go off to separate colleges. Let's make it a real adventure. One we'll remember."

Until they arrived in Puerto Cerrito, it had been a fairly uneventful week. Mexico seemed to be mostly bad roads, dirty hotels, and men who quietly leered at the three unchaperoned eighteen–year–old girls. The only

13

one who seemed to be thriving on the atmosphere was Suzanne, but Tina and Marie made her stay with them at every moment, afraid of what might happen if she went off on her own.

Puerto Cerrito was a small village with a colorful town square and a short main street that ran alongside the sea. Just outside of town was a beautiful expanse of white sand, which was the reason the girls had picked it as a place to spend the afternoon. Seeing her friends stretched out in the sun, relaxed for the first time since they left home, Suzanne knew an opportunity when she saw one.

"I'm thirsty," she announced. "I'm going to walk back to that little grocery and get a soda. Anybody want anything?"

"Suzanne, are you sure—"

"It's just right over there, Tina. You can watch me if you want." Suzanne zipped her white denim shorts on over her bikini bottom and pulled an embroidered Mexican blouse over her head. "I'll be back in a little while."

Knowing they would watch her, she walked deliberately into the shop and then slipped out a side door to head back towards town. There was really not much to see; most places were closed during the heat of the day. As she walked down the dusty road, a trail of hisses followed her and she began to realize that she was the main attraction in town. Her long, fiery auburn hair swinging in a braid down her back, her tight white shorts, and especially the damp spots where her bikini top pressed against the white cotton blouse, caused every man lazing in the shade of his porch or slouched in his doorway to sit up and take notice.

She was about to turn around and head back to the beach when a hand–lettered sign in a window caught her eye. "TATUAJE AQUI. TATTOO." A drawing of a man covered from head to toe in intricate skin art confirmed that the sign meant what she thought it did.

14

The idea intrigued her. What a perfectly wild thing to do. A little tattoo in a hidden spot that no one would see unless she chose to expose it. A memento that would make this uneventful trip to Mexico seem like the whirlwind adventure she had been hoping it would be.

"Interesada?"

"Si, mucho." Suzanne realized she had been spoken to in Spanish and had responded in the same language without thinking. But then all reasonable thought slipped away, as she gazed awe–struck at the man leaning against the doorway.

Her first thought was tall, dark and handsome, but then she decided he was not all that tall, just incredibly broad–shouldered and muscular. His liquid brown eyes had already given her body the once over and now appeared amused at her response. He ran his fingers through his thick, black hair and then tugged thoughtfully at his moustache.

"You want a tattoo for yourself?" he asked. She was surprised and pleased by how quickly she was able to mentally translate his question into English.

"Yes, just a tiny one." She showed him the size with her fingers. "Is it very expensive?"

"You will be able to afford it." He crossed his arms and added quite seriously, "A tattoo is forever, you know."

She nodded, overwhelmed by his presence. He was so much more masculine than anyone she had encountered in her sheltered high school years. He smelled of musky sweat and cigarettes and suddenly she was thinking that perhaps the adventure she was looking for involved more than a tattoo.

"Luis! Carlos! Rico! Vamanos. Ahora! Pronto!" Three men dragged themselves out the door, grumbling and cursing, but when they caught sight of Suzanne, they laughed and nodded wisely. They ambled down the road, clapping each other on the back and snickering.

The man gestured to the interior of the ramshackle building. "Pase, por favor."

"Gracias." Suzanne took a deep breath and preceded him into the dark storefront. She was in a narrow space that was apparently a waiting room. It contained a couple of wooden benches and a tattered copy of Penthouse. A dingy curtain ran the length of the area, separating the waiting room from the rest of the tiny building.

"Come back here," the man beckoned her, pulling the frayed string of a ceiling bulb to illuminate the room.

"Are you the one who does it?" she asked nervously.

"Yes, I am the tattoo artist. Please sit down." He gestured toward a plastic chair. He leaned against a table; the only other furnishings were some cardboard boxes which seemed to hold his tattooing apparatus. "Now, what would you like?"

"What do you mean?" Suzanne sat rigidly on the edge of the chair.

"A rose, a heart, someone's name..."

"Oh. Gee, I don't know." Frantically she tried to think, but her brain did not want to function in such close proximity to him.

"Where are your friends?" he asked idly.

For a second she was surprised, but then she realized that everyone in town had seen the three gringo girls at the market in the morning. "At the beach."

"It's only you who wants a tattoo then?"

"That's right. Oh, I know..." She wanted to say butterfly but she could not think of the word in Spanish. "A butterfly. Like this." She gestured with her hands. Finally he gave her a stub of a pencil and she drew it on the leg of her shorts.

"Ah, la mariposa!" He nodded his approval. "A good choice. Now where do you want it?"

Suzanne took a deep breath. "Right here." She pointed to the side of her hip.

16

His eyebrows raised. "You don't mind taking your pants off for me to do it?"

"No, it's all right, I have my bathing suit on," she replied rapidly, unzipping her shorts and pulling them down a fraction to show him the lime green daisy print of her bikini bottom.

"I see. Okay, show me where you want it."

Suzanne felt much more naked than she expected once she had wiggled out of her shorts. She pulled up the hem of her shirt and pointed to her right hip. "Maybe up here, under the suit, so it won't show."

He nodded, his face giving nothing away. "Bueno. Stand up here on the chair so I can reach it more easily."

Her heart pounding excitedly, she did as he requested.

"I'm going to draw it on first," he explained. "My equipment is not up–to–date. Now you will have to pull the side of your suit up and hold your shirt away. Perhaps you had better just remove the shirt, if you don't mind. You have the top to your suit on, I can see that." He indicated the damp spots on the front of her blouse.

As she slowly lifted the blouse above her head she wondered what her parents would think if they knew where she was and what she was doing. Well, if this was being bad, it was time she found out for herself what was so bad about it.

As she looked around for someplace to hang the shirt, she heard a low whistle and a sigh.

"Madre de Dios!" He groaned. "Que magnifico!" His eyes were riveted to the round curve of her breasts rising above the ruffled edge of her bikini. He closed his eyes and shook himself. "Okay, the butterfly."

Suzanne gulped and pulled up the side of her suit again, exposing an area of very white, untanned skin. The Mexican touched the place with his fingertips. "So smooth," he murmured, running his fingers down the side of her thigh. "You have beautiful skin."

He began to draw the outline of a butterfly on her hip. "How does that look to you?" When he straightened up, his eyes were just even with her bikini top and Suzanne felt embarrassed to see that her nipples were now so erect that they were showing through the stretchy fabric.

She was so nervous that her legs began to shake visibly and she grabbed the back of the chair for support. But she had no intention of backing out now; she wanted to go through with this, to whatever conclusion occurred.

He shook his head. "You are shaking too much for me to do this with you standing up. Perhaps if you lie on the table—" he lifted her up with a swift motion and set her down lightly on the crude wooden table behind him. For the brief second that she was pressed against him, Suzanne felt as though someone had set a match to all the sexual places in her body. She had never been this aroused by the clumsy gropings of her high school boyfriends at the drive–in.

Sitting on the edge of the table, she felt the perspiration beading up on her skin; a trickle of sweat ran down her side, another worked its way between her breasts. She had not been aware of the heat in the tiny room until now. She watched him unbutton his shirt and use it to wipe his brow. In fascination and fear she could not tear her eyes away from the coarse, dark hairs that covered his chest.

"What color would you like the butterfly?" he asked as he gently guided her down onto her back.

His question startled her. She had nearly forgotten about the tattoo. It was uncomfortable lying there with her legs dangling off the table and she pulled her knees up so that her feet rested against the edge.

"A monarch butterfly. Orange and black. The color of my hair."

"This hair?" He lifted the end of her braid to his lips. "Or this hair?" The fingers of his other hand pulled at one of the dark red curls escaping from the front edge of her bathing suit bottom. "I have never seen hair this color," he murmured wrapping it tightly around one finger. "It is very unusual."

His eyes came up to meet hers questioningly. As he held her gaze, she suddenly felt his fingers inside her bikini bottom, running through her hair, stroking and pulling.

"I cannot do your tattoo unless you are perfectly relaxed and still," he said. "Do you still want it?"

"Yes," she murmured, not sure what she was agreeing to.

"Then we must release this tension in your body somehow." One of his fingers was probing lower now and its sudden penetration made her gasp and close her eyes. Just as quickly, he slipped it out again. With both hands he pulled her to a sitting position and then reaching behind, undid the catch of her top.

"You will breathe much easier," he said and then it was his turn to gasp.

Unconsciously she pulled her arms up to cover herself. Making a clucking sound with his tongue, he eased them down so he could admire the shape and dimension of her breasts. Despite the heat, Suzanne felt goose bumps as his fingertips caressed her already erect nipples until they grew harder and larger than she had ever believed possible. "Increíble," he murmured. "Quiero chuparte." Although she did not understand his words, she shivered at his tone. Finally he returned her to her position on her back.

"This is a perfect place for a butterfly," he muttered to himself, tracing an invisible outline with his finger on the flat space between her breasts which now moved up and down rapidly with her breathing.

"Are you sure you really want this?" he asked again as he hooked his thumbs through her bikini bottom and tugged it free.

19

"Yes," she whispered with fists clenched and eyes tightly closed, as he explored the moist area between her legs, gently rubbing and pulling.

"And how about this? Do you want this too?"

She opened her eyes and looked down at the view between her legs. He had dropped his pants; his swollen penis looked enormous and it was much longer than she ever had expected it to be. She could not believe it could fit inside her.

She tried to back away but there was no room to move. He grabbed her around the waist and pulled her towards him, her legs finding their own way around his hips as he found his way inside her, pushing and pushing until finally disappearing deep within. She cried out and dug her fingernails into his shoulders at the immediate pain.

"Not the first time?" he said in surprise. She nodded and turned her face away.

"Madre de Dios! What have I done?" He began to pull himself out of her but she stopped him.

"No." Her command was almost inaudible. "I want it. It feels good now."

"Okay, my fiery butterfly. You asked for it." His lips closed around her right nipple. Just when she thought she could not take the pleasurable pain for another second, he switched to the left side, leaving the first one wet and tingling. And still he remained inside her, hard and throbbing. Overwhelmed by the intensity of these new sensations, Suzanne was swept along and did not protest.

She was still very excited when he pulled out of her and collapsed to his knees exhausted, his face resting against her leg. She was disappointed that they were finished already.

After a moment he stood up and pulled on his pants. "Your friends will be looking for you."

She could not bear to let Tina and Marie enter her thoughts. They belonged to another time, when she had been a girl in a black and white world that she did not want to return to. "I don't care," she declared defiantly, throwing her arms about his neck and bringing his lips down to meet her own.

Startled at first by her show of passion, he returned her kiss with equal fervor. "You'd better go now," he said pushing her away. With a last longing look at her heavy, ripe breasts, he turned and began to roll himself a cigarette.

Suzanne knew what she had to do. She reached for her blouse and shorts without bothering with the bikini. "I'll be back in a minute," she said, grabbing her purse.

"I'm not going anywhere," he replied with lazy amusement.

Blinded momentarily by the bright sunlight in the street, Suzanne did not immediately see Tina's white Buick cruising slowly towards her up the street. "Where have you been?" the two girls shouted at her. "We've been looking everywhere for you!"

Instead of answering or getting into the car, Suzanne walked around to the back and opened the trunk. Flinging up the top of her suitcase, she began hastily stuffing clothes and toiletries into a woven straw bag. Angry and curious, Tina and Marie got out to see what she was doing, but Suzanne was already slamming the lid of the trunk. When she turned, they staring opened-mouth at the neck of her blouse. Looking down she discovered that not only was she wearing the blouse inside out and backwards, but now that she wore no bathing suit, her dark, enlarged nipples showed clearly through the thin white cotton.

"I'm not going with you," she announced. "Go on without me. I'm staying here for a while."

Marie burst into tears. "What's wrong with you, Suzanne? What's happened to you? We can't leave you here. We can't even speak Spanish!"

"And what'll we tell your parents?" Tina blurted out fearfully.

21

"Look, why don't you guys just head straight north? You've even got time to see the Grand Canyon and take some pictures to prove you were there before you go home. I've got something I've got to do here. Tell my parents I'll be back in time for the fall semester."

Slinging the straw bag over her shoulder, she turned and started back towards the tattoo parlor.

"Suzanne! Stop! Don't do this!"

"I'll be all right!" She shouted over her shoulder. "I can take care of myself!"

"Forget it, Marie. She's gone crazy. If she wants to fight off Mexican lechers on her own, let her." Tina slammed the car door in disgust and started up the engine. But even she stared in amazement, along with everyone else in the village, as Suzanne disappear into the dark doorway of the shabby building a hundred yards away.

He was still sitting where she had left him, staring into space, the cigarette burning aimlessly between his thumb and forefinger. He seemed startled to see her. "You came back."

"I said I would. I still want that tattoo, you know."

He stared at her in disbelief.

"What's all this?" he asked, indicating the heavy bag she dropped on the floor.

"I've left them," she replied simply. "Is there some place I can stay around here?"

"You want to stay here? In Puerto Cerrito?"

She nodded and then as he watched, she whisked her shirt over her head and came towards him. "I want to do it again." She pressed his face between her breasts.

He laughed delightedly and slapped her behind. "It must be my lucky day." He kissed her and stood up. "Come. The tattoo can wait. I know a place where you can stay and it's much more comfortable than here. Cover yourself and let's go."

As he led her out the back door to a rusty pick–up truck with no windshield, he turned to her suddenly. "I don't even know your name, butterfly."

"Suzanne. And yours?"

"Raoul. Susanna..." He rolled the name over his tongue, giving it a Latin inflection. "It's a nice enough name but I already think of you as mi mariposa de fuego. My fiery butterfly, ready to spread her wings for me..." He squeezed her crotch meaningfully and Suzanne blushed but did not flinch. Wrenching open the door of the truck, he helped her up onto the torn seat. "We'd better hurry," he said, "or we may have to stop along the way."

Suzanne groaned and sat up in bed, drenched with sweat, her heart pounding. She had been eighteen again, actually feeling the lusty excitement she had felt on the first day with Raoul. A further wave of memories had her dashing for the bathroom and dry heaving over the toilet. If only she could have known the ending of the story then, like she did now.

CHAPTER TWO

Although it was only August, in northern Vermont the nights were already beginning to grow cooler. Sarah shivered a little as she walked around the inn closing windows and shutting off lights. There had been a late crowd at the bar; she'd had trouble getting rid of them after last call and they hadn't tipped her very well. Usually she enjoyed her work but tonight she was in a bad mood. Her feet hurt and her back ached and for a few exhausted moments she wished she were anything but a bartender.

As she checked the front door to make sure it was locked, she was surprised to see a light still on in the living room. As far as she knew there were no guests staying upstairs and Woody had been going to bed early the last few weeks. Stepping inside the doorway to flick the wall switch, she realized that, strangely enough, Woody was still awake.

"Woody, what are you doing up at this time of night? It's nearly two a.m." Sarah scolded him gently. Woody had not been looking well lately. She thought that perhaps the endless work of running the West Jordan Inn had finally begun to catch up with him. His usual ruddy face seemed pale. Beneath his mane of gray corkscrew curls, his forehead seemed perpetually wrinkled in concern.

Woody looked up at her with a dazed expression in his eyes. He was sitting on the couch with what appeared to be an old embroidered scarf spread across his knees. "Sarah. I thought you would have gone home

24

by now..." His words drifted off. He seemed to be seeing right through her.

"Are you all right?" Sarah was worried. He was not acting like himself at all. "What is that thing on your lap?"

He cleared his throat and said, "Can you sit and talk for a moment? There are a few things I need to tell you about."

This was so unlike Woody that Sarah did not hesitate. "Sure. Let me get a drink. I'll be right back."

She quickly grabbed her half–finished Margarita off the bar and hurried back into the living room. It had to be something serious or Woody would not be awake and wanting to talk at this time of night. Sinking into an overstuffed armchair across from him, she kicked off her shoes and put her feet up on a footstool, uttering a sigh of relief.

"So. Shoot. What's up?"

"Well, for starters, this came in the mail today." Woody held up the old scarf. Sarah could see now that it was quite large, more like a shawl. Although it was very faded, it had probably been a beautiful piece of work years ago. Exotic birds and tropical flowers were elaborately embroidered around all four edges, in colors that must have been brilliant before they were bleached by numerous washings, sun–dryings and time. Stretching from one corner to the center of the square of fabric were several monarch butterflies that appeared to have been added as an afterthought. Cleverly graduated in size, they appeared to be fluttering off into the distance.

"What is it?"

"Well, if I'm not mistaken–" Woody was speaking very slowly as though the words did not come easily to him – "it is very similar to a shawl that belonged to a girl, a woman, I was quite close to once a long time ago."

"Really?" Sarah waited for him to go on. She had a feeling she was about to learn something about her close friend and boss that she had never known before.

"I haven't seen her or this shawl in almost twenty five years. A few months ago I ordered a catalog from this sweater company down in Emporia–"

"Newfield's."

"You've heard of them?"

"I've seen their catalog. Beautiful stuff, but out of my price range. So go on."

"Well, I thought it would be nice to have around for guests to look at in the fall. Anyway, today I go to the post office and pick up an envelope from them. I open it, expecting to see a catalog and instead there's this. No note or anything." Rubbing the worn fabric between his fingers, Woody shook his head in disbelief.

"You're kidding! How strange! What are you going to do?"

"Well, I immediately called the company and asked them if there was anyone who worked there named Suzanne. That was her name, the girl I– knew."

Sarah snapped her fingers suddenly. "Suzanne from Newfield's! She called here a few days ago looking for you."

"What? Why didn't you tell me?" Woody's voice had an unusually hysterical pitch to it that made Sarah nervous.

"It sounded like some telephone solicitation. I mean, she asked for Mrs. Foster. I didn't figure it was anybody who knew you. Anyway, she said she was going to call back. Did you talk to her today?"

"You spoke to Suzanne."

"Woody! What is going on? Didn't you get a hold of her today?"

"They said she was gone. Said she had left sick a few days ago and then never came back. When I asked for her home number they put me through to the owner! Can you believe that? He grilled me as to who I was and how I knew Suzanne and finally told me that she apparently left town quite suddenly and nobody knew where she was. Jesus Christ, I can't believe she would call here and then do this to me again after twenty five years! Especially now."

Sarah slowly sipped her drink before speaking. "Is this someone you were in love with once, Woody?"

"This is the only person I was ever in love with! After Suzanne, I never came close to what I had with her again. Why do you think I'm still a bachelor at 54?"

It was a question Sarah had often wondered about during the three years she had known and worked for Woody. She had learned about his adolescent infatuation with her own mother who had been ten years older than him and married at the time. But he didn't like to talk about his past and she had respected that. Until now.

"Where did you meet Suzanne?"

"I met her in Mexico in the early sixties during my motorcycle days. You know, I had been in Mexico at the time your mother died when you were a baby and I still had a lot of guilt about it. For years I felt as though it might not have happened if I had been around."

"Woody, you know that's—"

He held up his hand to stop her. "I know it's crazy but that was how I felt. Every time I came back home to West Jordan, her ghost seemed to be haunting me and after a few months I would up and leave again. But I always avoided Mexico. Superstitious I guess. Finally I decided the only way to exorcise the feeling was to face it head on. It was during that trip to Mexico that I met Suzanne."

"Is she Mexican?"

"No, she was American. Living with some macho Mexican who acted like he owned her. She wasn't married to him and he treated her like shit, but for some reason she couldn't leave him. She was young, Christ, she couldn't have been more than twenty when I

27

knew her and she'd been there for a couple of years already!"

"Was she in love with you? No, I'm sorry, I shouldn't have asked you that. Go on."

Woody shrugged and traced the outline of one of the embroidered birds with a finger. "She told me she was in love with me and I believed her. Looking back on it, I don't know why. Maybe because she was so beautiful."

"Really? What did she look like?"

"So gorgeous she literally took your breath away. I'm not kidding! She had this long, straight auburn hair that hung down to her butt, chocolate brown eyes, and these big luscious lips that made you want to kiss her forever." Woody gave an embarrassed chuckle. "I know you probably don't want to hear this, but not only was she beautiful, she had this incredibly sexy body as well. She had these great breasts, real full and perfectly shaped and the rest of her was all curves and dimples–"

"Okay, okay. So go on." Uncomfortable with Woody's description of beauty, Sarah tossed her short, dark hair and awkwardly shifted the position of her own angular body.

"She said she wanted to come back to the States with me but she needed a few months to get the money together. I always had the feeling she was involved in something illegal. This guy she was living with would disappear for days, weeks, at a time leaving her all alone in this shack just off the beach. He'd have a few of his compadres check up on her now and then, bring her food or whatever. But she didn't seem to mind the poor conditions she lived in. I got the feeling she had grown up quite wealthy and that it was all sort of a game to her, like camping out. She enjoyed making something out of nothing, very resourceful and extremely bright.

"I hated that she kept me sneaking in and out of there but since her boyfriend was away more than he was home, it didn't bother me very often. This shawl was our signal flag. When it was thrown casually over the back of a chair outside the door, it meant the coast was clear. When it was hanging like a curtain over a string across the window, it meant go away."

And what did it mean in an envelope twenty–five years later? Sarah sucked on an ice cube from the bottom of her drink and waited for Woody to go on.

"I called home one night and found out my father had died suddenly. I had to fly home immediately. When I went to say goodbye to Suzanne, the red flag was in the window. I was so mad, that I waited outside by the outhouse until she came out, so that we could at least say goodbye. I told her I was leaving my motorcycle in the care of my landlady and would be back in a few months to pick it up and take her back to the States with me. She said she would be ready.

"It took me longer to get back to Mexico than I thought it would. By the time I returned, Suzanne was gone and the shack was completely abandoned. Most people didn't seem to have any idea what had happened to her; the ones who did know, weren't talking. I didn't speak Spanish well enough to really pursue it. Finally, I got on my bike and rode straight home. I've been here ever since."

In the silence that followed, Sarah could not say what she was thinking. She couldn't tell Woody that she thought he was foolish to have wasted his entire life being true to the memory of some flighty girl who never even tried to contact him for twenty–five years.

"Now you've gotten me off the track here, Sarah. There is a completely different topic I need to discuss with you. Well, it's sort of connected." Woody looked nervous suddenly. He cracked his knuckles a few times and cleared his throat.

"What is it?"

"Well, I've got to close the inn down for a few months."

"What?" Sarah sat up rigidly. The sad but cozy mood of nostalgia Woody had created was instantly gone. "At this time of year? But the next two months are your biggest money makers!"

"I know, but I have no choice. I have to go into the hospital next week. They're operating on me for cancer."

"Cancer. Oh, Woody. I had no idea." Sarah felt as though she were spiraling down a long dark hole. Swallowing the lump forming in her throat, she stammered, "How– how long have you known? How bad is it?"

"I've known for a few weeks but I guess I've had it for a while. The doctors think it's fairly well advanced. I'll almost certainly be going through chemotherapy afterwards as well." Woody's voice shook slightly as he spoke but his tone indicated that he had accepted the situation and was dealing with it. "I thought about keeping the inn open, hiring someone to do the cooking but I think I would spend all my time worrying about it and would not be able to concentrate on getting well."

"I'm sure that's a wise decision." Sarah was afraid to put any emotion into her voice. "Does anybody else know?"

"Just my cousin, Frances. She's coming down to take care of me when I get out of the hospital."

"But I could have taken care of you–"

He cut her off. "Frances thrives on this kind of stuff. She would have been hurt if I didn't ask her. Now, I know you're probably going to be strapped financially, but you should be able to collect unemployment and I'm planning to make up the difference to you–"

"Woody! Here you are with cancer talking about what YOU can do for ME." Sarah laughed a little and dashed away a couple of tears that were running down one cheek. "Forget about me. Tell me what I can do for you."

"Well, there is one thing..."

"What?"

"I want you to help me find Suzanne. I know it sounds stupid, but for some reason it's the most important thing to me right now."

Sarah sat back dumbfounded. He might as well have asked her to bring him the crown jewels. "How can I do that?" she asked in a tiny voice. "I wouldn't know where to begin."

"But you have a good friend who is really skilled at digging up information and finding missing people." Woody gave her a pale but devilish smile. "And I bet he'd be delighted to hear from you."

"You mean Tyler?" Sarah flushed as angry thoughts and feelings filled her head. "You mean, Tyler Mackenzie, Investigative Journalist?" she continued mockingly. "No way! That bastard hasn't called me in six months! I mean, it's not that I don't want to help you," she quickly apologized, "But I'd rather not involve my own stormy love life, if you don't mind."

"You're crazy! You know Tyler is wild about you. You told me yourself that it was you who told him not to call you anymore."

"Well, someone as hyperactive as Tyler must have another girlfriend by now. Our ideas about how to conduct a long distance relationship were just too different. I'm sure Tyler will help you if you call him and tell him your situation. Really, Woody, I'll be happy to help you out in any other way; I'll cook your meals, I'll empty your bedpan, but don't ask me to call Tyler."

Woody knew the look of desperation in her eyes was caused by the fear that she would have to face the truth about the feelings for Tyler she had been denying. Getting them together to work out their differences was almost as important to him as finding Suzanne. If he didn't make it through this ordeal, he at least wanted to know Sarah was reconciled with the man who sparked her fire the way no one else did.

Sarah was crying openly now. "God, Woody. I'm so sorry this is happening to you. I didn't mean to yell at you just now. I mean, you're as close to a family as I've got. You've been like a father to me—"

"Please, not that ruthless gambler who destroyed your family's fortune. At least say I've been like a mother to you." He handed her a box of tissues.

She laughed in spite of herself and blew her nose. "I'm being a selfish little fool, aren't I? You just tell me what you want me to do for you and I'll do it. I'll even help you find that old girlfriend of yours if that's what you want."

"Actually, I was hoping you could help me get this place ready to shut down. I've never closed the inn for any length of time before. It's going to take a bit of work. Why don't you come by around noon tomorrow? And now you better go on home and get some sleep."

Woody locked the door behind her and watched her start up her car. But by the time Sarah had pulled out of the parking lot, he was already on the telephone. "Manhattan...The last name is Mackenzie, first name Tyler..."

Although she knew Tyler would probably turn up sooner or later, Sarah was still not prepared for the flood of emotions that swept over her at the first sight of him.

She was a few minutes late getting to the inn that afternoon and without stopping to greet Woody, she went immediately to unlock the door of the Night Heron lounge and set up the bar. The lounge had been given its name because of the large stained glass window behind the bar which featured several red–eyed night herons wading through a marsh. Sarah's mother, Winnie Scupper, had made the window thirty–five years ago, before Sarah was born, as payment for a large dinner tab that her husband had welched on. Working in front of it always made Sarah feel a little closer to the mother she had never known.

32

Carrying a small chalkboard, she raced into the kitchen to find out what the dinner specials were and there he was, as painfully good–looking as ever. He was sitting on a stool with his trusty notebook opened on his lap, his gold Cross pen poised above it, listening to Woody talk as he chopped vegetables for salads.

Tyler's hair, longer and curlier than it had been six months before, was a burnished shade of gold that, along with the bronze color of his skin, suggested he had spent more than a few hours relaxing in the sun during the summer months. He had shaved off his beard, revealing the squareness of his chin and the creases in his cheeks that became deep dimples when he smiled. Now he sported a moustache which lent his boyish face an air of educated sophistication. He was wearing a stunning batik print shirt and a pair of loose fitting khaki shorts that displayed just how tan his long, lanky limbs really were.

Sarah stopped short and gasped in dismay, the swinging doors catching her from behind. She was not ready for this confrontation; she could not remember any of the witty, stinging remarks she had wanted to greet Tyler with. Instead, all she could think of was that she had not washed her hair and that in her favorite, but faded, Hawaiian shirt and denim skirt, she looked like a used dishcloth in comparison to him.

"Hey, Sarah, what's happening?" Tyler rose to greet her with open arms and a big smile on his handsome face. Clutching the chalkboard protectively across her chest, she accepted his hug without returning it. "What's wrong?"

"Nothing, I–" She wanted to tell him how angry he had made her by not contacting her all these months, but all she could say was, "I just wasn't expecting to see you, that's all."

"Woody didn't tell you I was coming up today?" Tyler took a few steps back and looked from one to the other of them.

"No, he didn't." Sarah tried hard not to flash a dirty look at Woody, but she could not keep the cynicism out of her voice. "He must have wanted to surprise me."

"Well, I came as soon as I could get away. I have to admit," he added in a loud, conspiratorial whisper, "I could barely wait to get here after he told me you were going to work with me to locate Suzanne."

Sarah's jaw dropped and this time her eyes shot daggers at Woody, but he had discreetly turned his back on the two of them and did not catch her expression. But what could she say? She had promised him she would do anything for him. He was suffering from cancer; all she was suffering from was a high strung, over–motivated, workaholic ex–boyfriend who drove her crazy with desire whenever he was around and crazy with the empty space he left in her life when he wasn't. If it would help Woody, she could live with that for a few more weeks of her life.

"I did say I would do that, didn't I?" Sarah's voice seemed to be returning from a distant place. "Well, I won't have anything else to do while the inn is closed."

The wounded expression that appeared in Tyler's amber eyes as a result of her callous tone gave her a little thrill of triumph. Yet, at the same time, she hated hurting this man who cared so deeply for her in his own erratic way, not realizing how much pain he caused her at the same time.

"Woody, what are the dinner specials?" Sarah turned her concentration to the chalkboard in front of her.

"Chicken Cacciatore, Cheese Enchiladas, Grilled Reuben Sandwich. Soup is Clam Chowder."

"So, Tyler," Sarah said after an uncomfortable moment of silence as she carefully wrote the specials on the board in pink chalk. "When do we start?"

As usual, talking about his latest project perked him right up. "I'm going down to Emporia tomorrow to Newfield's Woolens. It seems like the best place to begin. It's the only current information we have on Suzanne. Other than the fact that she's disappeared." He laughed a little and shook his head. "This is a fabulous challenge, Woody. I can't wait to get started."

"It's after four, Sarah," Woody said meaningfully.

"Oops. Gotta go. See you later, Tyler." Sarah disappeared through the swinging doors.

"Well, Woody." Tyler stood up and stretched stiffly. "You got a room upstairs I can use tonight? Looks like I might be needing a place to stay."

CHAPTER THREE

Tyler had too much on his mind to notice how scenic the drive was between West Jordan and Emporia. For the hundredth time he glanced down at the Newfield's Woolens catalog on the seat next to him, trying to imagine every possible scenario he might run into when he got there. There was a small picture of the building on the inside cover which gave the impression that Newfield's was a personal, country–store type of business, although the high priced inventory seemed to indicate otherwise.

He had already decided to pretend he was Suzanne's cousin from New York, sent by the family in California to find out what might have happened to her. At first he had planned to be her brother but decided against that idea as unsafe because she might not have a brother or if she did, someone might know him. As a family member, it would not look suspicious if he visited her house – he could even say he had a key. As long as he was cautious, the idea should work. The problem was he knew so little about Suzanne; it was entirely possible that he could blow his whole cover with a wrong answer.

To keep from becoming too nervous, every few miles he tried to take his mind off the immediate future by thinking about something else. But his thoughts always took the depressing turn to Sarah and how she was acting towards him.

They had met almost three years ago, when he had come to West Jordan to do a story on Sarah's mother, Winnie Scupper, the famous stained glass artist who had mysteriously fallen from a bridge and died when Sarah was just an infant. He had been living with another woman at the time, but the chemistry between

Sarah and him had been overpowering. He let his New York life slip into oblivion as he found reason after reason to stay in Vermont. He was soon involved with unraveling the circumstances surrounding her mother's death as well as helping her to recover a missing part of her family's fortune.

Unfortunately, when it was all over, Sarah had not been interested in moving back to the city with him. They had tried to see each other as often as possible, but Tyler was sometimes involved in researching stories that took him far away for weeks at a time. He had a way of throwing himself into each new project with a wholehearted passion. This enthusiastic energy made him one of the best in his field, but it also tended to make everything and everyone else shrivel up and fade into the background. When he had to cut his last visit short because of a lead on a supposed cover–up of a nuclear waste dump on Long Island, Sarah had told him in no uncertain terms that she'd had enough of their on–again/off–again relationship.

She said she needed someone she could count on seeing more regularly than him. She did not understand, nor did she believe, that when he became totally immersed in his work that he really did not have time for much else, or for other women. True, women were easily infatuated with his appearance, but he knew better than to get involved with most of them. In the last six months he'd had a few lonely assignments, staying in cookie–cutter motels on the outskirts of factory towns. His longing for Sarah had got the better of him a couple of times. Once he'd let a woman pick him up in a bar, but that had proven so empty and unsatisfactory that he only felt worse afterwards. At home he tried to turn a friendship with a woman he knew into something more, but it just didn't ignite him the way Sarah could.

Somehow he had to win her back.

He was so self–absorbed that he drove right through Emporia without realizing it. As he looked for a place to turn around, he saw a large sign with the red and green Newfield's logo on it and he knew he had inadvertently arrived.

The fact that the large parking lot marked "Employees Only" was virtually empty made him realize that Saturday may not have been the best day to start this challenge. Across the street there was a small Newfield's outlet store that was bustling with touristy looking customers. Tyler decided to take his chances that someone would be working in the office building on a Saturday.

The building had been cleverly designed to fit in with the rest of the Victorian buildings on Emporia's Main Street. An old, two–story white house with green shutters and a long porch was what a sightseer speeding by would see, but this was merely a facade for the office building stretching out behind it. This was further connected to a large, metal prefab warehouse building in the rear with garage doors and loading docks leading out onto what appeared to be Emporia's only other street.

Tyler tried the main entrance and was surprised to find the door open. Directly inside the entrance he was greeted by a bird–like, nasal–voiced girl who was sitting behind the receptionist desk reading a romance novel with a lurid pink cover.

"If you're another reporter, you can just march back out. Mr. Newfield has already given his statement to the press and I'm not allowed to tell you anything."

Tyler was taken aback at having his profession guessed before he'd even spoken a word. Then he realized this was a practiced remark given to everyone. "But I– I'm Suzanne's cousin–"

"Oh. Sorry." The girl giggled and covered her mouth self–consciously. "I thought you were here about

Esta Variance. You know, the telephone operator who died of a drug overdose yesterday."

Tyler nodded as though he knew what she was referring to, wondering what kind of situation he was walking in on.

"Police told us not to talk to anyone about it. Place was swarming with cops and reporters yesterday. That's why I gotta work on Saturday, my day off. Keep the public outta the building." Suddenly aware that she was probably saying more than she should, she abruptly changed the subject. "Suzanne doesn't work here anymore, you know."

"She doesn't?" Tyler tried to keep his tone expressionless.

"No, she just left one day with a stomach ache and never came back. Boy, Mr. Newfield was pissed! You know, Suzanne was like his private secretary, well, she was his friend too, I mean not his girlfriend, she was too old for that, I mean–" the little receptionist blushed as she stumbled on her words. "I mean, he likes younger girls as his girlfriends. Anyway, he must be hoping she'll come back because he hasn't hired anyone to take her place yet, and now with Esta gone we're really shorthanded."

"Well, I've got to find out where she is." Tyler leaned forward and gave the girl a charming, intimate look. "Maybe you could help me– I'm sorry, what's your name?"

"Diane." She shrugged her narrow shoulders. "Sure, but I don't know how. I didn't know her very well."

"Could you call Mr. Newfield so I could talk to him?"

Her face brightened. "Oh, he's supposed to be coming in this morning. Why don't you go up and wait in his office? I'll call his house and tell him you're here. It's just right up those stairs."

As he walked up the carpeted stairs, Tyler congratulated himself on setting the wheels into perfect motion. Not only would he get to talk to Nicholas Newfield himself, he would have a chance to poke around his office beforehand.

The president of Newfield's Woolens apparently needed his private secretary back badly. The expensively furnished office was in grand disarray. Wrinkled clothes hung over a chair in the corner, the large executive desk was piled high with papers, files and various other objects. A couple of sweaters were spread out on the floor as though they were being appraised. Although the sun was shining brightly outside, the blinds were tightly drawn on all the windows, making the office as dark and stuffy as a sick room.

After a quarter of an hour of illicit poking, he deduced that Nicholas had two children (their school photos were on his desk), he was divorced from their mother (wedding picture was removed from frame and shoved in bottom drawer), he liked to entertain (two bottles of expensive champagne were chilling in a small refrigerator), he frequently played video games on his computer and rarely looked at the daily sales reports gathering dust on the floor next to his chair.

One item in particular fascinated him. On the left hand side of the desk, face down on a stack of sales agreements, was a framed black and white photograph. It was grainy blow–up of a monarch butterfly tattooed on what appeared to be someone's buttock or hip or thigh. It was a very artistic, almost erotic effect caught by a sharp lens, with the whiteness of the skin standing out against dark, unfocused shadows and the fine lines of the butterfly etched across the enlarged pores and tiny hairs.

The sound of a door opening startled him and with a swift guilty motion he replaced the photograph where he had found it. By the time Diane was in the room he was innocently studying a watercolor hung on the wall which turned out to be an architect's rendering of the planned expansion of Newfield's Woolens in the summer of 1982.

"I talked to Mr. Newfield. He said he'd changed his mind about coming in today but that you should go over to his house. You ever been there?"

Tyler was amused by her small–town naiveté. "No, I haven't. Can you give me directions?"

"Well, wait till you see his place! It's really something. I hope you brought your bathing suit because it's got a fabulous pool. He lets us employees swim up there on summer afternoons. One of our company benefits." As she talked she was drawing him a map on the back of an envelope. "See, it's up here, on top of a hill. It has a great view too."

Tyler had not really expected to be as impressed with the Newfield place as he was. The house was enormous and sprawling with wings and solariums added on randomly, connected directly to the house or by breezeways. Perched on a rolling hillside, which had been landscaped to perfection, it would have been more suitable as a large country inn than the private home of a single, middle–aged man. As he approached the house he could hear splashing and shouting from the rear, indicating the location of the pool and that Nicholas was not spending a hot Saturday in August alone.

On an impulse, he followed a flagstone path through a sculpted flower garden until he reached the back of the house where the pool was. Instead of the busty bathing beauties he expected, there were two rather overweight girls and a slim, flat–chested one all trying to stay afloat on the same inflatable raft. Two small boys wearing inner tubes with Donald Duck heads played in the shallow end.

41

When he opened the gate and walked in, the girls shrieked gleefully and dumped themselves into water up to their necks.

"I'm looking for Mr. Newfield," he shouted to them.

"He's inside." One of them pointed to a wall of sliding glass doors. Tyler found himself peering into a spacious living room with extensive but casual furnishings. There were plenty of couches and comfortable chairs, a large fireplace with a sheepskin rug in front of it and a number of round tables placed at intimate intervals. There seemed to be an unusual amount of artwork decorating the walls and most of the flat, available surfaces.

"You'll have to go in and shout for him," the same girl told him. "It's a big house."

Sliding the nearest glass door aside, he stepped into the air–conditioned coolness of the darkened interior. He called hello a few times and then, in his usual fashion, busied himself with inspecting his surroundings before his host arrived.

His educated guess was that Nicholas had done some entertaining the night before. A few bar glasses sat on the mantel and on the end tables, one still half full of watery looking liquor. Some damp towels were piled on a chair and a light on the CD player indicated that its power had never been turned off. An orange bikini top was draped over the back of a couch and several cushions were scattered on the floor.

"Oh, hi. I didn't hear you come in." A large man was coming towards him from the interior of the house with his hand extended. His wet hair was slicked back and the white, terry cloth robe tied snugly around his expansive middle indicated he had just stepped from the shower. "Nicholas Newfield. You must be Suzanne's cousin."

"Tyler Mackenzie." As he shook the proffered hand, Tyler noted the bloodshot eyes and red cheeks of this friendly man.

"Can I offer you some coffee? It's just finished brewing." Nicholas was hastily flinging the cushions back onto the couch as he spoke. "Kind of a late night," he apologized with a meaningful laugh. "This damn murder investigation – I suppose Diane told you? Anyway, I really needed to cut loose last night. I'm just getting up now." Sweeping the damp towels into his arms, he asked, "Cream and sugar?"

"Just cream." Tyler shook his head as he watched him climb a couple of steps and disappear down a hall. Instead of dragging around with a hangover, the man seemed to be in higher gear than he himself was.

By the time Nicholas had returned with the coffee, Tyler had done a quick perusal of the artwork on the wall and learned that most of it seemed to be done by Nicholas himself. He seemed to dabble in all forms, modern, impressionistic, collage, even photography. Most of them dated from the sixties and early seventies. Art student, Tyler concluded. Several of the paintings contained images of a woman with very large, round breasts and curvaceous hips which he had been about to write off as a young man's sexual fantasy until he came to a group of three black and white photographs.

He was immediately struck by the stark erotic quality all three shared. He could not decide if it was the photographer's skill, the young woman's provocative poses or a combination of both. Was it the way she tossed her long hair and thrust out her extraordinary breasts or the way her filmy garments had been carefully arranged to expose and tantalize?

In one picture she was standing in knee–high prairie grass wearing a gauzy white blouse and full skirt. A stiff wind blew her hair out behind her, whipped her unbuttoned blouse open on one side to expose a voluptuous breast and lifted her skirt so high that the curve of her buttocks was clearly outlined. Her eyes were closed and the smile on her lips indicated she enjoyed the way the wind felt on her bare skin.

43

In the next one she was posed against a crumbling stone wall like an ancient Greek statue. Her hair was piled on her head which was turned in profile, her body was draped in a sheet that fell open at all the right places. She looked as pale and beautiful as a Venus de Milo.

In the final one she was wearing a sort of harem costume created of sheer white scarves arranged in just the right way to tantalize the imagination. Another scarf, covering her face in the traditional fashion, left nothing exposed but her laughing, teasing eyes.

"Does it bother you to see her that way?"

Tyler swallowed guiltily, caught in his voyeurism. He laughed nervously. "These pictures are exceptional," he remarked tearing his eyes from them to accept his coffee.

"I just wondered if it bothered you to see your cousin posed like that. I never knew just how puritanical the family was."

Tyler choked, unable to hide his reaction. He was glad that his flaming cheeks would be construed as familial embarrassment. "I wasn't looking at the face," he admitted turning away. "And to tell you the truth, I haven't seen Suzanne since I was ten. At that age you don't notice things like–" he made a few significant hand gestures.

Nicholas roared with laughter. "Like tits and ass?"

Tyler laughed with him and sipped his coffee, assessing the dangerous position he had put himself in. This man obviously knew Suzanne very well. It was going to be difficult to pull this charade off.

"So if you haven't seen Suzanne since you were ten, what are you doing here now?" Nicholas made himself comfortable on one of the couches and scrutinized Tyler with interest.

"I'm on a mission for the family." He was at least ready for this question. "The rest of them are in California, I'm the only one on the East coast and my aunt has this idea that Vermont is just a short hop from New York City. They're all a little worried because they haven't been able to get in touch with Suzanne for a few weeks now and when they found out she quit her job as well, she asked me to come up here and check things out."

"Worried about their investment in the little house in the country no doubt," Nicholas muttered more to himself than to Tyler but it told Tyler something he hadn't known. "Suzanne didn't quit her job, she just disappeared. I haven't even filled the position yet; I keep hoping she'll come back. Of course now that we've lost Esta as well, I'm going to have to do something...Guess we'll have to start interviewing for at least one new employee..." He drifted off into his thoughts.

"Have the police been notified of Suzanne's disappearance?"

Nicholas gave him an odd look. "Considering her past, I wouldn't think that would be a particularly good idea, would you?"

"Well, no, I guess not. Of course, you probably know more about that than I do. How far do you guys go back?"

"Oh, late sixties. Back to my art school days. Those were wild and wonderful times; guess you're too young to have been involved. I was a restless young man, always looking to try something new. Suzanne was the only one who could keep up with me." His eyes wandered to the photographs on the wall. "My God, she was beautiful back then. I hired her to model for me for an independent project I was doing for my sculpture class and well, I just fell in love with her. There were women before her and lots of women since, but none of them ever had an impact on my life the way she did."

"So do you think she left town of her own free will?"

"So to speak." Nicholas frowned. "When I knew her back in the sixties she was chased by demons of some sort from her past. Always jumped when someone knocked at the door, used to wake up in the night screaming. Then she went off one morning and I never saw her again until she showed up in my office here about ten years ago looking for a job."

"Weren't you worried back then when she disappeared like that?"

"Well, yes and no. I mean, those were hang–loose days, you know. If your girlfriend didn't come home for a few nights, you got high and slept with someone else and figured she was doing the same." Nicholas sat up and leaned forward with an earnest expression on his ruddy face." To be perfectly honest, I'm not sure how much I should tell you. I don't think she ever told her family what she was doing during most of her life before she settled down into a quiet and respectable lifestyle up here."

The two men eyed each other for a moment, trying to decide how far they could trust each other. "You're right," Tyler said finally. "She never told us much of anything, or at least no one ever told me. But I thought it might be helpful in trying to locate her if I knew something of her past history. I mean, maybe she's just staying with old friends someplace. All I remember is that she spent some time in Mexico after high school and nobody was very happy about it."

Nicholas shook his head pensively. "She would never talk about it. I think something really terrible happened there. She had a lot of pent–up anger that she needed a release for. And eventually it got her into a lot of trouble."

"How's that?"

"Oh, she became very political in a radical, anti–establishment way. I guess a lot of people were that way back then, but she took it to extremes. Violent extremes. Personally, I never understood it and she kept her politics out of our relationship."

A noise from the hallway made them both look up. A slim, dark haired girl stood in the doorway, wearing only a high–cut orange bikini bottom. She shook her shaggy bangs out of a pair of large, sleepy brown eyes as she stood in the doorway with one hand on her hip and pouted. Her smooth, youthful breasts had a perky, upward curve and no visible tan lines. "Oh, there you are, Nicky. I wondered where you'd gone."

"I have company right now, Marta. Why don't you go out to the pool for a while?" Nicholas shot Tyler an apologetic look which bordered on mischievous.

"Oh, all right. But I can't stay all day, you know." As she strutted past them, Nicholas grabbed her arm.

"I told you that you had to wear a suit during the day."

"Well, I can't find the top."

"I think it's on that chair over there." Tyler pointed across the room.

From beneath her thick fringe of hair, Marta regarded Tyler with sudden interest. "Is he going to be here tonight too?"

With an almost parental authority, Nicholas led her over to the bikini top and helped her put it on. "I'm going to get tan lines," she complained.

"Then lie in the shade." He kissed her at the door. "I'll see you in a little while." Patting her half–exposed rump, he gently shoved her outside, sliding the heavy glass into place behind her. "Not too smart," he commented, turning back to Tyler with a grin. "But she's a hot little number. You know, I don't see much family resemblance between you and Suzanne. How did you say you were related?"

His sudden question caught Tyler slightly off guard. "Oh. Uh, her mother and my mother were sisters. I take after my father's side of the family."

Nicholas was rummaging around in a drawer as Tyler spoke. He came forward flipping the pages of a photo album. "I've got a recent picture of her here

47

somewhere. Taken at the company picnic we had up here last summer. Oh, here it is. Looks a little more mature than the saucy wench on the wall, doesn't she?"

Tyler stared in amazement at the snapshot. It showed a matronly Suzanne in a one piece, flowered swimsuit, floating merrily in Nicholas's pool astride an inflatable dolphin. Everything about her seemed softer and fuller and although she was laughing, there was sadness in her eyes. "What happened to her red hair?"

"Faded away along with her figure. Happens to many of us when we reach our forties." He patted his own stomach.

As usual, Tyler's sharp eyes sought out the curious details. "What's this thing here on her hip?" he asked, already certain of the answer.

Nicholas laughed. "Believe it or not, that's a tattoo. It's always been there; I mean, she had it before I knew her in college. I think she got it in Mexico. Believe me, on her smooth, young body, it was very sexy. But I shouldn't be talking about your cousin to you this way." Nicholas stood up. "Look, I don't know what to tell you. I called a few people, checked a few places and I came up with zip. I even went over to her house to see if there were dirty dishes in the sink. You know, like if she had been kidnapped or something, the house would still be a mess."

Tyler nodded, making a mental note of the fact that Nicholas had a key to Suzanne's house.

"But it was perfectly clean. Spotless. Her suitcase was gone and there were some empty hangers in the closet. Her car was not there. It looked to me as though she had left of her own free will. And all I can say, is I hope God helps her if she needs it. Now if you'll excuse me, I do have some weekend house guests..."

The interview was definitely over. As Tyler rose, he cursed the fact that Nicholas had already had access to Suzanne's environment and whatever helpful clues there might be to her whereabouts.

"Well, thanks for your time—"

"Listen, no problem. How long you going to be around for?"

"I had planned to stay the weekend but—"

"Then why don't you come by tonight? I'm having a little party, sort of blowing out the stops before my kids come up on Monday and I have to behave for a week. Some French girls I know are coming down from Montreal and I think you might find them, shall we say, interesting." Nicholas raised his eyebrows provocatively.

"Well, sure, maybe I will. I'll see how I feel." It was certainly an invitation to catch Nicholas with his guard down. Even though his openness and generosity seemed authentic, there was still something about the man that Tyler's instincts did not trust.

He left the house the way he had come, slipping out by the gate to the pool and heading down the flagstone path to where his car was parked. But as his hand touched the door handle, he stopped short, realizing he had forgotten to ask Nicholas for directions to Suzanne's house.

Retracing his steps, he let himself back in through the sliding glass door. Nicholas was nowhere in sight. After a few minutes of tentative calling, he climbed up the short flight of stairs that led to the rest of the enormous building.

He was in a long dark hallway floored in brick—red quarry tiles. To his left an archway seemed to lead into a kitchen. To the right were several closed doors and then an open one at the far end from which came the gurgling sound of water and laughing, high pitched voices.

Much as he knew he should turn and go, he was drawn towards that open door. As he approached it, the air became increasingly warmer and moister. A quick peek around the corner of the doorway told him all he needed to know.

49

A woman and a man were seated in a sunken hot tub which was bubbling at full blast. Another woman was stretched out naked on her side on the tiles behind them, idly combing the wet hair of the woman in the water.

Embarrassed, Tyler sped quickly and quietly back towards the kitchen and collided with Nicholas in the entrance way.

"Oh! I thought you'd gone!" Nicholas's face was flushed and he sniffed a few times nervously.

"Sorry to surprise you but I seem to have lost the directions my aunt gave me to Suzanne's house. I thought—"

"Of course. Come in here. I'll draw you a map."

Tyler followed him into an ultra—modern kitchen done in black and white. His eyes swept quickly over the room, trying to learn more about Nicholas in the few additional seconds he had here. Another nervous sniff brought his gaze sharply back to Nicholas's face. He noticed now a few grains of what looked like white dust lingering around one of Nicholas's nostrils.

Tyler grimaced and nodded to himself. It all made perfect sense, including Nicholas's high— spirited behavior when he first arrived. But it hardly gave him any more confidence in the truth of what he had learned. He was sure now that there was a lot that Nicholas wasn't telling him and never would. But he knew a way he could find out a lot more. If only Sarah would cooperate.

CHAPTER FOUR

"West Jordan Inn."

"Sarah? It's me. Tyler."

"Who? Tyler? I'm sorry, I'm having trouble hearing. We're having a Last–Night–Open party here. I'll be with you in a minute, Red! Where are you?" Loud music and clinking glasses punctuated her words.

"I'm in Emporia. At Suzanne's house. Listen, I need you to come down here tomorrow."

"Tyler, it's Saturday night, I've got a full bar, a full dining room, I'm probably not going to get out of here until 3 in the morning and you call me to tell me that you need to see me? Don't you ever think of anyone but yourself?"

"Oh, get off your self–righteous trip, Sarah! This isn't for me, it's for Woody, remember?" There was a silence at the other end of the line. "Are you there?"

"I'm here. What do you want me to do?"

"There's a job opening up at Newfield's and I need you to be there first thing Monday morning to apply for it."

"But Woody's going into the hospital on Monday!"

"You know Woody will want you to come down here. I need your help."

"Look, Tyler, I've got to go–"

"Okay. So, I'll see you here for supper tomorrow night around seven. Now let me talk to Woody in the kitchen. I'll give him directions so you can find this place."

He gave Woody a brief rundown of what had transpired so far, gave him directions to Suzanne's for Sarah and wished him luck with his surgery. He was

51

about to hang up when a question struck him. "Woody, tell me something. When you knew her, did she have a monarch butterfly tattooed on her hip?"

After a stunned pause, Woody spoke slowly. "However would you know about that?"

"I've seen a picture of it. Just checking to make sure it's the same Suzanne, you know, identifying marks and all that."

When he hung up the phone, Tyler was confident that Woody would make sure that Sarah would be in Emporia by the next night. He poured himself another glass of wine and sat carefully back on Suzanne's couch.

He was having a difficult time feeling relaxed in this house he had broken into. By law he was guilty of breaking and entering as well as trespassing, even if it was for a good cause. But each little noise made him jump. He would fantasize that it was Suzanne coming home and he could just put her in the car with him and drive back to West Jordan and everyone would live happily ever after.

He was also uneasy about how effortless the break–in had been. It was obvious that someone had climbed through the same window before him. The screen came off easily with a minimum of prying and the double hung window behind it was unlocked and slid up without a hitch. A few traces of dried mud on the floor had confirmed his suspicion. He could not imagine the portly Nicholas hoisting himself over the sill and, although he did not believe everything Nicholas said, he did believe him when he said he had a key.

The house itself was a gem with lots of windows, woodwork and highly polished hardwood floors. Half of the second story had been removed to make a cathedral ceiling in the living room. In fact most of the walls between the small, old fashioned rooms had been removed, giving an airy, open feeling to the space. Even the bedroom upstairs was more like a loft with a wide railing that overlooked the downstairs living area. The only room with a door was the bathroom which was decorated with handmade ceramic tiles in desert tones.

Personal and private were words that came to mind. Tyler noted that there were no beds other than the double bed in the loft, indicating that Suzanne did not have overnight company very often. But most of his afternoon had been fruitless as far as learning why Suzanne had disappeared so suddenly. He had noted a complete absence of mementos or pictures from the past. Not a childhood photograph, not a high school yearbook, no antique jewelry. Not even a current snapshot of herself anywhere. Of course, he figured, she might have taken those things with her, wherever it was she'd gone.

In a desk drawer he had found her mortgage payment book which was registered under the names of Harold Emerson and Suzanne Laveaux. The last payment had been made August 10th, a few days before she had vanished. He wondered how easily it would be to get a telephone listing for Harold Emerson in San Diego, or if Suzanne's parents even still lived there. He found the title to her car, a silver blue VW Jetta, and a payment book for that as well. But no birth certificates, passports or checkbooks. There was a postcard from Portugal signed Mom and Dad and a Christmas card from someone named Andrea.

The best he had found was a shoe box of canceled checks neatly arranged in chronological order for the last seven years. Tomorrow he would go through those and see if they shed any light on things. But right now he felt exhausted and depressed and not sure what to do next.

He was sure there was more to be learned from Nicholas if only he could figure out how. If Sarah could get a job inside Newfield's she could probably gain access to a lot of information that he never could. If he didn't leave here on Monday, he was going to have to make himself very scarce or find a plausible excuse for hanging around.

The least he could do was go to Nicholas's Saturday night party. It could only be enlightening and a couple of "interesting" French–Canadian girls might take his mind off Sarah.

When he finally awoke the next day, he was sprawled on the couch, fully dressed with a headache that wouldn't quit. He had no idea of how he had arrived back at Suzanne's but his car keys on the floor next to him indicated that he must have driven. The gray light and steady rain outdoors gave no indication of what time it was and he was surprised to see by his watch that it was almost noon. Groaning, he closed his eyes and tried to remember the evening's events. He had a vague memory of being in the hot tub with those French–Canadian girls and he surely hadn't been wearing any clothes. He thought he must've passed out shortly after that.

_ Tyler rolled off the couch onto the floor and tried to stand up. He did not want the rest of the night to come back to him. Staggering into the bathroom, he splashed cold water onto his face and peered at himself in the mirror. There were puffy bags beneath his eyes and his hair stood out from his head at odd angles. I look like shit, he thought, and then, as he stared as his moustache, something else came back to him...somebody saying that his moustache tickled...

Groaning again, he stripped off his clothes and climbed into the shower. While half of his brain tried desperately to recall the previous night, the other half didn't want to remember at all. He felt he at least had to recall whether or not he'd had sex with anyone. He could not believe he could have gotten so drunk as to forget if he had. And yet he still had no recollection of driving home.

He hated losing track of hours of his life like that. If he had learned any more about Nicholas, he had already forgotten it by now. Toweling himself dry, he trailed wet footprints up the stairs in search of his suitcase and some fresh clothes.

His suitcase was not standing neatly against the wall where he had left it. Cursing for the umpteenth time, he turned to find it open on the bed, his clothes in an unsightly heap as though someone had hurriedly dumped them inside. Frowning, he approached it warily. Hungover or not, he knew himself well enough to know that this was not his style. Someone else had obviously been here looking for something, possible clues to his identity or clues to Suzanne's whereabouts.

But who and when?

For a moment he stood still, shivering and naked, wondering if someone was in the house right now, watching and waiting. But no sound came to him except his own rapid breathing and the sound of water dripping off the eaves as the rain outside slacked off to a drizzle.

Exhaling, he gingerly extracted a T–shirt and jeans from the pile. Once dressed, he did not feel quite as vulnerable and began poking more boldly through his belongings, trying to ascertain if anything was missing. As he accounted for everything his fuzzy mind could think of, it came to him that perhaps he had not driven himself home. Perhaps he had been escorted by someone curious to know more about him. Someone like Nicholas?

He shook his head. It didn't jive somehow. The hasty way the clothes had been stuffed back into the suitcase made it seem as though someone had been surprised in the middle of their search and had beat a fast track for the door. Perhaps they had been hard at it when Tyler himself came home, whatever time that was.

But the question of who and why burned in his mind as he made himself some toast and coffee. Improbable solutions came and went. There was even the possibility that it could have been Suzanne herself.

The ringing of the telephone on the wall next to him made his heart leap again. As he contemplated whether or not to answer it, a tape machine up in the bedroom loft kicked in. A tape machine – why hadn't he thought of it before? Someone as private as Suzanne was sure to screen all her calls before she answered them.

By the time he found it, the caller had already hung up. Tyler rewound the nearly full tape and pushed play. Munching his toast, he settled back against the pillows to see what it might reveal.

The first few calls were from Nicholas. "Suzanne, if you are there, please pick up. I'm starting to get worried." Then there were several hang–ups and then finally another message.

"Suzanne, it's Dad and it's Sunday afternoon. Haven't heard from you for a while and we just wanted to let you know that we're leaving tomorrow for that Southeast Asian tour we told you about. Singapore, Bangkok, Hong Kong, the whole shebang. We'll be gone until September 15th. We'll send you a card. Call us tonight if you get a chance."

Damn. So much for contacting her parents. At least he wouldn't have to worry about them blowing his cover for a few weeks.

There were two more hang–ups and then another message. "I'm still waiting for August's check." It was a gruff, humorless male voice. "I'm assuming it must have gotten lost in the mail because I know you couldn't possibly want to end up in the slammer again."

Holy shit. Tyler put down his coffee cup and replayed the last call again. What could it mean? If he could figure out the meaning, it might have everything to do with Suzanne's disappearance. By the amount of noise in the background, it sounded like the caller was in a public phone booth somewhere like a bus station.

Unable to make anything of it, he moved on. The Emporia Bookbarn called to say that the book Suzanne had ordered was in. Dr Simon's office called to remind her about a dentist appointment. The next message was from Dr. Simon's office again to remind her that she had missed her appointment and to please reschedule.

He finally reached the last message – the call that had come less than an hour ago. "Hi, this is Andrea. Just wanted to see how you were doing and let you know I've moved and have a new phone number. 612–555–3459. Call me some time!"

Flipping quickly through the phone book, Tyler discovered that Andrea's new area code was in Minnesota now. But that was all he knew about her. At least her phone number was a place to start. Everything else seemed like a dead end.

But it was nearly two o'clock and he had his own life to worry about. Sarah would be here in a few hours and he wanted to be ready for her.

By the time Sarah's Subaru station wagon pulled into the driveway, Tyler had finished setting up a romantic dinner perfect enough to melt any woman's heart. He wiped the morning's rain off the wrought iron table and chairs on the deck and then moved them out into the center of Suzanne's perennial garden, setting two places with ceramic plates and wine goblets he'd found in the china closet. The vegetable garden, unharvested for weeks, yielded a sumptuous salad as well as all the ingredients for gazpacho and ratatouille. A bottle of wine was chilling in the refrigerator and swordfish was marinating for the grill.

Sarah, however, was not the type to be swept off her feet by flowers, wine and atmosphere. Despite the beauty of the hollyhocks, lilies and coreopsis, and the delicious feast Tyler had prepared, the conversation was stiff between the two former lovers. Sarah did not seem at all ready to pick up where they had left off six months previously and was as wary as ever of Tyler's natural charm. When Tyler pointed out how the evening light made the rain–soaked leaves glisten, Sarah swatted at a mosquito and commented that the rain had brought the bugs out.

In Tyler's opinion, she had never looked better and he told her so over and over again until she bluntly told him to "can the corn." She was wearing a full–skirted sundress in a print of tiny purple, blue and red flowers with a fitted bodice that displayed her long, slim waistline. It was held up by thin straps that revealed her strong shoulders and bare back. Her dark hair was held off her face by a purple headband making it easy to admire her high cheekbones and the tilt of her large gray eyes.

Sarah's stony response to his loving gaze caused him to change the subject abruptly. "So. What does this garden tell you about Suzanne?"

"Is this a quiz?"

"Oh, come on, Sarah, lighten up. We're supposed to be working together on this."

She scowled at him for a moment over her wine goblet before downing the contents and pushing it towards him for a refill. Looking around thoughtfully, she said, "Well, these are perennials, so she obviously planned to be around here for a while...The vegetable garden certainly needs some tending. I guess what this tells me is that she wasn't planning this disappearance or she wouldn't have planted all these tomatoes and cucumbers and things that need to be eaten in August. Someone who loves gardening as much as she apparently does wouldn't leave their garden at this time of year."

Tyler grinned ruefully at her quick deductive reasoning. It was a rare occasion when he could outsmart her.

"Don't you feel creepy staying here in her house? I mean, what if she shows up all of the sudden? How would you feel if you came home and found a strange woman sleeping in your bed?" In spite of her vendetta,

Sarah could not help but laugh at the look on Tyler's face at her question. "Never mind. Stupid comparison." A few more gulps of wine and there was a rosy flush to her cheeks. "So tell me about this job you want me to apply for."

He quickly filled her in on Esta Variance, the young telephone operator who had died of a drug overdose. "Apparently it came as a surprise to everyone she worked with. I guess she wasn't the type you would associate with deadly drugs." He went on to tell her about the party at Nicholas' that he had attended where designer drugs had been the focus of the evening for most of the guests and then about the strange phone call that indicated Suzanne had been in jail once for something.

Sarah was only half listening. "A telephone operator? You mean, take mail orders over the telephone? But I've never done anything like that! They'd never hire me."

"They will when they see the resume we're going to put together for you."

"I don't know about this, Tyler. I'm not the great impostor, I mean... impersonator that you are."

Tyler reddened slightly at the implied double meaning in her words. "You won't have to be anyone but yourself, Sarah. We'll just alter your work history to make you an applicant they can't refuse. Truthfully, the job I'd like to see you fill is Suzanne's, but I'm sure Nicholas is going to keep that open awhile. But we'll make you a perfect executive secretary while we're at it. More wine?"

"There. Is that professional or what?" Tyler handed Sarah the two page resume that his laptop computer and portable printer had produced on Suzanne's coffee table. He sat back and relaxed into the cushions of the comfortable couch and watched her read.

Working together had eased the tension between them as Tyler had hoped it would. His leg, pressing against Sarah's as she sat next to him reading, set sparks leaping in his heart as well as other parts of his body. But before he could seriously begin hoping about the outcome of the evening, she put down the resume and stood up.

"Well, I guess I'll go out for a few hours."

"What? Go out where?" He sat up in amazement at her announcement.

"I don't know. To the local bar I guess. There must be one. I need to sit anonymously and drink some tequila and think." She fished in her shoulder bag until she found a comb to run through her thick hair.

He did not need to voice his disappointment for her to respond to it.

"Look, my whole life has just collapsed for a few months, all right? I don't know where I stand on anything. I don't know if life will ever be the same again. I just need some space right now." She slung her handbag over her shoulder and grabbed a sweater off the back of a chair. "Besides, I'm on a weird schedule."

"So?" His belligerent, one word response expressed all his anger and hurt in a neat package.

"So don't wait up." And she was gone.

"Damn." Tyler clenched his fists, trying to control his urge to smash his wine goblet against the wall. He had barely managed to crack the surface of the ice castle surrounding Sarah; she would not let him reach in and touch her. He threw his head back against the couch and closed his eyes. Well, he knew one way to get to her. Later.

Sarah didn't have to worry about choosing the wrong place to have a drink. Rusty's Cafe was the only bar in town open on a Sunday night and nothing to write home about. Decorated with plastic beer signs and baseball caps, it was as tacky as flypaper on a summer afternoon. A TV was poorly tuned in to a Red Sox game, which the bartender watched from the end of the bar where he chain–smoked Camels and guzzled Diet Pepsi. The only other patrons besides Sarah were an overweight middle–aged man in a salmon–colored golf shirt and matching shorts accompanied by two women. Both women had hair dyed the same shade of blonde, styled in a way reminiscent of Farrah Fawcett. They wore matching sleeveless sweaters of glittering gold and black yarn that barely accommodated their breasts, the size and kind of which seemed to enter a room minutes before the rest of the body.

Sarah was homesick for the West Jordan Inn already.

Tired and depressed, she rummaged in her purse for change for the cigarette machine. Tyler would shit if he knew she was smoking again, but what did she care what Tyler thought.

"Here you go, babe." A handful of quarters came sliding down the bar towards her.

"Thanks, but I'm not your babe, buddy." Sarah shot the quarters back at him and waved a dollar bill at the bartender.

"Touchy, aren't we? Then I guess I'm not your buddy, BABE." His two companions twittered appreciatively.

She could feel their eyes burning into her backside as she fiddled with the cigarette machine. She tried to maintain an air of indifference as she puffed her cigarette and sipped her drink, but her natural self–confidence seemed to be eroding bit by bit in this new, strange environment. Stress was making her girlish and sensitive; the wrong word from the right person would probably send her over the edge. She could not keep up this tough facade much longer.

One of the glitter blondes pulled at the neckline of her sweater and looked down at herself. "Oooh, sunburn," she announced in a squeaky voice.

"Oooh, me too," echoed the other one, peering down her own sweater.

"I warned you girls, oh, excuse me, women–" he threw a meaningful glance at Sarah, "but you insisted on showing off all afternoon."

"Oh, Nicky, you loved every minute of it." The left blonde gave him a reproachful smooch on the cheek.

Sarah focused on the air space over their heads, pretending to watch the TV. She had a feeling they were about to put on a show for her benefit and she didn't feel removed enough tonight to enjoy people–watching from her usual cynical distance. Besides that, she always felt uncomfortable around well–endowed women who drew attention to themselves and their "assets."

"Ouch, this is really starting to hurt," the right–hand Farrah complained, holding the scratchy sweater away from her chest.

"I guess I'll just have to rub something cool onto your tits tonight, won't I?"

"I bet I'm more sunburned than you are!" Farrah #1 pulled up her sweater to expose one enormous and painfully pink breast. Sarah could not help but stare. Even the bartender tore his gaze away from the tube to ogle.

The man they called Nicky laughed merrily as Farrah #2 lifted her sweater to compare. "Girls, girls! This is not the Riviera! You're embarrassing the other customers! Besides it's hot enough in here already."

Sarah had to laugh. "Don't worry about me! I'm not offended." Astonished maybe, but not offended. At least this ridiculous trio was taking her mind off her own troubles. She ordered another tequila.

"That one's on me. George, add the pretty girl's drink to my tab."

"Look–"

"Don't give me any women's lib crap, darling. I'd still be buying you a drink if you were a guy. Set me up again while you're at it, George." Sarah's own experience told her Nicky had had more than enough to drink already.

"Thanks, but I can take care of myself."

"What's that supposed to mean, sweetheart? I don't understand why a beautiful girl like you, who's got everything going for her, has to give a well-meaning guy like me a hard time. If I wasn't already here with these two gorgeous babes, I could probably show you a good time like you've probably never seen."

"George, why don't you give the man a tall glass of ice water on me?"

"What am I supposed to do with this?"

"Soak your schlong in it until you cool off a little. You come on way too hot for me, mister."

Nicky's jaw dropped open. A tense hush dropped like a curtain over the bar for a few seconds. His companions looked at him expectantly and were surprised when he burst into a huge belly laugh. "If I wasn't so drunk I'd play hardball with you, lady. But right now you render me speechless."

Tyler sat up suddenly and blinked. He had no idea how long he'd been asleep on the couch but his watch said it was 1:15. The lights were still blazing – apparently Sarah had not come home yet.

He had spent the evening going through Suzanne's canceled checks. Just as he began to get bored, a new pattern started to emerge that caught his attention.

On the first of every month Suzanne had paid her electric bill, her car payment and her gas bill. On the tenth she paid the mortgage on the house. On twentieth she paid the telephone bill and her credit card bills. But suddenly, into the third year there was a change in the order of things. The telephone payment shifted to the tenth and on the twentieth a new check was added each month, made out to someone named Luther Dross for $100. On each check the words "Loan Repayment" were written on the explanation line in the lower left corner.

After a couple of years the amount suddenly shot up to $200 and by the current year it was up to $250. So far Suzanne had repaid Luther Dross over $9,000.

There was no question in Tyler's mind that Luther had been the caller on the answering machine.

He flipped one of the checks over. Beneath Luther's signature was a bank stamp from a Credit Union in Chicago. A quick survey revealed that all of Luther's checks had been cashed at the same bank. Still no closer to an answer but very close to a headache, Tyler had shut his eyes for a few minutes to think. And now it was 1:15 and Sarah was not even home yet.

"Damn." He stood up and stretched and then paced the floor until a noise from the loft stopped him in his tracks. There it was again, a little gasp or a wheeze, unmistakably human. He looked around for something to defend himself with and then armed with the empty wine bottle, he tiptoed up the stairs.

When the bed came into view, he breathed easier, resting for moment on the top step so his heart could return to its normal rhythm.

Sarah was stretched out across the bed, her face buried in her arms. Her back shook as another sob forced its way out of her and she gulped air trying to control it.

"Sarah! What's wrong?" He sat on the bed beside her.

"Nothing." Her reply was muffled as she wiped her eyes on her arm and her nose with the back of her hand before sitting up. "I'm just being a wimp, that's all."

He handed her a tissue from the nightstand. "Wimp is the last word I'd ever use to describe you. Why don't you tell me what's going on here?"

"It's nothing." She closed her eyes as another tear wiggled its way down her cheek. When Tyler reached over to wipe it away, several more rapidly took its place. He pulled her towards him and held her close, as she tried to explain her sadness into his shoulder. He caught the words "alone" and "scared" and the rest really didn't matter to him.

"Don't be. I'm here with you. You're safe." He only half believed it himself but knew it was what she needed to hear. Holding her against his chest made his whole body ache for her. Inside he was crying out that he loved her and wanted to have sex now, but he heard himself saying "Lay down, I'll rub your back."

With uncharacteristic meekness, she obeyed him. When he unzipped the back of her sundress, he saw that she was wearing the strapless black and purple lace bra and matching underpants from Victoria's Secret he had sent her for Valentine's Day. He grinned to himself knowingly as he massaged her tight muscles. Sarah did not wear fancy underwear every day and he was sure it was no accident that she had this set on right now. Underneath it all, she wanted a reunion as much as he did.

"Tyler?" She did not lift her head or open her eyes. "How many woman have you slept with since I last saw you?"

"Since Friday night?" His own joke made him swallow guiltily. He still could not remember much about the previous evening.

"You know what I mean. In the last six months."

"None. Well, maybe one. But it might just as well have been none, if you know what I mean."

She nodded. "Me too. I mean, I tried it but it seemed so...stupid. It wasn't worth it. It just made me angrier."

"At me? Why?"

"Because I can't live with you and I can't live without you."

Minutes later that the sundress fell to a crumpled heap on the floor; the lace bra and underpants followed shortly thereafter.

It was nearly dawn when Tyler finally drifted off to sleep with his body curled protectively around Sarah's. He wanted to stay like this always, nestled as close as possible to this woman he adored. There had to be a way they could make things work.

"Don't leave me, Tyler."

"I won't," he whispered. It was an empty promise but at least it came from the heart.

CHAPTER FIVE

It was high noon, and hot and steamy in the loft, by the time they finally got up for the day. Before her bare feet even touched the floor, Sarah was on the telephone to the Jordan Regional Hospital checking on Woody's condition.

"He's out of surgery and in the recovery room," she announced with a sigh of relief. "That's all the nurse would tell me. He'll be in ICU later."

A night of sex always improved Sarah's mood, as Tyler had known it would. After the news that Woody had at least made it through surgery, she was in high spirits, ready to take on the adventurous task at hand.

"We can't keep staying here," she remarked through a mouthful of cream cheese and tomato omelet. "I don't feel right about it."

"Let's just take one step at time. First let's see if we can get you inside Newfield's. If you get a job there, we'll look for an apartment or something." The thought of a dumpy, rent–by–the–week apartment did not appeal to Tyler. He was beginning to feel very much at home in Suzanne's cozy little house.

"But we could be arrested for trespassing–"

"Oh, come on, I'm her long lost cousin Tyler Mackenzie from the Mackenzie side of her mother's family. Who's going to question that?"

It was nearly two by the time Sarah was ready to go.

"For some reason I had pictured you dashing off to this job interview at nine in the morning. I guess I forgot who I was dealing with." Tyler gave her a peck on the cheek as she headed out the door. "Let's just hope the position isn't filled yet."

"Do I look like executive secretary material?" She gave a twirl on the stone walkway outside. She was wearing an ivory linen shirt and a straight black skirt.

"I don't think I've ever seen you wear high heels before. It's a very impressive sight."

"Well, I'm roasting in these nylons. Goodbye." Sarah's long strides up the path could be construed as either confidence or arrogance. Or maybe a bit of both.

"Mr. Newfield will see you now. Go up those stairs and turn left. It's the wooden paneled door at the end of the hall."

Sarah's confidence seemed to be seeping away as the interview grew closer. A snag that suddenly appeared on the knee of her right stocking undermined her poise even further. She was sure the broken thumbnail on her left hand would give away her entire charade.

She knocked on the massive office door, which was totally out of character with the economical appearance of the rest of the building.

"Come in! I'll be with you in a minute!" When the intimidating male voice boomed at her, she almost turned and ran. Feeling a bit like Dorothy visiting the Wizard, she pushed open the heavy door.

The office was still as cluttered and disorganized as Tyler has described it to her. Nicholas Newfield was tipped back in his expensive, contour–cushioned desk chair, talking on the telephone with his feet up on a pile of computer printouts. A pricey–looking sport jacket was tossed carelessly on the floor beside him and he was struggling to loosen his silk tie as he talked. There was something familiar about his profile that she couldn't quite place.

"Damn it, June! All right, all right. Drop them here at the office at five. Goodbye. Damn," he repeated as he hung up the phone and turned to face her. "Sorry about that. So you're here about the job—"

It was hard to say whose face turned a brighter crimson or whose jaw dropped farther. Sarah wished the carpet beneath her feet would become enchanted and fly her far away. Tyler had prepared her for decadence and self–indulgence, but never in her wildest speculations had she imagined that Nicholas Newfield would turn out to be the drunken fool she had insulted at the bar the previous night.

Nicholas broke the astonished silence with an enormous belly laugh. After a moment, Sarah could not help but join in. "I'm sorry," he said finally, wiping his eyes. "I just never expected–"

"*You* never expected! What about me? I'm the one applying for a job!"

Nicholas laughed again and then indicated the empty chair opposite his desk. "Please, sit down, Miss–"

"Scupper. Sarah Scupper. Can't we just pretend we've never met?"

"Believe me, I'd love to. You've seen a side of me I try to hide from my employees. I like to keep my sordid private life from interfering with my business. Please excuse this mess, Miss Scupper– I mean, MS. Scupper–"

"Sarah is fine."

"Sarah then. My secretary was called away suddenly about a month ago and I haven't been able to keep on top of things."

"Called away?"

"Personal problems. I don't know when she'll be back."

"Well, I'm here because I heard the executive secretary position was open."

"Really?" Nicholas's eyes narrowed, observing her with a shrewdness that had been masked the night before. "Where did you hear that?"

"Around town." Sarah tried to keep the nervous quiver out of her voice. "I've just moved here, I'm staying with a girlfriend. When I mentioned to some friends of hers that I was applying for a phone operator's job here, they told me that your secretary had left and you'd probably be needing one. I'm well–qualified as you can see from my resume..."

He glanced over the careful lies she and Tyler had worked out the night before. "Well, as unprofessional as it seems, I'm still expecting that Suzanne might come back and I'd like the job to stay open for her. Obviously, if she doesn't show up soon, I'll have to at least hire someone temporarily but I don't know if you'd be interested in a job that might only last a week or two. Would you be?"

"Truthfully, I'd be interested in any job right now, even if it only lasted for one day. I'd be glad to work for you under the condition that I would have to quit if your secretary returned."

Nicholas snapped his fingers suddenly. "How do you feel about kids?"

"Kids? What do you mean?"

"My kids are coming to visit for a week and I have no one to look after them. Suzanne always arranged all that for me. I have important meetings nearly every day through Friday and I can't be home. I need someone with spunk who could keep them in line. Something tells me you could do that." He grinned and Sarah had a glimpse of what Nicholas might have been like as a younger man, maybe a little mischievous and impulsive.

But she would have taken an office job over babysitting any day. She didn't know anything about taking care of kids. "How old are they?" she asked uncertainly.

"Shannon's nine, Nathaniel is eleven. You don't have to worry, there are no diapers involved. They're good kids, but they fight if they get bored. Mostly they're happy to swim in the pool all day. Would you mind spending the week at my house? It's quite large; you'd have your own room and bathroom."

"I haven't said I'd do it yet." Sarah knew this was a perfect opportunity and that Tyler would tell her to jump at it. To have free reign in Nicholas's house while he was at work... Tyler would have a field day snooping around. He had assured her that Nicholas knew more than he was admitting to about Suzanne's disappearance and Sarah had a feeling that under the right circumstances, she could get Nicholas to talk.

"But you will. Because I'll pay you a lot and if Suzanne hasn't come back by Monday, I'll let you have her job until she does." He seemed quite excited that he had so neatly solved his own problems. He wrote a dollar amount on a slip of paper and flashed it at her.

Sarah gulped. She knew she could not refuse. It was odd how much the idea of managing two children scared her when handling a bar full of drunken loggers didn't faze her in the least.

"Okay. When do I start?"

"They show up at five." He looked at his watch. "Damn, it's already three. I'll probably just take them out for burgers for supper. Why don't you come by around seven or eight tonight and get settled in?"

"Tonight?" Sarah had been looking forward to another cozy and satisfying evening in bed with Tyler. "I– I already have plans–" She knew Tyler would tell her to just go for it. He had certainly left her high and dry more than once when a lead on an exciting story came his way. "But I'll see what I can do."

"I just thought it would be easier – I have to be gone by eight in the morning and I'd like to show you around the place. You know, like where the freezer is, the emergency phone numbers, how to use the hot tub..."

The implication in the last phrase was unmistakable. Sarah shuddered at the thought and decided to lay it right on the line. "Let's just get this straight," she said squarely, trying to meet his amused expression with a stern one of her own. "You're hiring me to take care of your kids, not your house, or your laundry or you. Right?"

71

"Believe me, I can take care of myself. And just so you know, I make it a policy not to fool around with my employees. If we hadn't previously met on other, more social, territory, that question wouldn't even come up. Besides, I'm sure a desirable young woman such as yourself already has a boyfriend."

"That's right. I do." Her cheeks were burning again.

"Well, you'll have to bring him around some evening. We can all party together."

Sarah merely nodded. There was no way Tyler would come visit as her boyfriend; to Nicholas he was Suzanne's cousin on her mother's side. Her head began to throb at the thought of it. She had barely begun this charade and it was a tangled web already.

In her rearview mirror, she could see the battered gray Buick following her up the wooded road back to Suzanne's house, but she did not think anything of it. She was surprised, however, when it backed into the drive behind her.

She had not even removed her key from the ignition by the time a tall figure in black T–shirt and jeans was looming at the open window on the driver's side of the car. Before she could look up at his face, a flash of silver at waist level caught her eye. She gasped in astonishment; no one had ever pointed a revolver at her before.

"Get out." The command was growled with an impatient wave of the gun.

This could not be happening to her. Things like this only happened in the movies or in books.

Sarah looked down at her bare feet; she had removed her high heels and stockings in the parking lot of Newfield's. Whatever happened, she was probably better off without them.

"Now!"

72

Her hands were shaking so much she could barely get the door open. Where was Tyler? Why didn't he noticed what was happening in the driveway?

"Don't even think about screaming for your boyfriend." She glanced quickly at the face of the man who was prodding her towards the Buick with the hard steel of the revolver. He had long stringy blond hair that hung limply around a lean face that had once fought a losing battle with acne. "Because I'll blow you both away."

"What do you want with me?" she managed to sputter as he shoved her, face down onto the back seat of the car.

"I don't want nothin' with you. It's Fred what's been looking for you." He was lashing her hands behind her back now with what felt like plastic twine. He was fast. Within seconds he had her ankles tied also. "Only you probably know him as Rico."

He threw a sheet over her, leaped into the driver's seat and took off, the tires spinning wildly on gravel.

Sarah could not remember ever meeting anyone named Rico in her entire life. Her own hot breath came back at her as her face pressed against the car seat, and she tried desperately to imagine what was about to happen to her. But the ideas that came to her were too scary; to calm herself down, she tried to picture that Tyler was speeding after them in his own car, ready to rescue her as soon as they stopped moving. Finally she ceased thinking entirely and just tried to use her senses to figure out what was going on.

They did not travel more than ten minutes before the car slowed to a halt. More than likely they were in the village of Emporia, judging from the sporadic sounds of traffic in the background. She heard the car door slam and knowing she was alone, she was tempted to scream for help. Her clothing was soaked through with sweat; she rubbed her damp face against the seat and tried to roll over on her back.

73

Mere seconds had passed when she heard the murmur of two voices approaching the car again. Then the door near her head opened and the sheet was immediately whisked off her body. Sarah blinked and squinted in the afternoon sunlight.

"Ay, majadero! Quien es esta?"

"I told you to speak Anglo to me. What the hell is the problem now? I brought the girl. Now give me the dough and I'm outa here."

"Who the fuck is this, pendejo? This is not the woman I am looking for! I told you blonde and fatty. Are you fucking blind?"

Sarah lay perfectly still, afraid to move in the tense atmosphere surrounding her.

"So she probably dyed her hair! She's the one who came back to the house last night, the one who fucked her boyfriend until dawn like I told you. Look at her face before you jump the gun, buddy."

One pair of rough hands grabbed Sarah's shoulder and rolled her on her back, while another hand slapped itself across her eyes. "We don't need her to see our faces. I'm telling you this is not Suzanne."

Sarah flinched as her shirt was ripped open, the buttons flying wildly into the air. "No," she gasped.

"See? I told you Suzanne had big tits, I mean really big. Not in one million years is this her. Hey! Chica! What is your name?"

"Sarah." Sarah's voice was no more than a croak.

"Sarah, where is Suzanne?"

"Who?"

"Suzanne. La mujer – the woman who owns the house where you stay."

"I don't know."

Tears came to her eyes as one of the men smacked her hard across the face.

"Where is Suzanne?"

"I don't know. Please. Stop. I really don't know."

"Why do you stay at her house then?"

"Realtor rented it to us... don't know the owner..." She was not as faint as her voice sounded but her head was spinning and her cheeks ached where she had been slapped.

As suddenly as she had been grabbed, Sarah was released and made to roll on her face again.

"Take her back, you idiot! This is trouble I don't need!"

"You want me to get rid of her?"

"No, I don't need a botched–up murder on my hands. Just drop her some place on the road and make her walk back."

"What about my money?"

"What money? You have not done the job yet!"

Please, Sarah begged silently. Give him some money and let me go.

"Then you take her back, you Mexican maniac." She heard the clink of car keys on pavement and then a house door slamming shut a few feet away.

Grumbling to himself, the "Mexican maniac" climbed into the driver seat and started up the car. As he drove, he bellowed instructions over the back seat to Sarah.

"When I drop you off you must not look at me or this car or even move until I have drive away. Comprende? And let me tell you something more. If you go to the police and try to make them come after me, you will be very sorry. I will make sure that you and your pretty boyfriend will never fuck again and that might mean something much worse than killing. You understand me? DO YOU?"

"Yes," she whispered and then afraid he had not heard her she shouted. "YES."

She sat on the side of the road for a very long time, sobbing with relief. Now that her ordeal was over, she was shaking too much to walk. Until he had dropped her off, Fred or Rico, or whoever he was, had repeated his threats making them more elaborate each time. She did not know if he was all hot air but she certainly was not going to find out.

No traffic had passed her by the time she stood up. She was glad of this because she knew she was not far from Suzanne's house and her appearance would surely have brought up a few questions. She tied her ripped linen blouse in a knot above her waist and limped along the gravel and dirt road, wincing every now and then as her bare feet hit sharp rocks.

As she rounded the last curve, she saw Tyler walking down the hill towards her, his impatience obvious in his stride.

"Where have you been?" he called. "I've been looking all over the place for you! What did you do, go for a walk or something?"

Sarah merely waved, suddenly too overcome with emotion to speak. They were nearly face to face before Tyler realized that something was wrong.

"My God, what happened to you?" He gripped her at arm's length as he stared at her ruined blouse and her tear-stained face and then gingerly touched her swollen cheeks. "Holy shit. Sarah. What happened?"

Sarah threw her arms around his neck and buried her face in the warm, familiar smell of his shoulder.

"Holy shit," Tyler repeated when she had finished her story. They were sitting in Suzanne's porch swing; Sarah's head was in his lap, he held a bag of ice against her face. "In all my years of investigating stories, nothing like that has ever happened to me. I'm so sorry. I didn't think there would be any danger involved when I asked you to come here. I guess we should probably pack up and go to a motel." He shuddered, thinking of those two thugs watching him and Sarah make love.

"Damn. What time is it? I nearly forgot. You never asked me how my interview went." Sarah gave Tyler as secretive and triumphant a grin as she could muster before relaying the earlier events of the afternoon.

"Way to go, Sarah!" Tyler could not express how relieved he was that she would be sequestered away on Nicholas's estate for the next week. He told her now that the reason he had missed seeing her drive in after the interview was because he had been on the phone to his editor in New York. "I have to go back to the city in a few days and at least I'll know you'll be safe up there." His mind flashed on the wild party he had attended on Saturday night. "Hanging out with a couple of kids, I mean."

"But I'm supposed to be there tonight."

"Oh." He squeezed her hand, the immediacy of their situation sinking in. One night together and they were off in their separate directions again, the desire increased rather than satisfied. "How's your face?"

"Cold. It feels okay. I don't think it'll bruise much. They didn't really punch me, just slapped me hard. How does it look?"

"Red. A little streaky." He stroked her temples, his own fingers trembling a little.

Sarah sat up suddenly. "You won't stay here alone after I leave, will you?"

"I'll be all right. I can take care of myself."

"Tyler, he had a gun. G–U–N, gun." When he did not respond, she went on. "Look, I won't sleep a wink if I know you're here."

"Then you can call me in the middle of the night and tell me how much you love me." Tyler stood up and sat on the porch railing facing her. "Now let's talk about what you should be looking for at Nicholas's house. And how you're going to sneak me in while he's at work."

After Sarah was gone that evening, Tyler decided it was time to do some constructive investigating. From beneath the bed, he retrieved the piece of paper on which he had jotted Andrea's new phone number. He stretched out on the bed and watched a couple of flies mating on the windowsill as he tried to figure out his approach with Andrea. The old cousin angle might not be the best way to go about it. Friends might be more likely to conceal information about their unlawful activities from family members than from other friends.

In the end, he decided to just play it straight.

"Is Andrea there?"

"This is Andrea. Who's calling?"

"My name is Tyler Mackenzie and I'm trying to find an old friend of yours, Suzanne Laveaux? Or maybe you know her as Suzanne Emerson?"

"What do you want with Suzanne?" Andrea's voice had become instantly guarded.

"Well, first of all, I wondered if you'd seen her. She disappeared a few weeks ago and no one seems to know where she is."

"Who are you? How do you know Suzanne?" Andrea was taking no chances.

"Well, this is going to sound dumb, but I'm a friend of a really old friend of hers, Woody Foster, and he's dying of cancer—" Tyler didn't mind stretching the truth a little for the cause – "and I'm trying to locate Suzanne for him. Did she ever mention him to you?"

"Look, I'm sorry. The name doesn't ring any bells for me."

"She met him in Mexico in the 60's and they fell in love. Did she ever tell you about that?"

The silence on the other end was so complete that for a moment he thought she'd hung up.

"No, she did not," Andrea replied finally. "What do you know about me?"

"Not a thing. I got your phone number off of her message machine and I thought maybe you could help me out."

"Well, I wish I could but I don't see how I can. Now you have me worried. How long as she been gone?"

78

"About three weeks. What I was hoping is that maybe you could fill me in on her past. We think she must be running from something or someone and if we can figure out what it is, we might be able to find her."

There was another dead pause. "I don't know how much I can tell you or how much Suzanne would want me to tell you."

Unconsciously, Tyler straightened up, his pencil poised on an empty page of his notebook. "Let's start with how you know her. Where did you meet?"

Andrea let out a long sigh. "We met in prison, all right? But don't expect any details."

"What was she in for?"

"That's the part I'm not telling you. Suzanne has a right to privacy and I'm not about to violate it."

"What prison were you in?

"You think I'm stupid enough to tell you that if I don't want to violate Suzanne's privacy? If you knew where we were, you'd easily be able to find out what we did."

Tyler cursed himself for not separating the last two questions so that she wouldn't have made the connection.

"So when did she get released?"

"Oh, I'd say nine or ten years ago. Then she moved to Vermont where she's been ever since. Where are you calling from?"

"Vermont. When was the last time you saw her?"

"Not for several years now. She came by to see me a couple of times while I was still inside, but after I got out we kind of went our own separate ways."

"So what about before you met her? Did she ever talk much about her past?"

"Oh, some. I guess before she put on the extra weight she was something to look at. Told me how she used to model for an art student – what was his name..."

"Nicholas?"

79

"Yeah, that was it. Same guy she works for now, right? And about being a topless dancer in San Francisco. She really let men exploit her for her body."

Tyler's imagination seemed stuck on the thought of the young Suzanne as a topless dancer in San Francisco, but he pressed forward. "What about Mexico? Did she ever talk about what happened there?"

"Never. I didn't even know she'd been there."

"How about a guy named Luther Dross? Did she ever mention him?"

Andrea chuckled disgustedly. "Luther, yeah. I heard about Luther. Someone she hoped never to see again, from what I understood."

"Really? But didn't he loan her money for school?"

"Money for school? Where'd you ever get that idea? As far as I know, Suzanne never went to college. Well, I guess she took a few courses while we were doing time but those didn't cost anything."

"Then why do you think she's sending him a check every month to pay back a school loan?" Tyler quickly outlined what he had discovered in Suzanne's canceled checks and about the phone call from Luther.

"That son of a bitch. Don't you get it? It's extortion. He must be blackmailing her. She must really be scared if he can keep upping the amount like that. Shit. That pisses me off."

Andrea was on his side now without question.

"So how does she know Luther?"

"All I can tell you is they were in some kind of underground movement together in the late 60s."

"All you WILL tell me or all you want to tell me?"

"I don't know much about it. It was not a happy time in her life and Suzanne didn't like to talk about the bad times. I do know Luther was the one who got her into that topless dancing gig. He wouldn't be blackmailing her about that, would he? Maybe he's got pictures he's threatening to expose or something." At least Andrea's mind was working in the right direction now.

"I sort of doubt it. Nicholas, her old friend and current boss, has all kinds of pictures of her displayed in his house here and Suzanne doesn't seem to mind."

"He does? You mean, like porno?"

No, I wouldn't call them porno. I mean, she's naked but... No, they're definitely not pornography."

"Yeah, well, maybe Luther has some that are. That bastard."

"Any idea where Luther might live now? Did he ever try to contact Suzanne while she was in jail?"

"Oh, all the time, but she never answered his letters."

"Do you remember where he wrote from?"

Andrea's laughter bordered on cackling. "Leavenworth, I think it was."

"He was in prison too?"

"And don't ask me what for."

"Look, his checks are all cashed by a bank in Illinois. Does that ring any bells for you?"

"Yeah, that's where Chicago is, right? I think Suzanne mentioned they did hole up in Chicago for a while right before they got busted."

So they had been into something illegal together. The blackmailing possibilities seemed endless to Tyler now. As well as a very definite reason why Suzanne might have disappeared. But what did Luther have to do with this Mexican guy who was looking for Suzanne?

Tyler thanked Andrea for all her help and assured her that everything she had told him would remain confidential. He also asked that if she remembered anything else or changed her mind about what she considered Suzanne's privacy, to please call him right away, day or night.

"So what does this guy Woody want with Suzanne after all these years?" she asked him right before

81

hanging up. "Because if he thinks she's coming back to him, he's probably in for a big surprise."

As usual she did not elaborate and Tyler spent the rest of the night wondering what she could have meant.

CHAPTER SIX

The job was not as bad as Sarah had expected; in fact, it wasn't bad at all. It was the closest thing to a paid vacation that she'd had in years. Once she realized that Nicholas's kids were old enough to be spoken to like adults, and that there really was no level she had to come down to, everything was fine.

Together they played Monopoly, they played Risk, they played poker. They all swam in the pool, or Shannon and Nathaniel swam and Sarah snoozed in the sun. The kids played video games and Sarah read. There was a woman who came in and cleaned every day so she didn't even have to worry about that. One afternoon she piled them in her car and drove up to visit Woody in the hospital. Woody was doing okay, but he was not excited about having to start chemotherapy.

Little lies came easier and easier to Sarah. After the experience of the first few days was behind her, she called Tyler. During that time he had been frantically trying to finish up an article about the bands who had played at Woodstock and where they were today. He'd done his research before coming to Vermont but had procrastinated on the writing. Now it was due in New York on Friday.

"So what have you found out?" he asked eagerly.

"Not much. I did get him to talk about her last night but he either doesn't know or is not admitting much about where she might be. How about you?"

"Not much. Luther Dross called again last night. This time his message was basically 'Pay up or I tell all.' I wanted to pick up the phone and say 'I'll pay up – just tell me all.' I think this guy may be our keystone. If I can figure out where he lives, a trip to Chicago might be in order."

"Really?"

"Well, I don't know what else to do. Do you think I can come up there today and poke around?"

"Oh, I think we can arrange a trade of some sort." Sarah grinned. "We're going out to rent some videos soon. Once I plug the kids into the TV, the coast should be clear for a while."

By noon "Raiders of the Lost Ark" had them captivated in the living room. Sarah waited outside the gate for Tyler and then slipped him in the side door near the hot tub.

The smell of chlorinated water made Tyler's head spin for a moment as he tried in vain to recall once more how Saturday evening had ended.

"What's the matter?"

"Nothing. Did he offer you any coke last night?"

"You mean, coke like cocaine coke? For Chrissake, I'm his babysitter, Tyler."

"Just asking. Where's his bedroom?"

"Don't you mean, where's my bedroom? Let's do my part of this deal first." Sarah led him upstairs and down another hall.

Tyler laughed quietly as they entered Sarah's room. When it came to sex, once you got Sarah started, she was like a bear with honey. She just never seemed to get enough. Although it hurt his masculine pride to admit that she could outscrew him any day, it was the truth and he loved every minute of it.

"We're not staying up here all afternoon," he warned her as he unbuttoned his shirt. "I've got work to do."

"You sure do," she laughed as she pulled him down on the bed.

Forty–five minutes later, he had his shorts and shirt back on and was tiptoeing across the hall to the master bedroom. Sarah had slipped into her bathing suit and then headed downstairs to make sure the children were busy. "You've only got an hour," she hissed at him. "Then I want you to come in the front door and meet the kids so they know you are my boyfriend and may show up again."

Nicholas's bedroom was ultra–modern and smelled new, like a furniture salesroom. His headboard was chrome and glass and matched the nightstands and bedside lamps. The bed had black and white print sheets and several large throw pillows that matched the deep garnet red of the thick, wall–to–wall carpeting. There was nothing female about the interior design, unless you counted the drawer he found in the wardrobe that was full of crotchless underpants, garter belts and peekaboo teddies. They were too small to fit Nicholas so it was unlikely he was a cross–dresser. Tyler realized that after his previous encounter with the man, there was nothing he would put past him.

The mirrored wardrobe extended across one entire wall and seemed much too large for a single man. Half of it was empty, reminding Tyler that Nicholas had been married once, which probably accounted for the amount of extra closet space.

One of the nightstand drawers was full of drug paraphernalia, but this did not tell Tyler anything he didn't know. He thought the hand gun he found was a bit excessive for a small town in Vermont, but everything about Nicholas was a bit excessive.

He was not sure what he was looking for – something that implicated Nicholas in Suzanne's disappearance, a clue to where she might be. Instead he found himself staring at a round chrome and glass pedestal on which stood a sculpture of two naked bodies, a man entwined around a woman from behind so that the voluptuous curves of the woman's body were displayed to full advantage. He knew instinctively that it was Suzanne, once upon a time and long ago, as was the painting on the wall above the bed. It depicted a young woman from the waist up, her large breasts thrusting outward, her face expressing the throes of passion, her red hair flying wildly across the canvas. Nicholas's bedroom seemed to defy the visitor to find any indication that he might have ever shared the room with a wife.

He needed to find a desk – there had to be an office in the house somewhere. A place where credit card receipts and telephone bills were kept. Creeping down the stairs he found what he was looking for to the left of the kitchen. Judging from the disorderly heap of magazines on the chair and the unfiled papers strewn across the desk, it was not a room that appeared to be used very often. But it didn't take Tyler long to find the pile of current, unpaid bills beneath an amethyst geode used as a paperweight.

Last month's telephone bill was close to the surface. He copied down any suspicious numbers and locations. The most interesting were a couple of collect calls, one early in the morning from Houston and one later that same evening from Burlington. There were a couple of international calls to Charlestown, Nevis, a place he had never heard of before.

An American Express statement yielded some interesting facts as well. On the same day that Suzanne supposedly disappeared, Nicholas had used his credit card at a local bank for a large cash advance. There was also a charge a few days earlier from American Airlines, probably a couple of airline tickets. There was a charge from the Waldorf–Astoria for a two night stay and from some well–known New York City restaurants. The rest seemed fairly mundane; mail order catalogs, car repairs, and a number of charges to the Emporia Florist Shop.

A loud hiss from the doorway made the sweat break out on his brow. "What the hell do you think you're doing? The movie is almost over!"

"I'm sorry!" Tyler replaced the bills and slipped out of the door behind Sarah.

"Just get to the front door quickly and knock like you just got here." Sarah pushed him in the right direction and then stood in the hallway where she could keep one eye on the kids in the living room and still see the front door.

Tyler gave her a mischievous grin and then, without even going outside, knocked on the inside of the door.

"Wha– I'll get it!" Sarah called dashing to open the door.

Nathaniel was behind her in a matter of seconds. "Who is it?"

"Oh, Nathaniel, this is my boyfriend, Ty——uh,ger. Tiger." The warning look in Tyler's eyes had barely stopped her.

"Tiger? What kinda name is that?" Nathaniel eyed him suspiciously.

"You know, Tiger, like Tony the Tiger? Tony's my real name, Tiger's just my nickname. Sarah likes to call me that." Tyler made a big show of kissing Sarah on the lips. "How are you, sweetie? How's it going for you here?"

"It's illegal to drive without shoes, you know."

"What?" Tyler followed Nathaniel's gaze to his own bare feet. He'd left his shoes upstairs in Sarah's room. "Oh, I just left them in the car. So I wouldn't forget them. Sarah told me there's a really nice pool here. I thought I might get invited to go swimming."

"Sure. I'll invite you."

Sarah shook her head in amazement at how easily Tyler always managed to break the ice with strangers. While he horsed around in the pool with the children, she retrieved his shoes and deposited them in his car. It was too bad that he had already played his own charade with Nicholas. It would have been fun if he could have hung out here openly with her.

Later that evening, with a snifter of cognac and his AT & T calling card, Tyler tried to make sense of the puzzle pieces he had brought home. The phone numbers in Houston and Burlington both turned out to be airport phone booths. Probably somebody calling from Houston to say they would arrive in Burlington that evening and then calling to be picked up at the airport. Most likely it was not Suzanne, as this person would have been coming to Vermont rather than leaving.

Tyler was surprised to learn that Nevis was a small island in the Caribbean, a sister island to St. Kitts. He was not a geography wizard, but he was fairly well traveled and yet he had never heard of Nevis before. His calls there yielded information far more interesting than the airport phone booths had.

"Poinsettia Plantation. Can I help you?" A rich voice with a melodious Caribbean accent answered the phone.

"Yes. I was wondering if you can tell me if you have a guest by the name of Suzanne Laveaux."

"One moment, please." There was a long pause and Tyler thought about the international message units being charged to his phone bill as the minutes ticked by.

"Thank you for holding, sir. We have no one by that name registered here at the hotel."

"How about Suzanne Emerson?"

"No, we have no guests with the last name of Emerson either."

"Do you have any reservations under the name of Nicholas Newfield then?"

Tyler was surprised to hear an amused snort come across the line. "Mr. Newfield? Now why would he make a reservation at his own hotel, mon? Maybe it is time I ask what your name is."

"John Sebastian." The name of the popular 60s musician sprang out of his Woodstock story notes and onto his lips. Tyler's fast–acting brain was still trying to digest the fact that Nicholas owned a hotel in the Caribbean. "I'm a business associate of Nick's. I'm supposed to meet with him down there sometime this fall but I've forgotten the dates he said he'd reserved for me. When do you expect him again?"

"Mr. Newfield is expected here a week from next Monday. Would you like me to reserve a room for you, Mr. Sebastian?"

"I'll have my secretary get back to you about that. Uh, speaking of secretaries, does Nick usually bring his with him?"

"Bring his secretary with him to the Plantation? He does not usually bring his stateside work to Nevis, Mr. Sebastian. When he is here, he relaxes and tends to the business of the inn."

"I see. Well, when you talk to him, give him my regards and tell him I'll be seeing him soon."

He cut the connection, but kept his finger on the button. That had been an enlightening call but he was no closer to finding Suzanne. On a long shot, he dialed another number.

"Information. What city please?"

"Chicago. The number for a Luther Dross."

"Do you have a street address?"

"I think it's Lakeshore Drive." The tony neighborhood along Lake Michigan was the only Chicago address Tyler could think of.

"No, I'm sorry. The only Luther Dross I have is on Clinton."

"I'll take that number."

What now? He stared at the phone number in front of him, trying to figure out what to say.

"Is Sarah there? Tell her Tiger is on the phone."

"Tiger? What's up?"

"Sarah, I'm going to have to drive back to the city tomorrow."

"You are? Shit. When are you coming back?"

"I'm not sure. Listen, I just talked to Luther Dross. I'm flying out to Chicago on Sunday to interview him."

"You're kidding. How'd you ever manage that?"

Tyler grinned. "I told him I was doing an article for Mother Jones magazine on underground leaders of the sixties and how they stood on the issues now."

"You stroked his ego and he fell for it?"

"I also told him I'd pay him. Will you be all right on your own for a while?"

"Tyl– I've been on my own for the last six months. What do you think?"

He did not bring up the two men who had abducted her. "I'll call you tomorrow night."

"I'm going up to see Woody tomorrow night." He could hear her defense mechanisms grinding into place.

"Then I'll call you on Friday morning. I'll be back up here as soon as I can. When I come back, we'll look for an apartment or something to rent in Emporia so we can hang out together, okay?"

"Okay. But how long are we going to keep this up? I mean, what if we never come up with any answers?"

"As long as it takes. We'll find her, I know we will. Oh, and I thought you might want to know that Nicholas is supposedly leaving for Nevis Monday after next."

"What's Nevis?"

"It's an island in the Caribbean where he owns a hotel. See if you can get him to talk about it. It might lead to something."

Later that night, after the children had gone to bed, Sarah tried to figure out a way to bring up the subject of Nevis. She was curled up in a corner of one of the long sofas in Nicholas's living room, sipping a drink, listening to him ramble on about the trouble he was having importing some sweaters knit from the wool of rare New Zealand sheep.

"So I guess you travel a lot looking for new items for your catalog." She managed to squeeze in her lead when he stopped for breath.

"Some. Most of the people come to me. There are a few places I return to every year, you know, Scotland, Ireland, Peru..."

"Do you ever get to the Caribbean?"

Nicholas laughed. "Quite a bit actually. I own a hotel down there on a beautiful little island called Nevis. Bought an old sugar plantation on the side of an extinct volcano and fixed it up into a high class resort. Suzanne helped me get it organized; I probably couldn't have done it without her. That's where I retreat to when I have time to get away. Someday I'll probably retire there."

Sarah sighed. "Sounds heavenly. I've always wanted to spend some time in the Caribbean."

Nicholas scrutinized her silently and stirred the ice cubes in his glass. Sarah wondered if she sounded phony. Maybe he just thought she was fishing for an invitation. Probably people did that to him all the time.

Any chance that Suzanne—" Sarah stopped as Nicholas shook his head.

"No, I called down there right after she disappeared. The staff said they hadn't seen her." Nicholas dismissed the subject abruptly. "When I was kissing Shannon good night she told me she thought your boyfriend was `real cute'."

Sarah blushed. "He's so good–looking it's almost sickening. Sometimes he doesn't look real."

He laughed. "Then you must be quite a pair. When do I get to meet this guy?"

"He called earlier and told me he had to go out of town for the next week, so I don't know." Shit, she thought desperately. Now he's going to ask me what Tyler does for a living and why he travels. She changed the subject again as quickly as he had. "So judging from this room, you used to be quite the artiste. Doesn't it bother you that your kids are looking at pictures like those?" She waved a hand at the erotic photographs of Suzanne. She reminded herself that she was not

91

supposed to know they were Suzanne. Tyler had told her about them, not Nicholas. "And I mean, they really look at them."

Nicholas laughed again. "They've seen those pictures all their lives. It would seem pretty senseless to take them down now. Those photographs aren't going to hurt them – after all, they're 'ahhhrt'." He stood up and walked over to one of the photographs and stared at it pensively. "I just hope they never realize that Aunt Suzanne is the one who modeled for these."

"Suzanne modeled for those? Is that right? You two must go back a long way."

"All the way."

"So your relationship was pretty intimate back then."

"Very. Never matched it again. So far that is." He snapped out of his reverie and winked lasciviously at Sarah. "And believe me, I've never stopped trying."

"Would you mind very much telling me about how you ever met her?"

Nicholas sat down on the couch and put his hands behind his head. "Actually I'd probably enjoy it. It's something I haven't thought about in a long time. But I hope explicit sexuality doesn't disturb you." Closing his eyes, he began, "The first time I saw Suzanne she was rummaging in the refrigerator for a midnight snack, although it was probably more like 2 a.m. All she was wearing was a big white T–shirt...."

"My God, who are you? Do you live here now?"

Suzanne straightened up and looked behind her. A broad shouldered man and a petite blonde woman were staring at her. His brown hair was as long as hers was short. They both wore heavy backpacks and clothes that looked none too clean.

"Helen, look at her. What a perfect model she'll make for that Venus I want to do. Tell me that you live here and that you'll model for my sculpture."

"Nicholas, we're not even home two minutes and you're already making an asshole of yourself. Give me the key to the room. I've been up for thirty–six hours and I'm going to bed."

"Helen and I are a little sick of each other," Nicholas confided as he slipped his backpack off, sat down on a kitchen chair, and continued to gaze at a stupefied Suzanne. "We've been traveling in Europe together all summer and the holes in our relationship are almost too big to patch up. Shit, has anyone ever told you how extraordinarily beautiful you are? Of course they have, all the time, I'm sure. If I wasn't so wiped out I'd like to take you up to my studio right now and start working. You don't mind modeling in the nude, do you? You don't have to worry. I won't try to sleep with you. I always keep a professional relationship with all my models and I pay them very well."

Suddenly he leaped to his feet. "I'm sorry. I'm just babbling away here and I haven't even introduced myself or asked your name. If I sound like I'm on speed, it's because I am. It's the only way I could stay awake on the drive from Chicago." He held out his hand. "I'm Nicholas Newfield. And you are...?"

Their working relationship began two days later, when Nicholas finally got over his jet lag and got out of bed. He led Suzanne up to the fourth floor of the building, which was a renovated attic that he rented as his studio. His relaxed and friendly manner put her completely at ease and when the time came, she had no inhibitions about her taking her clothes off in front of him. Although he continually voiced his admiration for her body, he was true to his word and never laid an unprofessional hand on her. There was lots of time to talk while she stood motionless for him in a variety of poses. She said he made her laugh in a way she had forgotten.

He used her as a model for all his classes, for drawing and photography as well as sculpture. Much of the time as she sat or lay perfectly still, he would keep up a running monologue. Sometimes he would describe in graphic detail how he would someday make love to her body. "You probably wonder why I don't jump you now. It's not just Helen. Helen's nearly out of the picture anyway. It's just that the anticipation can be nearly as erotic as the act. Holding off that climatic moment can make it that much more exciting when it happens."

The same words might have sounded perverse coming from another man's lips, but he assured her there was not a trace of harmful intent in his gentle body. They began to find the prospect of a full–blown relationship very exciting except for the damper Helen put on things.

Helen resented all the attention Nicholas paid to Suzanne and made no attempt to disguise it. Suzanne's name cropped up frequently in the nightly arguments Helen had with Nicholas. He knew Suzanne did not understand the responsibility he felt towards Helen. Nicholas himself was beginning to wonder why they stayed together.

Finally one night, things came to a head. Helen was at a night class and Nicholas and Suzanne had just finished a pizza and were sitting on the couch in the living room watching TV. Nicholas had lit up a joint but Suzanne had declined.

"Oh, come on. Loosen up. It'll help you relax. It'll put you in the same head space as me. We can have more fun."

Eventually his friendly persuasion was too much and she laughingly agreed. Soon she seemed very sleepy – she had been up since before dawn for her job as breakfast waitress at a diner.

"Here, lean back on me like this. That way we can both stretch out." Nicholas positioned her between his legs and leaned her back against his chest. The top of her head rested just beneath his chin and he buried his nose in her hair. "Mmmm...I could get used to this. Very cozy."

Suzanne closed her eyes and murmured her agreement as she drifted off to sleep.

His sense of eroticism always working overtime, Nicholas could not resist the temptation that was sleeping in his lap. He slipped a couple of ice cubes out of a glass of coke resting on the floor by the sofa. With an ice cube in each hand, he slid his fingers inside the oversized button–down shirt Suzanne had put on at the end of their afternoon session. With a motion sure to arouse, he rubbed the ice cubes on Suzanne's bare nipples. Suzanne gasped, her body tensed up and her eyelids fluttered open for a second. Then with a sigh of pleasure, she relaxed and gave herself up to the sensation. Cold water ran down her breasts and soaked through the shirt, making dark spots on the couch cushions. Nicholas unbuttoned her shirt and reached for more ice. He knew Suzanne could feel his penis hard against her back.

"So what's going on, guys? Another sexual experiment for the sake of art, Nicholas?"

At the sound of Helen's voice, Suzanne sat up guiltily and closed the wet shirt across her chest, an action that only intensified the sexual implications of the situation.

"Relax, Helen. Come sit down over here and take off your shirt and I'll do it you too." Nicholas patted the wet cushion in the center of the couch in a reckless sort of way.

"Go fuck yourself, Newfield. I don't care what you do now. I've had enough of you and your uncontrollable 'controlled sexuality'! I'm moving out. Now."

Helen stormed into their bedroom and Nicholas made no move to stop her.

"I guess we're in trouble now." Suzanne stood up. "I better go to bed."

Nicholas rose and pulled her soaking chest against his own, kissing her deeply and passionately. "I'll see you tomorrow. Don't forget we're driving out to that abandoned farm to take some photographs."

By five o'clock the next afternoon, they lay exhausted and content on a quilt in the middle of a meadow. After two hours of Nicholas's erotic photo direction, neither of them could hold back any longer. For the next three hours they had made love furiously and non–stop, giving and taking in inventive ways that Suzanne had never dreamed of.

Nicholas stood up, ending his story abruptly. "And that's how these photographs came into existence. Enough dwelling on the past. Any other questions?"

Taken in by his storytelling, Sarah was surprised that he would stop so suddenly. "So it's pretty odd that she would just up and leave without letting you know, isn't it?"

"Back then or now? That's how she did it twenty years ago. You think you know a person so well and then, bingo. You find out you never knew them at all. There's a whole bunch of Suzanne's life she's never talked about. Still. But you wouldn't recognize her today from these pictures. She's plump and middle–aged with short hair and flabby thighs. Breasts that size don't last forever either." He turned away from the wall suddenly. "Now I don't want to talk about Suzanne anymore. She's gone and I'm giving you her job on Monday."

Sarah found it suspicious how he didn't want to talk about Suzanne, but couldn't stop once he got started. "Monday is Labor Day," was the only neutral thing she could think of to say.

"Tuesday then. And you're welcome to stay on living here after the kids leave until you find a nice place of your own."

"Well, thank you, you're very generous."

He waved the compliment away. "No, I'm not. I enjoy your company. I just hope you realize this homey lifestyle isn't the way I normally live. As long you don't judge my vices, you can stay as long as you want."

Much as she would have liked to leave the whole scene in Emporia behind, she had a feeling that a lot more could be learned from Nicholas when he let his parenting mask drop again.

"Excuse me a second." Nicholas went into the kitchen to answer the telephone. Sarah looked at her watch. It was nearly 11:30, a late hour for anybody to be calling. She got up and pretended to study a small pen and ink drawing, obviously of Suzanne again, which was closer to the kitchen door.

"I told you that this week was out...Then meet me at the office tomorrow...Look, I think I'm going to have to stop doing business with you. It's just not working out for me...Yes, of course. It was excellent...All right. Come by in an hour...No, not up to the house. I'll meet you at the end of the driveway. But this is it, understand. After this we are finito, comprende?"

His Spanish sign–off sent a chill down Sarah's spine. It reminded her too much of having her shirt ripped open by rough hands and an ugly voice saying she was not Suzanne. It had to be more than a coincidence and the thought made her stomach churn.

"Rather late for a call, isn't it?" she chirped brightly when he returned.

"Oh, we're heading towards the weekend when this is usually a round–the–clock kind of place. Another drink?"

"No, I'm tired. I think I'll head for bed."

She made a big show of running the water in the bathroom and opening and shutting drawers. She even came downstairs in her bathrobe for a glass of water. Fifteen minutes later, she lay fully dressed beneath the covers in the dark, waiting to hear the click of the front door. She hated this spying business, but reminded herself that she was doing it for the two people who meant the most to her in the world.

She tried to keep remembering this fact as she stumbled down the driveway trying to follow Nicholas. The crunch of her feet on gravel sounded deafening in the still of the night. She quickly moved to the grass where she could trail him with a silent swish that did not overwhelm the sounds of the crickets and peeping frogs coming from the meadow above.

The headlights of a car turning into the drive made her dive for the underbrush before they were abruptly cut off. Luckily the engine was left running and its rumble covered her ouches as she disentangled raspberry branches from her hair. Unfortunately, it also made it nearly impossible for her to hear any of the conversation going on.

But when the interior light was switched on for a minute, she got a good view of the driver. Although she'd never had more than a blurred glimpse of him, she was sure it was the same Fred or Rico who had slapped her again and again in his frustrated struggle to find Suzanne.

Confused and terrified, she dashed through the darkness to the security of the warmly lit house. But she did not feel safe until she had locked the door to her bedroom and secured the latch on the window. Stripping off her damp clothes, she wrapped herself in her bathrobe and a blanket to stop the shivering. But it was not the cool Vermont night air that had set her teeth chattering. She knew now that she would have to stick this out until she got to the bottom of the connection between Nicholas and that sinister man.

During the next few days and over the Labor Day weekend, it was hard for Sarah to recall the fear she had experienced that night. They were a relaxed, comfortable family group and Sarah enjoyed watching Nicholas spend some "quality time" with his children, who seemed to dote on him when given the chance. There was no doubt that – whether it be playing hide and seek or snorting coke with naked women in a hot tub – this was a guy who liked to have fun.

Although she did her best to follow Tyler's instructions to get as chummy with Nicholas as possible without going to bed with him, she still felt empty-handed by the end of the weekend. By the time Shannon and Nathaniel had left tearfully with their mother, they had grown inordinately fond of their nanny and suggested loudly more than once that they wished their father would marry Sarah so that she would stay.

"Definitely not in the picture," she assured them laughing. "Don't forget I've got Tony the Tiger."

But the truth was that, the closer she got to Nicholas, the more she liked and trusted him. And the more puzzled she became over what the link was between him and Rico and Suzanne. Maybe he had hired Rico to find Suzanne for him and had decided to call the search off that night. As she carefully dressed for her first day of work in his office, she assured herself that had to be the answer. She had new worries to face in the next few hours like playing the charade of an experienced executive secretary.

Instinct told her that, because of her easy–going relationship with Nicholas and the familiar way he introduced her, everyone in the office immediately assumed they were lovers. This rumor became even more solid when the word got around that she was staying at his house. The women who answered the telephone and keypunched mail orders were friendly enough, but kept their distance with typical Yankee suspicion. Much as she wanted to end the nasty gossip, she felt it probably worked to her advantage. She couldn't afford to get too friendly with anybody at Newfield's – the truth might slip out unintentionally.

Nicholas was so disorganized that it was easy being his secretary. There was always something obvious that needed doing. The stereotypical dictation and typing she had expected were the least of her worries. Covering Nicholas's ass seemed to be her primary responsibility. He was never on time for appointments and admitted that he frequently stretched his business lunches far into the afternoon. Suzanne's business relationship with Nicholas had rested some place between angel and mother and Sarah was not sure how long her temperament could stand that part of the job.

But before she even had time to settle into a regular routine, the break she and Tyler had so eagerly awaited fell conveniently into her lap one morning.

"My God, Sarah, look at this." Nicholas was waving a calendar at her, which had recently come to the surface in their combined clean–up of his desk. "I forgot to tell you I'm going on vacation next week. Down to my hotel on Nevis."

"Really? For how long?"

"Two weeks. Suzanne and I were going to fly down together. She made all the arrangements with the airline. I don't even know what flight I'm supposed to be on. Damn." He grinned ruefully. "Would you mind...?"

"What travel agent do you use?"

"None. She usually booked directly with the airline and we would pick up the tickets at the airport. Call American. They fly into St. Kitts."

She had found the number and was dialing the phone when he pushed the button down on the receiver. She looked up questioningly.

"Do you want to come?"

She stared at him blankly.

"To Nevis. In Suzanne's place. I've already paid for her ticket. You can see the Caribbean the way you always dreamed."

Sarah's head spun with the sudden decision. Did this make sense? Should she follow Nicholas or stay behind and see what turned up? For now she had to say what he expected.

"Sure! I'd love to come! But what will people think – one week on the job and then two weeks paid vacation?" She knew exactly what they would think, the same thing that they did now.

"Do you care? I certainly don't. Okay, well, that's settled then. Have them change the name on her ticket to yours. Okay?" He looked at his watch. "I've got to go meet with the warehouse manager. I'll be back in about an hour."

Sarah was overcome with a sense of guilt as she placed the call again. Would she be shirking her duty to Woody by running off to the Caribbean? She knew that Woody would tell her to go for it – it was Tyler who would guilt trip her about it.

The hell with him. Life was too short.

"American Airlines reservations. Can I help you?"

"Yes, I'd like to confirm two reservations for Monday the 11th to St. Kitts from – shoot. I forgot to ask him what airport we were flying from."

"Well, maybe I can help you anyway." Sarah was relieved that the operator did not have the usual bored, disinterested voice, she sounded young and eager to please. "What day are you flying back from St. Kitts? There are only a few flights a day so maybe we can work this in reverse and find your reservations that way."

Sarah scanned the calendar frantically. "It looks like Sunday the 24th."

"And the names?"

"Nicholas Newfield and Suzanne Laveaux."

She could hear computer keys clicking and then a triumphant, "Aha! Here it is. Let's see...you are flying back to JFK and then on to Burlington, Vermont. Does that sound right?"

"Yes, that's it. So we must be leaving from there also."

"This is odd...Hold on a second, please. I'm only showing a reservation for Mr. Newfield on the 11th, although I am showing a reservation for both of you on the way back. Let me just check on something here...Yes, it seems the first portion of your ticket has been used, Miss Laveaux. On August 16th."

"It has?" Sarah spoke slowly, trying to comprehend the obvious. "I'm not Miss Laveaux, by the way. I guess she is already there. In that case–" she changed her voice to a more authoritarian tone– "Would you book another ticket please? Under the name of Sarah Scupper. Charge it to the same credit card held by Mr. Newfield." She had a hard time keeping the excitement out of her voice. "And does this flight leave JFK every day? I have another friend who needs to join us also."

Sarah waited impatiently for the beep on Tyler's answering machine. "Tyler, it's me. I haven't heard from you since you left for Chicago but I hope you're calling in for your messages. Listen carefully. Suzanne flew to St. Kitts the day after she disappeared. She may have gone to Nevis where Nicholas's hotel is. She knows Nicholas is expected there on Monday so she will probably disappear by then. Get yourself down there as soon as possible – American flies from JFK every day. I'll be there on Monday with Nicholas. And I hope you remember the name of his hotel because I haven't got a clue. Call me tonight. I..." The machine clicked off to a dial tone. "–miss you, damn it."

She hung up and then quickly dialed the number of the Jordan Regional Hospital.

CHAPTER SEVEN

CHICAGO, ILLINOIS – SEPTEMBER 3, 1989

Tyler was not all that surprised by the shabby tenement that Luther Dross lived in. On the plane ride to Chicago, he had pictured all the former 60s radicals he could think of and what they were doing now; Jane Fonda, Tom Hayden, Abbie Hoffman (he was dead, wasn't he?), Bobby Seale, Eldridge Cleaver, Charles Manson (well, that was stretching it). He remembered a friend of his older brother who had organized a demonstration against the Vietnam War back in high school. He worked on Wall Street now.

But apparently Luther Dross had never had the means to embrace middle class values as he aged. The building he lived in was as close to being condemned as any inhabited building could be. It was nearly impossible to compare Suzanne's pristine country cottage with this filthy, broken–down apartment house.

Tyler pressed the button marked *#3 Dross* in the entry way.

"Who's there?"

"Tyler Mackenzie from Mother Jones."

From his third floor apartment, Luther buzzed him in. Tyler quickly ascended the two flights of urine–stained stairs, trying not to breathe. The rats he expected to see scurrying around did not show their whiskered faces. Luther was waiting in the doorway for him.

"Pretty gross, isn't it? Keeps me humble." Luther did not extend a hand or introduce himself, but motioned Tyler quickly inside. Even Tyler, a veteran Manhattan–ite, was impressed by the number of locks and deadbolts that Luther reengaged on the inside of the door.

A quick glance at Luther's cluttered apartment gave the impression that the man had not changed his socks since college. Books and papers were piled high everywhere. Shelves and tables were built of cinderblocks and plywood – a tiny bedroom showed a mattress on the floor amid heaps of unwashed clothes. A large poster of Che Gueverra, the Cuban revolutionary, was tacked to the living room wall above a folded mattress that served as a couch.

"Cup of coffee?"

"Uh, sure." Tyler hastily turned back to assess Luther's own appearance as the man headed for the tiny kitchenette. He watched Luther rummage in a sink full of dirty dishes for a coffee cup which he hastily rinsed beneath a rusty faucet.

He was speed–freak thin, with long silvery hair contained in a loose ponytail. A denim workshirt and an old pair of Levis hung loosely on his tall, scarecrow frame. Battered wire–rimmed glasses perched on the long, rather pointed nose that dominated his narrow, sallow face. The wrinkles on his forehead seemed set in a perpetual frown.

Expecting instant, Tyler was pleasantly surprised by the rich taste of the coffee in the grungy mug. Obviously there were certain pleasures that Luther would not deny himself, even if he was down on his luck. "It's very good," he remarked, looking for a place to sit down.

Luther did not acknowledge the compliment or the fact that Tyler wanted a chair. He rested his elbows on the counter behind him and asked bluntly, "So how did you hear about me?"

Tyler stalled the question until he had cleared a place on the mattress/couch and set his coffee and shoulder bag on the floor. Pulling out his notebook and making sure his voice–activated tape recorder was ready inside the open bag, he settled back as comfortably as he could and replied vaguely, "Oh, your name came up in conversation. Let me put it this way, Mr. Dross—"

"Nobody calls me Mr. Dross except the parole board."

"Luther, then. This is a then–and–now article. Where you were then, where you are now."

Luther guffawed. "That's a good one, man. Nothing ever changes. It's a big circle. We're back to where we were, still fighting the same war."

Tyler blinked. "You mean the Vietnam War?"

"No, man. The war against the government. The establishment that still tries to run our lives as though we were robots of the state."

"Oh." Tyler shifted uncomfortably. "Well, let's start with back then. Why don't you tell me in your own words what people will remember you for?"

"It's not me that they should remember, man. It's the action that took place. The statement we made."

"And what was that action?"

"You know, all those draft boards we destroyed. All those young men we liberated from having to 'selectively serve' their country."

Tyler had a feeling Luther had been lost in his same 'circle' of rhetoric for years. "So who are the 'we' you keep referring to. You and who else?"

Luther laughed again and paced the length of the small kitchenette like a trapped animal. Or, Tyler reminded himself, someone had spent several years in a jail cell. "You sure you're not working for the CIA, man? I'm not about to start naming names now. That was one of the plea–bargaining tactics they tried when they finally caught up with me. I could have saved myself some years in the pen if I wanted to name names. Who are 'we?' We are the defenders of justice, the champions of freedom..."

105

For the next half hour Tyler was trapped in a web of words and phrases that Luther spun around him. The man was out there and never coming back. Too many drugs, too much running, too much prison – it was hard to pinpoint what Luther's problem was, but it was definitely too much of something. Every time he tried to get a definitive answer out of him, Luther would strike off on another philosophical tangent. He was certainly too spaced–out to have anything to do with Suzanne's disappearance. He couldn't even focus on one thought long enough to finish it. It was obvious that, no matter what Luther was blackmailing Suzanne about, he was using the money to pay his rent. There was no way this guy could hold down a job.

Finally Tyler decided to jump in feet first. "So you know who told me about you, Luther? A woman named Suzanne. Remember her?"

Luther's demeanor changed abruptly from coffeehouse prophet to bird of prey. "Suzanne? Where did you see her? I've been trying to reach her for the last month. When did you talk to her?"

"Really? She didn't mention that you two were in still in contact with one another."

"Well, we're not really. I just have something I want to talk to her about. And she owes me some money."

"You lent her some money?" Tyler made a large gesture of looking around the shabby apartment in disbelief.

"It's about something a long time ago. So what did she tell you? Hey, you're not putting her in your article, are you?"

"I might be. Why? What can you tell me about her? She was part of your 'we' back then, wasn't she?"

"She told you that?"

"And you both went to jail at the same time for the same crime – I mean, incident, right?" Tyler could see he finally had Luther on the defensive.

"I can't believe she talked to you," Luther muttered half to himself. "I can't believe she gave you my name and address. That lousy, betraying bitch. So that's what this is all about. That's why the money's stopped coming."

Luther was pacing again as he cursed Suzanne. Tyler was keeping his mouth shut, letting Luther come to his own conclusions. "After I kept her secrets all these damn years..." He stopped suddenly. With three long strides he was in front of Tyler, looking down on him. "Okay, you want a good story for your magazine, Mr. Reporter? I've got one for you."

Tyler held his breath and waited for Luther to continue.

"Okay, for starters, did she tell you about the Birds of Paradise Club where she used be a topless dancer in San Francisco?"

"Well, yes, I do know about that. Were you with her then?"

"Damn straight. I got her that job. What a set of jugs that woman had! Those honkers of hers were big enough to support us both in style while every guy in S.F. enjoyed them too. What a bunch of assholes, paying all that money to watch a broad bounce her big boobs around every night. At least I didn't have to pay to see them."

"So you were lovers."

"Yeah, I'm the dick she came home to every morning if that's what you mean."

"Where did you meet her?"

"I picked her up in Mexico where—"

Tyler jumped to his feet in astonishment. "You knew her in Mexico?"

"Yeah, what's the big deal? I was vacationing down there. That's where the cheap grass was. Hey – she didn't tell you about Mexico, did she?" Luther's long fingers gripped Tyler's arm.

"N–no. Why don't you tell me about it?" Luther's grip relaxed and Tyler sank down on the couch again and tried to appear calm. "What was she doing down there?"

"The story we were told was that she had broken up with her boyfriend and needed a ride back to the States. But as soon as we saw her, we knew who she was." Luther grinned, savoring the rapt attention of his audience.

"Who was she?" Tyler felt confused.

"A fugitive from the federales. We recognized her from a poster a guy had been circulating in a bar the night before. There was even a reward for her capture or information leading to her arrest."

Luther's eyes had glazed over as he tried to focus his jumping mind on this particular incident. "In those days we didn't even consider turning her in." The ubiquitous 'we' again. "We would have helped anybody run from the law. And besides she was one ripe tomato for the picking. She had more than enough juice for the both of us."

Forcing his thoughts off the image of "the both of us", Tyler asked, "What was she wanted for?"

Luther flicked his tongue over his dry lips. "Murder," he said dramatically. "She was wanted for murder. And still is."

Tyler sat there dumbfounded, unable to respond. Luther's face suddenly crumbled and he began pacing again, punching one fist into the palm of the other hand, spitting curses at Suzanne again.

"Who– whose murder?" Tyler managed to ask as he realized he was losing Luther again.

"I don't know. Who the fuck knows? Some Mexican. Who cares? I'm sure they still want her for it."

"Did she do it?"

"Who the fuck knows?" Luther was shouting now. "She wouldn't talk to us about it. She just trusted us. Like I trusted her. And she led you right to me..."

Behind his wire–rimmed lenses, Luther's eyes were dilating and beginning to look quite mad. "So, full circle. Bam! I'm leading them right to her." He peered at Tyler suspiciously. "I've seen you before, haven't I? Weren't you with those FBI pigs who picked us up in St. Louis?"

Tyler shoved his notebook in his bag and quickly stood up. "It was nice meeting you, Luther. Thanks for the interesting story about Suzanne. If you think of any more details, give me a call." He stopped at the door, faced with the multitude of locks. "Oh, one more thing." He talked as he turned knobs and unlocked dead bolts. "What exactly were the two of you sent to jail for?"

Luther opened his mouth as if to reply and instead began to laugh. As his laughter grew to maniacal proportions, Tyler slipped out and pulled the door shut behind him.

By the time he reached his rental car, Tyler knew what his next step had to be. He stopped at the first phone booth he saw and placed a collect call to Woody.

"Woody, I'm in a phone booth in a sketchy neighborhood in Chicago so I can't talk long. Just one quick question. What was the name of that town in Mexico where you met Suzanne and where the hell is it located?"

He ended up flying back to New York that night and leaving for Mexico in the morning. He wasn't able to change the return flight on his ticket from Chicago, he would have had to spend the night in a hotel and leave in the morning, and it turned out to be cheaper to fly round trip to Mexico City from Kennedy anyway. Besides the fact that he didn't have a change of clothes with him and wasn't dressed appropriately for a tropical climate.

It took two more plane changes after arriving in Mexico City and then a four hour drive in a rented car to reach the tiny village of Puerto Cerrito. It was nearly nine o'clock at night and by Tyler's inner clock, which was still on Eastern Standard Time, it was close to midnight. This investigative trip had made perfect sense to him on each of the successively smaller planes, but as he bounced along broken roads full of potholes at dusk, in a country where he did not speak the language, he began to question whether this journey could possibly be worth the effort.

He had convinced himself that it was the quickest way to find out who Suzanne had murdered and why. As he drove down the unlit country highway in the darkness, he had to remind himself over and over again that it still made sense. If he could find out who Suzanne was running from, and how they had suddenly gotten hot on her trail again after all these years, then it might help him locate Suzanne. Or it might convince Woody that finding Suzanne might not be all he had hoped and he would call the search off.

When he finally reached Puerto Cerrito, the dusty main street looked deserted. It hadn't changed much from Woody's description, but as he reached the edge of town he was glad to find a building that hadn't been there twenty–five years ago. Hotel de la Playa was a cinder block structure with four units upstairs and an open air snack bar downstairs. Romantic as sleeping in a hammock on the beach had sounded, a regular bed was what he really needed tonight.

The woman who showed him the room spoke as little English as he spoke Spanish, but with the help of a dictionary he had picked up at the airport they were able to communicate.

"Interpretor...interprete...es un interprete aqui? Persona habla ingles?"

"Oh, si. Un muchacha en otro partido del Puerto Cerrito."

"She can come here, aqui en la manana?"

"Oh, si, si, en la manana. Buenos noches, senor."

Totally exhausted, Tyler barely looked around the spartan room before flopping down on the bed and falling asleep.

In the early hours of daybreak he realized that the swish–swish he kept hearing was the sound of small waves breaking gently against the sand. When a chorus of roosters started up and he heard the braying of a donkey (or maybe it was burro, he never knew the difference), he decided he might as well get up.

The view from the window was breathtaking – a mile of windswept, deserted beach stretched around a cove of turquoise water. His need to be down there walking was suddenly greater than his need for a cup of coffee.

As he ambled slowly along the water's edge, he remembered Woody telling him about the shack where Suzanne had lived with her lover at the far end of the beach. Nodding greetings to the curious villagers who watched him from their dooryards or grazing fields, he was soon beyond the town limits and into a less inhabited area.

He had almost reached the end of the sand and was about to give up and turn back when he spied a rusty wire gate hanging loosely on its hinges. A narrow, overgrown path ran inland and he could just glimpse a section of tin roofing behind some trees.

Prying the gate open, he moved soundlessly over the hard packed dirt of the path. Coming into a clearing, he stopped short, unsure of himself.

There in front of him was a ramshackle cabin, sagging on its foundations with its door swinging open. It was just as Woody had described, except that now it seemed to be inhabited by chickens and tools. Behind it was a much larger house, made solidly of cement and painted a gay turquoise color. In the yard, an ageless woman was washing clothes in a metal washtub, a few dirty children playing at her feet.

111

"Mira, mama, mira!" One of them pointed at Tyler. The woman stood up suddenly, still holding a dripping pair of pants and a scrub brush.

"Buenos dias," Tyler volunteered one of his few Spanish phrases. "Habla ingles, por favor?"

Pulling one of her children close, she quickly rattled off something in a whisper and pushed the child towards the door of the house. "No hablo ingles. Mi esposo habla un poco—" she gestured toward the house behind her, "pero mi esposo es en el pueblo." She pointed back towards town.

She was telling him that someone who lived there who spoke English was in town. He wished he'd waited to bring along the interpreter the innkeeper had told him about.

"Thanks. Gracias. I'll be back." There was no point in staying. He'd go have some breakfast and return when he found someone to help him communicate. He hurried back down the path to the beach, conscious of all their eyes on him. Just before he reached the gate, he heard the sound of an engine starting up and then tearing its way out the yard.

Someone was in a big hurry to announce his visit. He wondered who and why.

His interpreter turned out to be a twelve year old girl with big round dark eyes, a long black braid and stick–like legs that showed beneath her worn, printed cotton dress. Her name was Maria and she had lived in Los Angeles with her mother for most of her childhood until she was sent home to live with her grandmother for reasons she did not disclose. The wad of pesos he offered her made her eyes shine. She was ready to start immediately.

By the time they returned to the house on the beach, the news of their arrival seemed to have preceded them. The mother of the children stood squarely in the door of the house, a couple of teenage

112

boys idled expectantly beneath a tree, a gray–haired woman sat in a lawn chair in the shade as though waiting for the show to begin.

"Ask them if this is the house where a woman named Suzanne lived back in the 60s."

Maria looked at him curiously and then repeated his question in Spanish. He was surprised at the uproar that followed. Everyone began speaking at once and the old woman shouted a string of ugly words and spit on the ground. Maria began to back away fearfully until Tyler grabbed her arm.

"What are they saying?"

"They say yes, she did live here. The grandmother is cursing her, saying she should rot in hell wherever she is."

"Ask her why."

"She says because she is a– a– bad woman." Maria was blushing from whatever word it was she couldn't say. "She also called her a murderer."

The old woman was ranting now and finally the younger one led her, crying and sobbing, into the house. The two young men took up the empty post of barring the door to the house.

"See if you can find out what that old woman's name is," Tyler urged.

"Senora Gonzalez, Juanita. The other one is her daughter–in–law, Rita. These two are her grandchildren and Rita is their aunt."

"Ask them if they know why she called Suzanne a murderer."

After a brief exchange, Maria shook her head. "They won't say. They say if you want to know, go to the police station."

"Do you know the way?"

Maria nodded and gestured for him to follow her.

The cop on duty was too young to have been around when Suzanne had been arrested. But he seemed to know something about her story. After hearing that Tyler was investigating an extradition case for the American government that had to do with Suzanne, he opened a desk drawer and pulled out a file of wrinkled and yellowed papers. Moving closer for a better look, Tyler saw that they were old "Wanted" posters. It did not take long for the cop to locate the one he was looking for.

"Esta es ella?" He held out the poster to Tyler.

It was a grainy enlargement of a young woman with long hair wearing a low cut, off the shoulder blouse that revealed quite a lot of her most identifiable features. Maria translated it for him.

"It says she is an escapee from this jail who is wanted for the murder of a Raoul Gonzalez. It says she was last seen in the Matehuala area."

"Gonzalez? Related to the old Gonzalez woman, Juanita?"

The cop nodded. "She is his widow."

"His widow?" No wonder she had freaked at the mention of Suzanne's name. "Why would Suzanne murder him?"

The cop shrugged his shoulders. "You would have to ask someone older than me. My father was in charge of this station at that time. He is retired now, but you can find him at home. He will know the details of the story."

Tyler looked around. "I'm curious how she was able to escape. Can you show me where the cells are?"

When he saw the barred door at the bottom of a dank stairwell, he shook his head. "How could she ever have gotten out of here?"

The young man shrugged again and looked away. "It happens. It can be done. Come. I will give you my father's name and address. It will make the old man feel important to tell you about it. It was the most talked about thing around town in those years."

Julio Rodriguez lived in what had to be one of the nicest houses in town. Fully landscaped, with a wraparound verandah and iron burglar bars on the windows, Julio had clearly not made his fortune on a Mexican policeman's salary.

They sat on the tiled verandah drinking cool beers and a soda for Maria. Julio stroked his white mustache as he remembered the high point of his career.

"Yes, I will always remember it. I was a good friend of Raoul's brother who was there when it happened."

"Do you have any idea why she did it?"

"She was Raoul's–" Julio looked at Maria as she translated and softened the word he had intended to use –"mistress. His lover. He was happily married to Juanita and they had several children already when Susanna came here. He kept her out at his beach shack, but everybody knew about her. One day he found out that she had been playing around behind his back. They had an argument and–" He held up his hands.

Tyler shook his head in disgust at the double standard. "She was his lover but he got mad when she had another lover."

"She was his property. He took care of her. Then this American playboy comes to town…"

"American? Did he say American?" Tyler sat up suddenly, the true implications of the story beginning to settle in.

"Yes, on a motorcycle, like Marlon Brando in 'The Wild Ones.' I have the video for my VCR."

"I– I still don't get it. He was mad at her but she killed him? She must have been provoked."

"She did not know her place, that one! Everyone talked about her, flaunting herself all over the place, wearing the bathing suit that is too small, sometimes not wearing the suit at all! A good woman does not act that way!"

"How did she do it, the actual killing?"

Julio was silent. "I don't remember. It didn't matter. Raoul was dead, leaving behind his wife and children with no means of support. The townspeople wanted to see her rot in jail and slowly suffer."

Tyler took a long slow swallow of his beer, as he absorbed all this astonishing information. "How did she escape?"

The old man shrugged in a gesture identical to that of his son. "I was not there the night it happened. When I come in the morning, they tell me she is gone."

"But how could she get out?" There was something very fishy about this part of the story.

"The guard claimed to have fallen asleep. It happens. We are a very quiet town here, especially back then. Hard to stay awake sometimes for nothing. Someone must have released her at that time and helped her to escape."

"But who would have done such a thing?"

"The American perhaps."

Fat chance, Tyler thought to himself. There are too many holes in this story.

"So why is your government investigating her?"

"What? Oh, she is wanted again for something and she seems to have disappeared. My investigation has led me here, but I'm afraid it isn't shedding much light on where she might be now. But I can't say as we'd be able to let you have her if and when we do find her."

Julio made a spitting sound. "It is a long time ago. What is past should stay past. The only ones who might care now are the Gonzalez family and a couple of Raoul's close friends. If your government punishes her well, the rest of us will be happy enough. But they have always wanted revenge."

Tyler bought Maria dinner at the hotel snack bar and gave her another handful of pesos, thanking her profusely. "There is just one more thing I need you to do. Do you mind?" She looked exhausted but still very excited by the day's events. The look on her face also indicated that by now she was struck with a bit of puppy love for Tyler and would do anything he asked.

"No, I am fine," she assured him.

"I just need to make a couple of telephone calls using my international calling card. One to my answering machine and one to set up my return flights for tomorrow."

She led him to an open telephone booth on the main street. There was only one message on his answering machine worth noting. The one from Sarah – about Suzanne flying to Nevis and about Tyler getting there as soon as possible.

Tyler slapped the side of his head in disgust. "Here I am flying all over the place trying to find her through her history and Sarah figures it out with one telephone call. Damn, I wonder if I can fly there from Mexico City?"

He wrote down the names "St. Kitts" and "Nevis" on a piece of paper and asked his twelve–year–old interpreter to see what she could do. "They say yes, you can fly there from Mexico City by changing planes in Puerto Rico. When do you want to go?"

"Tomorrow. As soon as possible. But even if I get up at dawn, with my two other plane changes, I probably won't get there before two or three. First have them figure out when my second plane gets to Mexico City – here, here's my ticket – and then take it from there."

His mind was racing with the thought of another global leap. Was there anything pressing in New York that couldn't be put off for a few more days? He didn't think so.

It seemed like a small eternity before Maria turned to him and said, "It can be done but it will take two days. You will have to spend the night in Mexico City."

"Great. Go ahead and book me."

After walking Maria home, Tyler stopped at a small taverna for another beer. He had plenty to think about and was able to easily shut out the Spanish conversation of the other men at the bar. He was surprised when one approached him with a big smile and asked in heavily accented English, "Your name?"

"Tyler Mackenzie. And yours?"

"Fernando. Usted es touristo? Tourist?"

"Si."

The man grinned some more but he seemed to have exhausted his repertoire of English. He shook Tyler's hand and said, "Hasta luego," and returned to his group of friends. The rest of them were watching Tyler intently but their expressions were not as friendly. Tyler saw Fernando repeat his name several times for them and they repeated it as if they were memorizing it.

Strange place, he thought as he quickly finished his beer. The information he had acquired here had been more than interesting, but he didn't know how much he would be able to tell Woody. Or whether it had any bearing on Suzanne's most recent disappearance.

CHAPTER EIGHT

CHARLESTOWN, NEVIS – SEPTEMBER 11, 1989

Tyler sat on a shabby kitchen chair on the second story verandah of the Sea View Guest House and watched the Monday morning ferry from St. Kitts come steaming into the Charlestown dock. He'd already been to the center of town and back to pick up coffee and a sweet roll for breakfast. As he balanced the coffee on his knee, he wished the Sea View was just a little more upscale, enough to have a rusting kitchen table on the verandah to match the chairs.

It was definitely a rundown place, but it had a certain West Indian charm, in a dumpy sort of way. His room was spacious but devoid of all furniture save the big double bed. The bed was solid with a firm foam mattress, the sheets were clean and he had a great view of the harbor without even getting up. What else mattered in the sunny Caribbean?

A real shower would be nice instead of a waist high metal pipe sticking out of the wall in the bathroom. And maybe a comfortable chair to sit in. But the price was right, which was the real reason Tyler had chosen this cheap, classic guesthouse.

When he had first stumbled off the ferry on Friday afternoon he had immediately hired a taxi to take him up to Poinsettia Plantation. Set high on the side of Mt. Nevis with a breathtaking view of the lush green island rolling down to the sea, it was everything that a world class hotel should be. With a price tag to match.

There were a handful of other beautiful inns hidden along the southern coast of Nevis, which he learned was called Gingerland. The only thing they lacked was beachfront property but he found, upon inquiring, that each hotel owned a piece of Pinney's Beach, the five mile sprawl of white sand and palm trees the ferry had passed on the way into town. But these hotels all ranged in price from $250 to $350 a night and Tyler could not bring himself to spend that kind of money when Woody was supposed to be footing the bill.

"Where do the local people from other islands stay when they come to town?" he asked his taxi driver. And that was how he had been directed to the Sea View.

When he discovered that beautiful Pinney's Beach was only a ten minute walk along a bougainvillea–lined path and a seaside cliff trail, he could not imagine why anyone would pay so much to stay in a stuffy, high–brow joint in the misty rain forest on the side of a mountain that was nearly always shrouded in clouds.

His double room was luxurious compared to the narrow, closet–like single–bed cells that lined the upstairs hallway. A Columbian fellow who had come over on the ferry with him was staying in one of them. A traveling West Indian salesmen was in another.

He had gone back up to the Poinsettia Plantation for a leisurely lunch the next day with his binoculars and bird book in hand. After buying the bird book at a shop in town, he had hastily broken down the binding and rubbed some dirt into it to make it appear well–worn. It was the best cover for spying on people and places in the Caribbean that he could think of.

Poinsettia Plantation was at the end of a long uphill drive lined with the colorful green and red–leafed bushes it had been named after. The large, white main building, apparently the former great house of an old plantation, was three stories high with porches that seemed to wrap around all four sides. Tucked into the hillside were cottages of varying sizes and off to one side was the ruin of an old stone sugar mill which had been restored to house a gift shop and restaurant. The pool and lounge chairs on the other side of the property seemed incongruous in this peaceful setting. It was hard to imagine Nicholas here and yet in some ways the atmosphere was not unlike his place in Vermont.

Tyler sat at a wrought iron table in the flagstone courtyard and sipped a daiquiri as slowly as he dared, watching the hotel guests arrive for lunch. Most of them were well over fifty–five and wore large straw hats and more clothing than the climate required in order to protect their aging skins from the hot sun. Old ladies carrying needlepoint work and hardback novels seemed to be in their element here. Unlike the young, bored honeymoon couple, who sat wrapped in beach towels, drinking rum punches and looking around anxiously as though they might miss the action if it ever got started.

"Which cottage is Miss Laveaux's?" he asked the young waiter who came by to take his order for lunch.

"Miss Laveaux?"

"Suzanne. A close friend of Mr. Newfield's."

"Ahh." His face lit up with recognition and then quickly clouded over. "I don't know," he said. "Have you chosen your luncheon yet?"

"Well, who would know?" Tyler persisted. He was fairly certain that all the employees of the inn had been instructed to cover for Suzanne. Hoping he'd found a weak link in the chain, he laid a twenty EC note on the table.

The waiter shook his head. "Ask at the front desk. Now what will you have? The curried chicken salad is a house specialty."

Tyler ate as slowly as he could, eavesdropping on the conversations around him, trying to think of a plan. Every time a bird chirped, he raised his binoculars to the trees and lowered them at a snail's pace so that he could observe the cottages in the distance.

"I come here every year at this time. Nicholas's parents were family friends of ours back in Missouri."

"Is that right? Well, I've been here several times over the past decade but usually in February.

Unfortunately my husband passed away this past winter–"

"Oh, I'm so sorry."

Tyler saw his opportunity and seized it. "Excuse me, ladies. Would you mind if I joined you for dessert and coffee?"

There wasn't a female senior citizen alive that could resist his winning smile and charming manners. Within moments he was chattering up a storm with the two older women, both of whom seem to grow rosy under his beaming attention. It took no time for him to say that he knew Nicholas and Suzanne from Vermont. He wondered if they had seen Suzanne during their stay this time. He hadn't been able to catch up with her yet.

"Suzanne? No, I haven't seen her but I've only been here two days. She keeps pretty much to herself when she can. The pretty turquoise cottage under the poinciana tree is hers. If she's home, the shutters will be open, so my guess is that she's not around. Why don't you ask Verleen at the reception? She's very close with Suzanne, she's sure to know when she'll be coming."

"It's a funny relationship she and Nicholas have, don't you think?" the other one chimed, in an effort to show that she was a regular guest also. "I thought she was his wife the first time I met them."

"Yes, I know what you mean. But I don't think she'd want to be his wife, do you? I mean, he's such a lady's man."

"Have you seen any green monkeys yet, Mr. Mackenzie?"

"Green monkeys?" Tyler wondered if this was the name of a rare bird endemic to Nevis that he should know about.

"Yes, they live all over the side of this mountain. They're not really green – I don't know how they came about their name. I'm sure you'll come across some in your birdwatching. They have such cute little faces."

"Oh, I always thought they looked kind of sad."

The conversation was drifting from the topic he was interested in and he only half listened to the rest of it as he plotted in his mind how to get inside Suzanne's cottage. He excused himself a few minutes later and went back to his own table to pay his bill. As he walked nonchalantly out of the courtyard in the direction of the rain forest, he was startled to see the Columbian from the Sea View sitting at a small table against a stone wall, wearing sunglasses and drinking a beer. He gave Tyler a friendly wave.

"Hey! Nice place, yes?"

"Yes, very nice. How did you get here, by taxi?"

"Bus. It stops at the bottom of the, uh, road." He waved a hand at the driveway. "Guidebook says good lunch here."

"Oh. Yes, mine was excellent. Hope you enjoy yours."

"Yes, thank you very much."

Nevis was a small island, Tyler reminded himself as he stopped to watch two hummingbirds feeding on a hibiscus hedge. He was bound to run into the same people over and over again. He would have to watch his step.

The old ladies had pointed out a path to him that headed into the forest and eventually worked its way up to the top of Mt. Nevis. Once safely hidden from public view, he veered off the path and hacked his way through vines and branches until he was directly behind the cottage pointed out to him as Suzanne's. A short distance away there appeared to be another well–worn path that led directly from the back of the little house and headed down the mountain towards the main road to town.

Surrounded by a tall croton hedge, the tiny backyard of the cottage was completely private. Tyler did not have to worry about anyone seeing him as he worked the latch on the back door with a screwdriver and a credit card. Nevis was apparently a safe place to

123

live, there were no burglar bars or dead bolts on the door and it was a relatively easy break–in.

At first glance it did not appear as though anyone had lived there for several months. There was one large bed/sitting room with a small kitchenette and bathroom off the back. The bed was neatly made, there were a few clothes hanging in the back of the closet, but Tyler had a feeling these clothes stayed here when Suzanne returned to Vermont. A musty smell hung in the air that reminded him of his family's summer house on Fire Island at the beginning of the season when the dampness of the ocean made the sheets and couches feel cold and clammy for a few days.

There was no food in the refrigerator and just a few canned goods on the shelf above it. There were no dishes in the dish drainer and the garbage can was empty.

The lack of dust made him suspicious however. If a house has not been occupied for some time a thin layer of dust should cover just about everything in sight. Unless of course one of the maids came in once a week and did a quick dusting. And watered the plants in the flower box on the porch. This was a hotel. Of course somebody took care of the place.

So that no stone would be left unturned, he poked his head into the bathroom. Immaculate again. As he turned to go, the slow drip of a faucet in the shower stall caught his attention. Reaching in automatically to turn it off, he found the shred of a clue he had been searching for. Beads of water clung to the shower walls and the floor of the shower was covered with small puddles and drops of water. The soap in the soap dish was wet.

There was no doubt in his mind that someone had taken a shower here in the last twenty–four hours. Someone with a key.

Sure enough, the path from the backyard led down to the main road that circled the island of Nevis. It was easy to catch a minibus back into Charlestown. Tyler wondered what he should do next. He had a very strong feeling that Suzanne was still somewhere on Nevis, but was staying away from the place where she was most likely to be found. She was probably staying some place without a shower, which could easily include 95% of the dwellings on the island.

The answer, of course, was to hide in the rain forest and stake out the cottage until she returned. Tyler did not relish the thought of camping in the bushes with the mosquitoes and stinging ants for hours on end. If she did come, it would most likely be under cover of darkness and spending a night in the jungle was even less appealing. He would do it if he had to. But first he would try to find an alternate plan.

He got off the bus at the town square where the banks and supermarket were. Now these were two good possibilities of places where Suzanne would eventually show up. He went into the supermarket and cruised the aisles while he thought. He bought a bag of local peanuts and then sat on a bench in the square, munching and watching the comings and goings of the tourists and locals.

It was Saturday afternoon; the banks were closed but the supermarket was doing a brisk weekend business. It was easy to tell the yacht people from the clothes they wore and the big boxes of food that they hauled away in the direction of the dock. The local women wore dresses and skirts, but the boat women always wore shorts. He saw the honeymoon couple from the plantation go by in a mini–moke, one of the roofless jeeps that looked like a toy car. The Columbian fellow sauntered down the street and gave Tyler a friendly wave.

Eventually the heat and dust got to him and he gave up his casual surveillance and headed for the beach. There was no question about it – he would have to go back to Suzanne's cottage and wait.

He had dinner that night at Unella's Restaurant, right next door to the Sea View. Open on three sides, it had the same panoramic view of the harbor and seemed a favorite of locals and tourists alike. He also noted the direct line of sight into his own room that anyone eating at Unella's could enjoy along with their food. He would have to remember to close the curtains when Sarah came to visit.

Tyler was beginning to have an uncomfortable feeling about the Columbian whose name he had learned was Diego. While Tyler ate parrotfish and rice and peas in the open air dining room, Diego sat at the bar indoors, drinking beer and watching a rerun of Star Trek. And watching Tyler, no doubt. He tried to pass it off as his naturally suspicious nature – Unella's was the predictable place to eat and drink if you lived next door – but he had run into Diego too many times by chance that day.

A few doors down a nightclub played disco music loud enough for everyone in town to hear it. Unable to sleep, Tyler sat in the darkness on the verandah of the Sea View, drinking beer, watching the twinkling lights of the sailboats bobbing in the harbor. Across the water, Basseterre, the capitol of St. Kitts, sparkled like a handful of bright jewels scattered across a black velvet landscape. Tomorrow he would turn the tables and follow Diego around. It would be interesting to see the outcome.

Charlestown was quiet on Sunday morning. The ferry stayed tied to the dock, the minibuses did not pass on the narrow main street. Tyler stayed in bed as long as he could, waiting for some sound indicating that Diego was awake. Finally his hunger got the best of him and he threw on a pair of shorts and a T–shirt and headed into town in search of breakfast.

When he was returning with a frozen half–pint of milk and a small loaf of banana bread, he passed Diego

126

going the opposite direction. They exchanged pleasantries about which shop was open on Sunday and then went on their separate ways.

Across the street from the Sea View, Tyler ducked behind an open gate overgrown with thick green vines. Eating the sweet bread and sipping icy milk, he stood waiting for Diego to return. As he suspected, no more than ten minutes passed before Diego came strolling briskly up the street, drinking an orange soda. He went inside the guest house but within five minutes he was hurrying back down the stairs, looking frantically in both directions. He looked at his watch, lit a cigarette and paced back and forth.

Finally it seemed to dawn on him that since he had not seen Tyler heading back into town, he must have gone off in the direction of the beach. Retrieving his beach towel from the clothesline on the verandah, Diego was off again.

Tyler squeezed the wad of plastic wrap that was left from the banana bread and grimaced as he walked quietly across the street. This certainly added another dimension to the picture. It was suddenly clear to him that Diego had probably followed him all the way to Nevis from one of his previous destinations. The question was why.

At dawn on Monday morning Tyler sat propped up in bed, going over his lists and outlines, trying to eliminate where Suzanne wouldn't be in an effort to figure out where she was. Sarah would be arriving late today and getting together with her was another problem that would need solving.

He sighed and let his gaze drift out over the harbor. The sailboats already showed signs of life. A few of them were getting ready to head out to sea; a man was lowering empty water containers to a woman in a dinghy; a rubber boat overflowing with hungry sailors revved up its outboard motor and made its way to the dock.

He needed to exchange some money this morning when the banks opened. He had thought staking out the bank was a good idea but this tiny island managed to support five banks and it would take a stroke of luck to pick the one that Suzanne might use. The bakery and the vegetable market seemed like better options.

Out on the water, two pelicans were diving for fish in the golden early morning light. Laughing to himself, he picked up his binoculars to watch them more closely. He was starting to enjoy his birdwatcher charade.

And then suddenly it came to him. He knew where Suzanne was staying. It made perfect sense. Now he just had to find her.

Tyler did not think that Nicholas would bring Sarah over on the ferry. A small, chartered plane was more his style. But on the off chance, he wandered down to the dock to meet the four o'clock boat. It was easy to hide himself behind the crowds that greeted the ferry each time it arrived. Dark glasses, a panama hat and his binoculars helped disguise him also. Without turning around, he knew that Diego was somewhere nearby, watching him and what he was doing.

He was surprised to see Sarah and Nicholas in the line of travelers waiting to get off the boat. Sarah had an odd beatific grin on her face as Nicholas leaned over, pointing out various places along the waterfront to her. With a protective gesture that made Tyler's stomach turn, Nicholas helped Sarah onto the dock, then led her to a spot away from the crowd where he left her to go in search of their luggage.

Seeing what might be his only opportunity, Tyler strolled casually to her side and then turning his back on her, raised his binoculars to the sea.

"Sarah, don't turn around, it's me, Tyler."

Sarah could not help but glance over her shoulder at him before shifting her gaze quickly to where Nicholas stood by the front of the ferry. "My God, Tyler. What are you doing here? What if he sees you?"

"He won't. Listen, I think I've found her. You've got to meet me tomorrow morning. I've got a lot to tell you about and I'm going to need your help."

"Where? How?" Sarah's voice expressed bewilderment and fatigue.

"Get yourself to town somehow. No, I know. Poinsettia has their own stretch of beach down from Pinney's. You're in the Caribbean, you must be dying to get right onto the beach and into the water. They must take a busload of guests there each day. At eleven o'clock take a walk back towards town along the sand. I'll be there just far enough away so no one will recognize me."

"Sarah! Cecil is here with the van for us! Let's go!" Nicholas's voice boomed across the clatter and chatter of the crowd.

"Okay?"

"Okay!"

When Tyler turned around she was already gone. He spotted her being helped into a van at the end of the dock along with an elderly couple. His stomach churned with the frustration of being so close to her and not being able to touch her or even speak to her. He wondered if she would have her own room at the inn and his cheeks flushed with fury at the thought of her possibly sharing a room or, worse yet, the same bed as sleazy Nicholas.

There was so much he had to share with Sarah. He hadn't spoken to her since before he went to Chicago and she had no idea that he'd even been to Mexico. He wondered how she would feel about continuing the search when she found out Suzanne had been a murderer on the lam for the last twenty–five years.

He forced his mind back to the task at hand. There was still work to be done before dark. If he kept his eyes open he could accomplish a lot in the next two hours.

Shortly after 11 a.m., Sarah's shadow eclipsed the hot sun shining down on Tyler's beach towel. He opened his eyes but before sitting up, he enjoyed a long, breathtaking look at Sarah in a skimpy black and pink flowered bikini.

"What's wrong?"

"Nothing. I guess I've just never seen you in a bikini before and I'm rendered speechless by the sight. Is that new?"

"Nicholas bought it for me. He seemed to think it was necessary equipment for the Caribbean. What do you think?"

"I think I want to throw you over my shoulder and carry you back to my humble room and screw your lovely brains out. What do you think?"

"Sounds like a good place to start. When'd you take up birdwatching?" Sarah knelt in the sand and thumbed through his West Indies bird book. "Or are you doing research on some rare species?"

"Yes, a middle–aged bird named Suzanne that migrated here from the northern U.S. and will only show herself to a very few trusted natives. Here – have a look." He handed her the binoculars.

"Look at what?"

"Look at that sailboat out there, the beat–up one that's getting a new coat of paint over the tail end where the name used to be. If everything I figure is correct, that's Suzanne sitting in that dinghy, vigorously wielding a paintbrush."

"But she's got black hair!"

"Fooled you too, didn't she?"

"But how can you be sure?"

Tyler gently removed the binoculars from Sarah's grasp and hung them around his neck. "There's a guy

130

who's been watching my every move and I don't want him to catch on that I'm not a birdwatcher. When we get back to my guesthouse we're going to break into his room and find out who he really is. Now walk with me like you just met me and let me tell you where I've been in the last week and why I think that woman is Suzanne."

By the time they reached the Sea View, Sarah was shaking her head in amazement. "I can't believe you actually went all the way to Puerto Cerrito last week. And I can't believe we're going to all this trouble for a woman who's been jailed for subversive activities in the U.S. and is wanted for murder in Mexico!"

"Sarah, from what I could guess, the argument might very well have been about her relationship with Woody. You don't know what the actual situation was. It could have been self–defense. Besides, I've seen the jail. Life on the run has to have been better than that."

Sarah grimaced and did not reply. She had not counted on there being a question of ethics involved with this search. But as she climbed the stairs, Tyler's fingers caressing on the small of her back reminded her of the other, more pressing, issues at hand.

"This place is more my style than yours, Mackenzie. Why aren't you staying some place classier?" Sarah's eyes roamed the bare wooden walls and floor of Tyler's room. Exhausted and satisfied, they were stretched out on the sheets, their naked bodies glistening with sweat from their amorous exertions.

"I'm getting rather fond of it actually. And it fit into Woody's budget. Do you have any idea what it costs to stay at that fancy–ass hotel where you are?"

"It doesn't matter. I'm friends with the owner."

"Does he come on to you ever, Sarah?"

"No, I told you, he doesn't want sex to ruin our relationship. Apparently he's got a couple of local girls who keep him more than happy while he's here, so I've been safely stashed away in my own room. You've got nothing to worry about, sweetheart." She kissed the line of golden hairs that ran down the center of his tan chest.

"Shhh. Listen." Light footsteps could be heard stopping for a moment outside Tyler's door and then continuing down the hall. "That's Diego now. Hear him? He's unlocking his room. Now what I need you to do is distract him while I go through his stuff. Think you can manage it?"

"I don't know, Tyler. I'm not as good at this cloak–and–dagger routine as you are."

"Oh, come on, you're pretty good at cloaking my dagger, baby." He grinned at her as he quickly slipped into his shorts. "Now put that little swimsuit on again and get out there and work your charms. Offer him one of the beers in that cooler over there. I know he won't refuse. Hurry. I hear him on the verandah now."

Tyler watched through the half–closed louvers of his porch–side window as Sarah arranged her slim torso and long legs against the railing of the verandah in front of Diego and struck up a conversation. Soon enough she was laughing at her own attempts at pigeon Spanish (which Tyler knew she actually spoke very well) and before long she was back in the room for the iced beers that Tyler had mentioned.

"What are you waiting for?" she hissed. "Get going."

"I wanted to make sure you really had him." From a small cooler he extracted two Carib lagers and a bottle opener.

"He thinks you're napping, so be quiet."

"Of course." It was not a time to argue with Sarah, who obviously did not enjoy these charades as much as he did. As soon as he heard the laughter start up again from the verandah, he crept down the hall to Diego's room.

Tyler knew that, when it was just himself and Diego in the building, Diego did not bother to lock his door. It opened easily with a telltale scraping sound that he prayed would not be detected by the merrymakers on the porch.

There was not much to search through. The narrow room was furnished in the same Spartan manner as Tyler's. He went immediately for the suitcase under the bed, looking through its pockets and hidden zipper compartments for passports or identifying papers. It took him but a few minutes to locate Diego's passport. He quickly flipped it open.

Diego Gonzalez was not Columbian at all but Mexican. Tyler knew now why the man had lied about his nationality and his name. When he slipped the passport back into its compartment, his hand came in contact with something else, which he pulled out for inspection. He whistled softly to himself when he saw what he was holding.

It was an old Polaroid snapshot, faded to a pale brown color from never having been fixed properly when it had been shot over twenty years before. It was a picture of two dark young men who looked very much alike and a girl. The girl stood in the middle with her arms around both men. She wore a low cut peasant blouse and a full skirt and an embroidered scarf covering her long hair. A loose strand of it seemed to reach beyond her waist. It was hard to see the details of their faces but the girl's voluptuous bustline was very familiar to him now. He had seen it so many times in the artwork on the walls of a house in Emporia, Vermont.

He flipped the old snapshot over. In spidery handwriting was written, "Diego, Susanna, Raoul, Octobre 1966."

Tyler had found what he had been looking for. He slipped it into his pants pocket and silently left the room

CHAPTER NINE

"Here she comes. Let's go."

Sarah tossed the binoculars on to the bed and picked up her shopping bag, heading for the stairs. Tyler locked the door behind them and stepped out on the verandah once more to verify that the black–haired woman was indeed rowing her dinghy towards the dock. Then he hurried to catch up with Sarah.

In the early morning hustle, it was easy to follow a shopper without being seen. Tyler checked a few times behind him to make sure that Diego was faithfully tailing them as usual. This morning's plan would not work without Diego.

Sarah had been horrified to learn that Diego's last name was Gonzalez. "From the family that wants revenge for the murder? Tyler, let's stop right now. I know Woody doesn't want to put our lives in danger over this. He already lost Suzanne to them once. How would he feel if he lost us too?"

But Tyler was too intrigued to back out now. Somehow this guy had managed to follow Tyler all the way to Nevis from Puerto Cerrito without being seen. He wasn't certain, but he thought Diego had even been settled in at the Sea View before Tyler himself had arrived.

"What if he's part of her plan?" Sarah suggested wildly, desperate to change Tyler's mind. "What if they planned to meet down here and run off together?"

"Don't be ridiculous. I'm sure she doesn't have a clue that he's here." Studying the old snapshot, Tyler had come up with an idea to prove that the woman on the boat was Suzanne and that she was not in cahoots with Diego.

Sarah and Tyler took turns discreetly shopping in the same stores as Suzanne while the other one waited outside to keep an eye on Diego. Sarah went into the grocery store, Tyler followed her into the hardware store and a small pharmacy, Sarah waited in line to buy bread at the bakery. Suzanne wore a large straw hat and sunglasses which she did not remove in any of the shops.

Finally, in the vegetable market Sarah found an opportunity to make conversation with her.

"Aren't these tomatoes just beautiful? I wonder if they taste as good as they look." She directed her remarks to Suzanne who was standing nearby, picking out a few choice tomatoes for herself.

"Believe me, they do. They're expensive but they're worth it." Her voice was lower and huskier than Sarah had expected.

"You know, up in Vermont we can never get our tomatoes to grow this big or this red."

"Really?" It was just a polite response obviously intended to indicate she didn't care about Sarah's tomatoes in Vermont.

"Tyler, come look at these tomatoes! They're worth taking a picture of."

Tyler suppressed a smile at the personality Sarah was displaying. He could tell that Suzanne was sizing him up behind the security of her dark glasses. While she watched, he acknowledged Diego's presence by greeting him coolly but she had no reaction. But when she saw him lift his camera to take a picture of Sarah and the tomatoes, she turned abruptly away and began picking over a pile of limes. For a few moments she took no notice of Diego standing nearby, picking his teeth and casually observing Sarah and Tyler as he pretended to examine a lime in the same stack.

Watching them over Tyler's shoulder, it was obvious to Sarah the moment that Suzanne recognized Diego. Her whole body stiffened and the blood instantly rose to her cheeks and then drained away just as quickly. It was not the look of someone who was expecting to meet somebody.

After studying the snapshot for some time, Tyler and Sarah decided that Diego Gonzalez looked almost exactly as he had in 1965. His face now had deep creases and lines in places that had once been smooth and there was just a hint of gray at the temples of his thick, wavy hair. He still had the same stocky, muscular build he had possessed as a young man.

Suzanne, on the other hand, due to natural and unnatural causes, looked nothing like she did back then. Her baggy khaki shorts and sleeveless chambray shirt did not conceal the soft middle-aged bulges beneath. Without her spectacular hair and body, she seemed like many other women of her age who have not been treated kindly by the passage of time. She did not rate more than a cursory glance from Diego, who shifted his gaze back to Tyler and Sarah.

Sarah knelt down to adjust her sandal. "She's recognized him," she murmured softly to Tyler.

Tyler moved across the aisle for a better vantage point. "Look at these mangoes, Sarah." He held one up for her to see just as Suzanne, with a trembling hand, knocked several limes to the floor.

Diego gallantly bent down to retrieve them and as he handed them to her, Suzanne's body froze once again. Tyler thought she was looking at the tattoo on Diego's wrist – it was a tarantula with a sinister appearance. Diego still showed no signs of recognition. As soon as he turned his back on Suzanne, she put down the limes and fled the market, a haunted look on her face.

As he watched her hurry away towards the dock, he remembered that Suzanne also had a tattoo, but in a much more private place.

They spent the rest of that day and most of the next taking turns watching Suzanne's boat from the verandah or the beach, trying to decide what to do.

"I wish we could read the name she painted on the boat," Sarah remarked to Tyler.

"I'm sure she anchored it that way so the name wouldn't be visible from shore." Tyler sat up and put his sunglasses on. "I tell you, this is the life, isn't it? Keeping a surveillance on somebody from one of the most beautiful beaches in the world. I know this is a big decision, but I think it's time to walk down to that beach bar and pick up a couple of tropical drinks."

"The wind's picking up. You know, I think you're wrong."

"About the drinks?"

"No, the boat. All the boats are facing the same way. See how they're all starting to shift position with the change in the wind?"

Tyler could see Sarah was right. All the yachts in the bay were moving, riggings clanking against masts and booms.

"I'll watch; you go get those drinks," she said, settling herself cross–legged on her beach towel. "See if you spot Diego lurking about anywhere. I'm afraid we're leading him right to her. I think we'd better find ourselves a ride out to meet her in the morning."

"Maybe we shouldn't wait that long. Maybe we ought to go after dark tonight."

Thoughtfully, Sarah nodded in agreement. They had already decided they had nothing to lose by approaching the woman they suspected was Suzanne. But by her reaction to Diego in the market, it was clear that she had not been planning a happy reunion with him on Nevis. For a few hours after exploring Diego's room the previous day, they had entertained the notion that Suzanne had secretly run off with the purpose of meeting Diego here. After some discussion, they decided

Diego would not be following Tyler around so intently if Suzanne had made plans with him already.

The sun was dropping lower in the sky, bathing the beach and its coconut palms in a golden wash of light. Looking at her watch, Sarah was startled to discover it was nearly five o'clock. She had barely crossed paths with Nicholas in the last two days. He had told her they had work to do at the inn, but first there had to be play and he hoped she didn't mind if his play did not include her for a few days. He was apparently into some kind of marathon menage–a–trois with a couple of local beauties. He had tossed Sarah the keys to his Land Rover and said he'd join her in a day or two.

Unfortunately, she felt too compelled to get this Suzanne thing out of the way before exploring the island. Woody had not sounded very good the last time she had called him. She knew that, sometimes, if dying people had a reason to live, their condition would take a turn for the better. From what Woody had told her, he could go either way. She hoped that this common–looking, dark–haired woman was really the exotic redhead from Woody's past.

A southerly wind had shifted the anchored sailboats nearly 180 degrees now. The freshly painted name on Suzanne's boat was almost in sight. Sarah watched eagerly through the binoculars, forgetting in her intensity to be discreet about where she was focusing.

"Unbelievable. Look at that. It's got to be her." Sarah bounced on her heels with anticipation. Unable to contain her excitement, she ran down the beach towards Tyler who was slowly ambling along the water's edge carrying two frothy banana daiquiris in plastic cups.

"Guess what? You're not going to believe what the name of the boat is! Here – switch with me and take a look." She relieved him of the drinks so he could hold the binoculars.

"What does it say? It's half in shadow – I can't read it very well. Water's Nymph? Watery Nymph...Wendy's Nymph...Woody's Nymph...Woody's Nymph?"

"Woody's Nymph! We've found her!" Sarah took a big sip out of each of the daiquiris that were sloshing over with her enthusiasm. "Now we can go out to dinner and celebrate. The search is over! First thing in the morning–" She stopped short when she caught the desperate look of warning in Tyler's eyes as he lowered the binoculars and tilted his head towards the trees behind him.

Leaning over he planted a kiss on her cheek and whispered, "Diego is just back there."

Sarah could only see his brown feet planted in the sand behind a large coconut palm. "Shit." Annoyed with her own indiscretion, she turned abruptly and headed back to her beach towel. The beach was nearly deserted at this time of day, and she tried to regain her joyful mood by admiring the natural beauty of her surroundings. Unsuccessful, she downed her drink in a few gulps and splashed into the warm, gentle waves for a last dip of the day.

From out in the turquoise water, she could see that Tyler was looking through the binoculars at a couple of shorebirds poking their long beaks into the sand. This birdwatching charade seemed to have gone to his head. She was never sure any more if he was just pretending to be interested in birds.

She floated along with the current until she could see the tree that Diego had been sitting behind, but he had vanished. There had to be a path out to the road from there; he was nowhere to be seen on the beach. She would be glad when all this craziness was over. It gave her the creeps to think someone was watching her all the time.

Sarah and Tyler watched the sunset and then strolled leisurely to the road where the jeep was parked. "Let's go back to my room and change our clothes and then drive up the coast to Oualie's for dinner," he suggested. "We need to figure out how we're going to present this situation to Suzanne and I want to be far enough away that I'm sure Diego won't be able to follow us."

"You know, I don't think we can wait any longer. I've been thinking that we ought to find a way to get out there tonight."

"Tonight?"

"I'm afraid we may have pointed her out to Diego this afternoon and besides, we know she recognized him yesterday. How much longer do you think she is going to hang around now that she knows he's here?"

Tyler considered what Sarah was saying. For Suzanne's own safety, they should probably make contact as quickly as possible.

"You're right. I'll go down to the dock right now and see if I can find us a way out there after dark. I'll meet you back at the guesthouse."

The Sea View was quiet and a quick peek through the keyhole assured Sarah that Diego was not in his room. She decided to wait until later to shower. Slipping on her sundress, she sat on one of the metal and vinyl chairs on the verandah and watched the twilight slowly envelop the harbor and the dock and the yachts bobbing at their moorings. Once she lifted the binoculars to check on Suzanne's boat. She could see a light on in the cabin and a dark shape sitting on deck watching the stars come out.

Strains of music and laughter drifted over from Unella's Restaurant next door along with the tantalizing smell of fried fish. It was all so very peaceful – the only unpleasantness was the gnawing hunger in her stomach and the uncomfortable chair she was sitting on.

Tyler returned just as darkness settled over the sea. He had waited at the dock until a likely couple had motored up in a rubber dinghy, dressed for dinner out.

Explaining the situation and assuring them he would be back before they returned from their five course supper at Montpelier Plantation, they agreed to let him borrow their boat.

"Unbelievable. You could talk a monkey into giving you his last banana," Sarah laughed as she quickly followed him back to the dock.

They had not thought to bring a flashlight but the dock was well lit and Tyler was able to start the outboard motor with only a minimal amount of trouble. They headed slowly out across the harbor in the direction of Woody's Nymph.

A loud explosion suddenly shattered the calm of the evening. Over the water, maybe half a mile away, up by Pinney's Beach, sparks and flaming timbers were raining down like fireworks. Behind them on the dock and all over town, people were racing to the edge of the harbor. Tyler cut the motor.

"A yacht! Somebody's yacht blew up!" She heard a man shout in explanation.

"Holy shit," Tyler muttered. "It can't be– it wasn't–"

"Oh, my God, I don't know, it really looked like it."

Several men jumped into a speedboat and sped past them, headed towards the burning wreckage.

"Go back," Sarah urged. "We shouldn't get in the way."

"No, we've got to find out. Everybody's headed out there. What difference will we make?"

"Look at the flames. It's too dangerous. Take the boat back to the dock and we'll drive the jeep out to Pinney's Beach."

Back on shore they found that the road to the beach was crowded with people running and shouting and the going was slow. In sleepy Charlestown this was a big event.

"Damn. It's too dark to see anything. How will we ever know?"

141

"Someone will know. The other boats must know. I'll ask around."

Sarah stayed with the open Land Rover while Tyler disappeared into the crowd on the shore. He was back in less than five minutes, a grim look on his face.

"It was her boat, wasn't it? Did they find her yet? Is she all right?"

Tyler shook his head. "No sign of her yet. Most of the local guys think the explosion was too big to be accidental."

Sarah looked out at the water where big searchlights were being set up in motorboats around the smoking remains of Woody's Nymph. Tyler put a comforting arm around her shoulder.

"They probably won't find anything until morning." He had refrained from saying "her body". "I don't think we're going to learn any more by hanging around here. Let's go."

Sarah did not move. "If it wasn't accidental, then who would have set it?"

"There's only one person I can think of. Driver, the Sea View, please. And step on it."

They waited in the darkness until midnight, eating take–out hamburgers from Unella's and drinking Carib Lager in Tyler's room, but Diego did not show. A heavy silence settled over them and grew into a dense depression as they realized how little chance there was that Suzanne had survived the explosion. They had failed Woody.

"How are we ever going to tell him?" Sarah moaned.

"Whatever you do, don't do it over the phone. Wait until you go back home to tell him in person. Maybe in another week or so, he'll be in better condition to handle the news."

They lapsed into silence again.

"I'm afraid to leave you here," Sarah said finally as she prepared to return to the Poinsettia. "Assuming Diego did do it, he knows you know Suzanne was on the boat. We virtually pointed it out to him. Wouldn't he take you out next?"

"Take me out?" Tyler laughed despite the tenseness of the situation. "You talk like a TV cop show, lady. Truthfully, I'm more worried about you driving back alone at this time of night than I am about myself."

"Then come with me. Nicholas will never know. He hasn't been awake before ten a.m. yet and we'll come back at dawn to see if the coast guard has found out anything."

Tyler swatted a mosquito on her arm. "I really think I ought to stay."

"And I really think you ought to come. Just think, you can take a real shower in the morning with hot water and everything..."

"Well, if you put it that way, I guess Diego's not going anywhere before morning. As long as we're back in town by dawn." Closing the louvers and locking the door, he followed her out to the street.

CHAPTER TEN

Tyler slipped out of Sarah's room just as the sunlight was beginning to bounce off the distant sea at the foot of Mt. Nevis. She was sleeping so soundly, he felt there was no point in waking her when he could easily run down the poinsettia–lined drive and catch a bus to town.

As he bounced along in a minibus full of school children wearing neatly pressed uniforms, he wondered if Nicholas should be considered a suspect in the explosion. Had he really been involved in a sex marathon for the last three days or was that just a cover? Tyler and Sarah had turned their backs on him completely – he could have been up to anything.

He knew that for some reason Sarah seemed to trust Nicholas, despite the fact she had seen him dealing with the Mexican who had slapped her around. When they had discussed it recently, Sarah had brushed it aside, saying Nicholas was definitely a substance abuser and that she was almost certain it had been some kind of drug deal. But Tyler thought there was still every reason to believe that Nicholas had known all along that Suzanne had run to Nevis and why. He may even have helped her do it.

It took only a few well–directed questions in town to find out that no body had been recovered from the wreckage. Apparently there was evidence, however, pointing to the fact that the owner, a middle–aged American woman, had been on the boat at the time. Something would wash up on the beach eventually along with the soggy, charred remains of the yacht to confirm her death, but for now the search had been called off. Hugo was taking precedence.

Tyler did not know who Hugo was. It was Diego that Tyler was concerned about. Diego who had followed him to Nevis, had lurked and eavesdropped, and was still carrying a twenty–five–year–old picture of himself and Suzanne. Only now Tyler was carrying it around. He had tucked it away in his notebook and now he checked to make sure it was still there. It might prove to be valuable evidence. He wondered if Diego had noticed it was missing yet.

His question was answered the moment he unlocked the door to his bedroom at the Sea View. Someone had unceremoniously gone through his belongings without bothering to replace them carefully. Luckily he had carried everything important with him – his money, his passport and his notebook were all safe in his day pack. The only thing missing was his camera which, of course, made the break–in look like a normal burglary.

Without stopping to consider the consequences, he was at Diego's door in a few long strides down the hall. He banged his fist on it and shouted, "Wake up, amigo! We have to talk!"

There was no response and he repeated his actions, finally kneeling to peek through the keyhole. It seemed that the room was unoccupied at the moment.

"Shit." Tyler leaned his head against the door frame, trying to figure what good it would do to confront Diego anyway. There was no way to prove he had done anything illegal unless he had a case of dynamite under his bed, which was highly unlikely. But it was Tyler's nature– he always wanted answers and more than that, he wanted justice. Just for his own satisfaction he needed to find Diego and get down to the facts, once and for all. He was probably just off having breakfast.

Tyler made the short walk downtown to The Confectionery, a bakery and cafe where the yacht people usually congregated for breakfast. He tried to start up a conversation more than once about the explosion of

145

Woody's Nymph, but was cut off or brushed aside for what was apparently a more important topic.

"Hugo is coming, man. And they say he's gonna be a big one." The leather–skinned, sun–bleached sailor was gulping down his coffee.

"Oh." Tyler batted the name around in his head again for a while before turning back to the sailor and asking, "Who's Hugo?"

"Hurricane Hugo. Started out as a tropical depression off the coast of South Africa and it's been building steam all the way across the Atlantic. It's supposed to hit here some time tomorrow night. That's why the coast guard called off the search for that lady you were asking about. They've got a lot of work to do. And so do I." He kicked back his chair abruptly and was gone.

A hurricane. Magazine pictures of destruction and chaos flashed through his mind. Damn it all, this was the icing on the cake. They would never find out any more about Suzanne's boat now. Anything that might have eventually washed softly ashore in the surf could possibly end up miles away, on a different island perhaps. He wondered whether he and Sarah should leave or stay.

He suddenly realized that the level of conversation in the room was loud and urgent. Some people were laughing and talking about hurricane parties, others had worry and distress written all over their faces.

"There you are. I've been looking all over for you."

Sarah was standing over him, tall and willowy and extremely sunny–looking in a yellow shirt and shorts that contrasted nicely with her tan skin and dark hair.

"Have you now? And I thought I had made a clean getaway."

"I want you to come back up to the plantation with me. I've been thinking about it and I think it's time we sat down with Nicholas and came clean about what we've been doing."

Tyler squinted up at her, trying to figure out what was racing through her head.

"We've got to tell him about Suzanne. He deserves to know."

Tyler nodded grimly.

"Besides, he may be able to tell us what connection that guy Rico has to Suzanne and help us to nail down Diego somehow. I'm sure Diego and Rico are working together on this." She was gripping the back of a chair as she talked, her fingers white with tension and stress.

"Okay. Let's go." Tyler grabbed his last piece of toast and stood up. "Besides, someone needs to drag him out of his sexual stupor and tell him that a hurricane is headed this way. He might want to batten down a few hatches at the inn."

They were surprised to find Nicholas eating breakfast on the flagstone terrace overlooking the sea. He was clean–shaven and his wet hair was neatly slicked back away from his face.

"Oh, there you are, Sarah. I knocked on your door to see if you wanted to join me for breakfast but apparently you were already gone. Well, pull up a chair. Who's your friend?" Nicholas was filling his mouth like a starving war–torn refugee who hadn't seen food for days.

Tyler cleared his throat. "We've met before. I'm Tyler Mackenzie."

Nicholas shaded his eyes and peered at Tyler's face. "Tyler Mackenzie...oh, yes. You're Suzanne's cousin, aren't you? You were at my house during that last party I had. The one with the French Canadian sweeties..." Nicholas chuckled to himself and then his gaze narrowed sharply. "Strange coincidence, you meeting Sarah here on Nevis." His tone indicated he did not think it was coincidental at all. "She happens to be your cousin's replacement at my office." He turned to Sarah. "But I suppose he already knows that."

147

A red flush crept over Sarah's face and she looked to Tyler for help. Tyler sat down in the wrought iron chair on Nicholas's left and leaned forward.

"Well, I've got to be straight with you, man. I'm not really Suzanne's cousin."

"Now why doesn't that surprise me? And what about you, Sarah? Who are you not really?"

Sarah seated herself on the edge of the chair on his right and took a deep breath. "We've got a lot of confessions to make to you, Nicholas. And we hope you've got some for us."

As they began to unfold their tale, Nicholas sat back in his chair looking purposely disinterested, his arms crossed over his chest, his mouth pursed with anger and contempt. But before long his expression had changed to one of incredulousness and after Sarah had related the story of her abduction, he began to look sick with disbelief. When Tyler told him finally about the boat blowing up, the color drained from his cheeks and tears sprang into his eyes.

"My God, it's my fault. It's all my fault." He covered his face with his hands.

Sarah laid a hand on his arm. "Now come on, Nicholas. Tyler and I feel that way too. We virtually pointed the boat out to Diego. We shouldn't have waited so long to make contact with her. There's a thousand ways any of us can take the blame."

"But this guy, Rico, who you said is also called Fred, he saw Suzanne in my office when he came to make a drop..." A couple of angry tears finally spilled over and made their way down Nicholas' face. "Suzanne left work that day and never came back. Don't you see? If it wasn't for this nasty habit of mine..." He used the red cloth napkin in his lap to blow his nose and wipe his face. "Well, I guess that's it. This time I stop for real. I can't keep letting people die because of my drug problem."

Sarah and Tyler exchanged glances again. Neither of them had been ready for Nicholas to fall apart on them like this. They had expected him to be angry with them at first and then, after some discussion, agreeable to helping them out. But there was no turning back now.

"People dying? What do you mean?" As usual, Tyler zeroed right in on the crucial question.

"Fred Martin, or Rico whoever he is, used one of the telephone operators on my staff at Newfield's as our middle man, so to speak. A few weeks later, she overdosed on coke and died."

"That was the same day I came by," Tyler spoke up.

"That's right. I had that blow–out party in an attempt to forget what was bothering me. I felt that indirectly it was entirely my fault. I mean, I didn't hold the coke up to her nose but if I hadn't agreed to the arrangement, she probably wouldn't have access to the stuff. That's what you heard Fred and I arguing about that night, Sarah."

"So have you ever met Diego?" Nicholas shook his head in response to Tyler's question. "There's little doubt that he and Fred/Rico–" Tyler chuckled a little as he put the names together–"Frederico. That's his name probably. As I was saying, I'm sure Diego and Frederico are in on this together. At least as far as hunting down Suzanne was concerned. Suzanne's reaction to Diego in the market confirmed that she recognized him and was frightened. The question is how do we prove that he killed her?"

"First of all, you ought to go back and break into his room again." Nicholas was staring pensively at the old snapshot that Tyler had pulled from his notebook at the appropriate moment of the story. "She would never talk about her time in Mexico to me. But sometimes she would wake up from nightmares screaming and begging in Spanish." He sat up suddenly. "I think I'd like to go

149

with you to find this guy. I have a few things I'd like to ask him myself."

"Mr. Newfield! So sorry to interrupt–"

Three pairs of eyes turned to look at a short, round gentleman with a jolly, sunburned face who was trying to get their attention. His short, round wife was a perfect match for him.

"My wife and I are going to check out this morning. We don't feel up to weathering a dead–on hurricane and we've managed to get ourselves on the evening flight out of St. Kitts–"

"Dead–on hurricane? What the devil are you talking about?"

"That's the other thing we thought we ought to tell you," Tyler added sheepishly. "There's a hurricane headed this way. It's supposed to hit here late Saturday night."

"Been on all the weather reports on television and radio. The experts are recommending that all tourists go home as soon as possible. I think the Boswells are checking out this morning also."

Damn it all. How could this be happening now?" Nicholas slammed down his coffee cup and stood up, suddenly very much in charge. "Tyler, I guess you're going to have to pursue that villain on your own today. Sarah, I'm going to need your help here. We've got to send all the guests packing and start making preparations for this damn storm. But first call American Airlines and get us seats on the last flight out tomorrow. We'll probably have to island hop to Puerto Rico or someplace. I'll pay whatever I have to. And get your boyfriend on the plane also."

"You don't want to weather it out here?" she asked in semi–seriousness. She was surprised Nicholas would let himself be frightened off by rain and wind.

"Are you out of your mind? I've got a business to run back in the states. It could be weeks before we could get another plane out of here after a hurricane rips through. It could be months before electricity and telephone might be restored." Nicholas turned to the elderly couple. "It's been a pleasure having you. Sorry you had to cut your visit short. Hope we see you again next year. Now if you'll excuse me..."

He hurried off in the direction of the office.

"I guess I'm off again too then." Tyler gave Sarah a quick squeeze. "I'll meet you back up here for supper."

Tyler returned around five in a state of complete frustration. He had spent all day trying to catch up with Diego to no avail. Laying around at the Sea View, he had found it difficult not to doze off. But he was afraid to venture very far from home base for fear of missing him. When he had strolled down to the grocery store to pick up an afternoon snack he had been thwarted by long lines of customers and empty shelves. He hated wasting precious time standing in line so he contented himself with an ice cream cone from a small shop on the way back.

Around three o'clock he could not keep his eyes open and next time he looked at his watch it was four. Cursing, he quickly checked Diego's room for any changes but there were none he could see. Diego was definitely hiding out somewhere. Tyler could not believe that, in the face of a hurricane, he would not come and retrieve his belongings before returning to his hideout or leaving the island. He had picked the lock on Diego's door as soon as he had arrived back from the Poinsettia. His passport and airline ticket back to New York were still in his suitcase and Tyler doubted that Diego would leave without them. Of course, anything was possible.

But now, sitting on the terrace having a sunset cocktail with Sarah, it was hard to imagine that a hurricane was coming. The still air hung over them, heavy and humid, the peaceful atmosphere broken only occasionally by the buzz of a hummingbird at a hibiscus flower or by the telltale banging of a hammer. By

151

promising a good day's wages, it had not been hard for Nicholas to round up a crew of local men to nail boards across the windows of the cottages and great house. More than half of the registered guests had departed and the remainder would be heading out in the morning.

"I helped move some of the priceless and very breakable antique china pieces out of the dining room and into the wine cellar," Sarah remarked. "You should see Nicholas's wine cellar, Tyler. Some of the varieties and vintages he has there are impressive even to an amateur like me. I'll show you. You can pick out a bottle for our dinner." She grinned. "At least we'll get to have one romantic night in the tropics together. Even if the windows of my room are boarded up already."

"Sarah, I can't spend the night. I've got to go back after we eat. I'm sure Diego will come back after dark and I've got to be there."

Her grin faded to a grimace. "We just can't ever seem to make it work out for us like normal people, can we?"

He patted her hand. "That's because we're not normal people, my dear."

Satiated on pumpkin soup, curried conch and fine wine, Tyler was sorry he couldn't finish the night off in bed with Sarah. But his persistence seemed to be paying off. The landlady at the Sea View told him that Diego had returned shortly after dark, had washed up and changed his clothes and was now next door in the bar at Unella's.

Music from an open air nightclub a few doors down was blasting loud enough to be heard anywhere in Charlestown. As he hurried up the steps to the restaurant, he wondered how he would possibly sleep tonight – getting drunk might be the only answer. There were more people eating out than he might have

152

expected, but the prospect of a hurricane seemed to put some people into a very social frame of mind.

He spotted Diego inside, seated at the small bar decorated with multicolored Christmas lights where the main focus of the patrons and bartender was a color T.V. Diego had one hand on his Carib Lager and the other on the bare knee of a young black woman sitting next to him. Provocatively dressed in a yellow mini skirt and a backless white halter top, with an eye out for foreign men, it was she who saw Tyler approaching them.

"Dis a frien' of yours?" she murmured to Diego as she openly assessed Tyler's possibilities.

"Hey, Diego, my man, what's happening?" Tyler swung himself up onto the last available barstool. "Haven't seen you in a while. Whatcha been up to?"

"Oh, nothing much. Falling in love with this chica bonita here, that's all." Diego squeezed her thigh. "How do you say it...getting a little pussy, maybe?" Although slightly slurred by large quantities of alcohol, Diego's English seemed to have improved vastly in the last twenty–four hours.

"Well, I wondered where you disappeared to last night." While Tyler ordered and paid for a Heineken, Diego smooched with his girlfriend in case Tyler hadn't believed their connection. "Ahem. Aren't you going to introduce me to your new love interest?"

"Shirella," the girl said, breaking instantly out of the embrace and extending her hand.

"Tyler. Pleased to meet you, Shirella. So did Diego light your fire last night? Oh, maybe that was a poor choice of words. I mean after Suzanne's boat blowing up and all." Holy shit, the words had just jumped right out of his mouth. Tyler hadn't meant to come to the point so fast, but after working all day towards this moment, he had just blurted it out without thinking.

153

Diego did not even look at him. Staring directly ahead at the air space above his beer, he said, "I don't know what you're talking about."

"Oh, come on, compadre. Shirella knows what I'm talking about. Everyone on the island knows about the yacht that exploded in the harbor last night." Tyler tried to catch Shirella's eye on the other side of Diego.

"What does that have to do with us and our loving?" Shirella stroked the inside of Diego's arm suggestively, making circles with her finger around the tattoo just above his wrist.

"It might interest you to know that the woman who died on that boat last night was an old friend of Diego's. Someone I think he's been trying to find for years." Tyler's gaze was fixated on the tarantula tattoo. It seemed significant to him but he could not think of why. All the alcohol he had consumed since five was beginning to catch up with him.

Diego was acting as though he didn't even hear what Tyler was saying. He kept his eyes focused somewhere below the T.V. and above his beer. His face had hardened into a firm, tight mask that displayed no emotion.

"Don't act like you don't know what I'm talking about, Diego. Unless you can come up with another good reason why you followed me down here all the way from New York and haven't stopped trailing me the entire week until last night."

Tyler still could not get a reaction from him. And then the meaning of the tattoo came back to him.

"Come on, Diego. I know you know Suzanne. She has – had– a tattoo also, a monarch butterfly, right here, way high up on her hip. I'm sure you remember it."

Much as he tried, Diego could not keep the shock from registering on his face as he turned to Tyler. "How could–" he caught himself and then stood up abruptly. "Time to go, Shirella."

154

Diego walked quickly out of the restaurant, leaving Shirella to collect her belongings and scramble after him on wobbly spike heels. Tyler was not far behind. It was difficult to see, but their arguing voices carried through the dark to lead him in the direction they had headed. He tried to keep a decent interval behind them. They passed the Sea View and turned up a side road that lead towards the mountain.

They stopped talking after a few minutes and Tyler quickened his pace, afraid of losing them. He was passing a yard fenced in by a wall of rusty, corrugated tin. When he came to the open gate he peered inside, wondering if they had turned off here to enter a darkened bungalow set back among a stand of young, lacy palms.

The next moment he felt as though he had banged the back of his head against a concrete wall although he could not imagine how he could possibly have done such a thing. Then the blackness of the night engulfed him as he crumpled to the ground.

CHAPTER ELEVEN

"I just don't understand why he hasn't shown up yet. It's nearly noon."

Sarah paced the long, empty front porch of Poinsettia Plantation. All the wicker chairs and rockers had been moved inside, as had the hanging plants and potted palms. Rain was beginning to fall from an ominously gray sky and the wind was picking up.

"I told him you had chartered the plane to St. Kitts for two p.m. He knows we're supposed to be at the airport at one."

"Maybe he's planning to meet us there." Nicholas counted up their bags that rested by the front steps. "Cecil! Get a move on it! We're ready!" He looked down at Sarah who had stopped moving and now stood firmly at the far end of the porch, peering earnestly through the rain for any signs of life on the driveway. "Don't get any ideas that I might let you stay here to wait for him, sister."

"Well, at least we have to stop in town and see if he's still at the Sea View. Maybe he overslept or something." It was a lame possibility but she was fishing for any reason now.

"Look, Sarah, it won't be the end of the world if he has to wait out the hurricane on the island. None of the natives have any choice. Now come on, here comes Cecil with the van. If it will make you happier, we'll stop and see what's up with Tyler."

"Of course it will make me happier, you idiot," she muttered under her breath.

She watched Cecil's muscular black arms effortlessly load the heavy suitcases into the back of the van. Cecil was Nicholas's manager and caretaker for the inn. He lived with his wife Marvella in a small stone cottage at the bottom of the driveway. Not only was he strong, intelligent and capable, but he had been born and raised on Nevis, so he knew exactly who and how to deal with any situation that might arise.

"Not to worry, Miss Scupper," he assured her. "We will stop and look for your boyfriend in Charlestown."

"Boy, I hope we can beat this storm out of here," Nicholas commented as the van bounced along the bumpy road in the driving rain.

"They saying now that it not to hit Nevis until nearly dawn. It coming by way of Guadaloupe."

"From the south. Shit. It'll probably be a direct hit on the plantation."

In the back seat Sarah clutched her shoulder bag with one hand and the door handle with the other. She was growing angrier by the minute, thinking about Tyler and how easily he got sidetracked and distracted sometimes. He was probably down at the beach watching the pelicans take cover from the storm or interviewing some young boys on the different ways they played marbles in the Caribbean.

"This is where he was staying?" Nicholas could not hide the astonishment in his voice. "Why would he stay in a dump like this?"

"Because Woody was paying. And because your prices are so outrageous. It's not that bad. No, don't come in. I can do this alone." Before Nicholas could protest, Sarah was dashing between raindrops and up the flight of stairs to the guest house.

The rain beat a loud, persistent rhythm on the metal roof and Sarah had to rap hard on Tyler's door to make herself heard. When there was no response, she tried the knob but the room was definitely locked up. She went out onto the verandah and peered in the louvered window. Tyler was not there and as far as she could tell everything was as it had always been; he had not done any packing.

157

"Damn!" She kicked the wall and bit her lip in frustration. In desperation, she ran down the hall and knocked on Diego's door and then tried the handle. The door swung easily open. The narrow room was empty except for the unmade bed, a decrepit chair and a rickety nightstand. Diego was definitely gone.

"Bad to worse." Sitting down on the bed, she hastily scrawled a note to Tyler on the back of an old bank deposit slip she found in her shoulder bag. "Our plane leaves St. Kitts for Puerto Rico at 3:30. Be there or be square. Where the hell are you anyway?"

Heading back out to the van, she tried to keep up her angry facade to cover the deep–seated worry beneath it. How many times had Tyler done things like this to her anyway? Too many to count. Since Suzanne was dead and now Diego was gone, he probably had decided to stay and do a story on the hurricane to make the trip worth his while. And he could have at least called and told her his change of plans, the shithead.

"Not there?"

"Not there. Let's get going." Her abrupt tone clearly indicated there was nothing more to be said about the situation. Cecil pulled the van away from the curb and continued on his way to the tiny airport in Newcastle.

The choppy five minute flight across the channel that separated Nevis and St. Kitts was enough to drain the color from Sarah's usually ruddy complexion. After checking in for their next flight, Nicholas seated her in the airport cafeteria and brought her a ginger ale.

"I'm glad we didn't take the ferry," he joked weakly. "The sea is already pretty rough. I'd hate to see what you'd look like after forty–five minutes on the water."

Sarah sipped her ginger ale and said nothing. Her eyes darted around the room, involuntarily looking for Tyler, not daring to admit to the subconscious hope that he would still show up. The airport was packed with noisy tourists, both excited and distraught about having to cut their vacations short at the lovely and expensive resorts of tropical St. Kitts.

"The couple in the room next to ours came down on one of those cheapo charter flights," she heard a woman at the next table say. "It's not scheduled to leave until tomorrow and their tickets are non–transferable to other airlines so they're just stuck. Of course their flight will be canceled. They may be here for weeks!" She laughed loudly and sipped more Planter's Punch through a straw.

Everyone's got their problems, Sarah thought and tried to shut out the conversation next to her by focusing on other groups of people around the room. All the tables were full and people were leaning against the walls or sitting on the floor. A single man carrying a beer picked his way through the crowd looking for an empty place to sit. Something about the pattern of his Aloha shirt looked familiar, but she couldn't see his face until he turned to scan their part of the cafeteria.

"Nicholas!" She grabbed his arm. "Look. It's him."

"Who? Tyler? He got here somehow?"

"No. Diego. Look over there by the window. In that flowered shirt." Diego had given up his search for a seat and was standing at the rain–streaked windows gazing out at the runway.

"Are you sure?"

"Positive. I talked to the guy several times."

"Well, maybe now it's my turn to talk to him." Sarah did not like the threatening undertone of Nicholas's voice. "I've got a few things I'd like to ask him." He stood up and kicked back his chair.

"Look, don't get too involved. Our flight boards in ten minutes." Sarah was anxious to leave the Caribbean and the whole fiasco surrounding Suzanne behind her.

"Here, take your ticket. If I'm not back in ten minutes, grab my flight bag and I'll meet you on the plane. Damn. Look, he's recognized you."

Diego had indeed focused his gaze on Sarah. When her eyes met his, an expression of horror froze on his face for a split second. Then he put down his beer on the narrow window ledge, and headed hastily for the exit.

"The guilty son of bitch. I'm out of here, Sarah. I've got some important business to take care of." At the same time Nicholas was speaking, the first boarding call for their flight came over the loudspeaker. "Listen, if I don't catch this flight, don't wait for me." He was shouting to her as he made his way across the crowded room. "I'll catch the next flight to Puerto Rico. The keys to the car are in the front pocket of my bag."

"The keys to the car..." she repeated aloud, not understanding. Then she realized he meant HIS car – the one they had left parked at the Burlington airport in Vermont.

Nicholas did not even attempt to analyze the primal impulse that set him flying after Diego. He did not think about what he would do or say when he finally caught up with him. For a few moments, however, he questioned his own sanity as he stood outside the airport, in the driving rain, trying desperately to find a cab to follow the one that Diego had just leaped into.

Usually there were a dozen idle drivers eagerly offering their services to any likely candidate. But no one was flying into St. Kitts today and the cabbies dropping off the anxious, departing tourists did not hang around, but returned as quickly as possible to the resort hotels looking for another fare.

Finally he managed to snare a ride, but the probability of catching up with Diego seemed slim. He explained the situation to Roderick, the cab driver, who nodded reassuringly. "No problem, mon. I know the taxi you are talking about. That would be Lester Brown's taxi and him a good friend of mine. Lester will tell us where he dropped this man off."

The better part of an hour went by as they crept forward. For some reason the traffic headed for Basseterre was nearly at a standstill. The three miles from the airport to town seemed endless, but Roderick assured him that Lester would be stuck in the jam also. They finally passed the root of the problem – a clogged drainage ditch had flooded a low spot in the road and cars were creeping through water that was a foot deep.

"Shades of things to come," murmured Nicholas. He was already beginning to feel like a fool for his actions but there was definitely no turning back at this point. The windshield wipers of the car could barely keep up with increasing strength of the storm.

"Lester usually park down by the wharf but the last ferry gone already. Maybe he in the square."

"Look, Roderick, this is probably just a wild goose chase I'm on. Let me pay you for your trouble and you can just take me back to the airport."

"They say not many more planes will be leaving today. You might – Look! What I tell you? There Lester be now." Roderick pulled up beside the battered blue Ford Cortina and rolled down his window. The two men shouted back and forth briefly, using the local patois that Nicholas could not understand.

"He drop him at a bar up on Cayon, he says." Roderick put his car in gear and took off again. "Most places closing up for the storm but this one, a small local place, it staying open to catch all the business."

A few minutes later he stopped in front of an old wooden, two story building, its louvered shutters tightly hasped across all the windows. Even through the pounding of the rain on the car, they could hear the raucous noise coming from within.

"You want me to come back and check for you in a bit, see if you want a ride to a hotel for the night? The Royal St. Kitts is staying open for those brave enough to stay. The casino can make a lot of money on a night like this."

"Sure. Thanks for all your help, mon." Nicholas tipped him heavily and made a dash for the open doorway.

A thick haze of smoke helped to shroud the underlying smells of dampness and sweat that overwhelmed the dark room. It was filled beyond capacity with men, most of them standing in small tight groups talking loud and fast in the local dialect which Nicholas could not translate. A huge group was packed in tightly around a table where four men played a violent version of dominoes, smacking their markers down with noisy thwacks of big, open palmed hands.

He spotted Diego in the corner of the room that was farthest from the door. He had acquired a bar stool somehow, perhaps through bribery, and was hunched over a beer, his back to the rest of the room. The bar was full of such restless, volatile energy that Nicholas decided to play it cool for a bit. It was definitely not a good place to pick a fight of the magnitude he was anticipating. Watching and waiting might give him the upper hand he needed.

Turning to a gangly barefoot teenage boy who hovered empty–handed by the doorway, he said, "Listen, kid, would you do me a favor? Buy me a beer and buy one for yourself too?" He pressed an EC bill into the boy's hand. With a nod of agreement and without a word, the ragged teenager was gone, slipping through the crowd effortlessly in a way Nicholas could never have pulled off.

A few hours later, Nicholas had very nearly lost sight of his mission. Other than Diego who was quite dark–skinned, he was the only white face among a sea of blacks and it had been difficult to keep his presence low key. He befriended a couple of over–six–footers who were occupying one of the only two booths in the room and with the promise of a few rounds, slipped in with

162

them. His teenage friend had been paid off to watch the door and let him know the minute Diego left the bar.

They had just graduated to straight shots of Cruzan Rum when the boy appeared at the booth. "Him goin' nah. But de starm it bad."

Nicholas surprised his companions with how quickly he leapt over them and towards the open door.

"You mustn't go out there, mon," several people warned him in various ways. "The rain will soak you. The wind will knock you down flat. This is a hurricane coming, mon, not a little drizzle."

A gust of wind and blast of cold water punctuated their remarks. Across the street Nicholas could see Diego huddled in a store entrance, taking a leak on the sidewalk. Nicholas turned back to the gawking crowd behind him. A yellow slicker hanging on the back of a chair caught his attention.

"Who's rain gear is this?" He grabbed it up and waved it high. "It's worth fifty EC to me right now and I'll see you get it back when I'm through with it."

The owner was at his side in a flash. "Neville Driscoll." His hand was out, eager for the money. "Not to worry, everybody know me, everybody know my slicker."

With hood drawn tight around his head, Nicholas stepped out into the driving rain just in time to see Diego dashing down the wet street, a lightweight windbreaker held over his head and shoulders like a cape. Diego did not run like a man being chased but like one who was trying to avoid being soaked to the bone. Nicholas caught up with him when he stopped in another entrance way to wipe the water out of his eyes.

Diego took one good look at Nicholas's face and was off again like a torpedo. He definitely had the physical advantage – the extra pounds and years of non–activity kept Nicholas from gaining an edge as they raced through the dark streets of Basseterre, splashing through deepening puddles and sliding on slick asphalt.

Although his lungs felt as though they were exploding, Nicholas forced himself on, using his anger as a catalyst, keeping a picture in his mind of Suzanne, youthful and beautiful and tormented, as she had been when he first knew her in college. But the fiery red color of the exploding boat as Tyler had described it to him kept blocking out the image, filling him with a savage energy he had never felt before in his life.

Several yards ahead of him, Diego came to a sudden stop as he rammed headfirst into what seemed to be a high chain link fence. Nicholas gained a few feet as Diego, momentarily stunned, took off towards the left. Nicholas could hear his feet crunching on gravel above the crashing waves of the sea.

Behind the fence was an imposing government warehouse of some sort and beyond that the raging storm–swept Caribbean. He had a feeling that they had reached a dead end. It was just a matter of time before Diego realized it too.

The darkness here seemed more enveloping than the area of town they had just left with its dim and random street lights. The sound of the ocean was disorienting and it was hard for Nicholas to follow Diego's actions clearly. When his cheek brushed hard against a stone wall, he knew that they had reached the end of the cul–de–sac. A few yards ahead a creak and a click gave Diego's hiding place away. He had obviously found a way to enter this unlit building they'd come up against. But it had to be darker inside than out. He wouldn't get far.

Nicholas fumbled for the penlight he always slipped in his shirt pocket before an airplane trip. Its tiny circle of light barely cut through the intensity of the rainy night. By playing it slowly across the side of the building, he was able to make out that it was an abandoned shell of an old colonial warehouse. Although the lower windows were tightly locked and shuttered, the windows of the upper story gaped ominously open like the empty eye sockets of a skeleton.

His light found the heavy wooden door, now rotting off of its hinges, with a sign tacked to it that Diego could not have seen before entering. "CONDEMNED BUILDING. GOVERNMENT PROPERTY. TRESPASSERS WILL BE ARRESTED."

Not tonight, Nicholas thought grimly, as he leaned on the door. Flicking off his penlight, he stepped inside.

It was impossible to hear anything over his own ragged breathing and pounding heart. The darkness surrounding him was nearly complete. The floor beneath his aching feet seemed to be hard–packed dirt. A scurrying sound nearby filled his head with images of enormous gray rats and he shivered instinctively. He might as well get to the business at hand.

"Diego! I know you're in here! Show me your face, you son of a bitch! We've got some talking to do." Nicholas flicked on his light and ran its thin beam around the corners of the room. The huge rats of his imagination came to life, squeaking and running for cover. "Whoa, momma. You see those rats, Diego? What's the word in Mexican for rats – los ratos? You want to spend the night with los ratos or you want to get this over with and talk to me? Now."

There was no reply as Nicholas explored the large empty space with his penlight. A wooden staircase at the opposite end of the open room led to the upper level. Beneath the staircase, the tan sleeve of a windbreaker shone like a beacon in the darkness.

A gust of wind off the sea rattled the shutters on the south side of the building. On the second floor, it lifted loose debris and moved it around, until it settled with a clatter on the ancient wooden floorboards. Nicholas focused his beam on the staircase and headed straight for it.

Within seconds, Diego was darting up the rickety stairs into the unknown spaces above. He tripped on something almost immediately, allowing Nicholas to come nearly even with him. Diego's fist shot out and made contact with Nicholas' shoulder. Nicholas reeled backwards just long enough for Diego to regain his footing and head for the farthest corner of the windswept room.

Nicholas ran his light around the upstairs of the abandoned warehouse, taking in the rotted floorboards beneath the open windows and the wet areas of the floor where the rain had forced its way through rust–worn places on the corrugated metal roof. The building shuddered ominously in the increasing wind; the roofing rattled mournfully.

"End of the line, Diego. There's no way out of here without coming back down these stairs." His shoulder pounded painfully and Nicholas wondered where his blustering bravery was coming from. Diego could probably knock his out–of–shape body down in no time with a few well–placed blows. But they'd both been through the metal detector at the airport and had their hand luggage searched. As long as there were no guns involved, Nicholas was willing to take his chances.

"I don't know what you want with me. I have done nothing wrong." Diego's teeth seemed to be chattering.

"Oh, come off it. No innocent man runs the way you just did."

"Your friend accused me of lies. I just wanted him to stop following me. He will be all right."

"What friend? I'm not talking about a guy. Don't try and weasel out of this, you bastard." Nicholas moved a few feet closer.

Diego backed away along the wall, stopping just short of an open window. Swiftly Nicholas reached down and picked up a rotten two–by–four that was lying at his feet. The rusty nails sticking out of it gleamed menacingly in the small circle of light.

"I said he'd be all right. It was just a little sleeping medicine."

"Who are we talking about?"

"The boyfriend of the girl at the airport. Tyler."

Nicholas groaned. "You son of a bitch." He took another step towards Diego holding his wooden weapon high. "Now tell me why you murdered Suzanne."

"Who?"

Nicholas slammed the piece of wood against the floor. "Don't play games with me." They were shouting now to compete with the roar of the wind and the crashing of the rain against the metal roof. "I saw that picture of you and her. I know you knew her in Mexico. I bet you didn't know I was her sweetheart after that. Was it you she used to have the nightmares about? Were you the one she was talking to in her sleep when she would scream, 'Please don't hurt me anymore!'?"

Diego face turned ashen for a few seconds. Then he spit on the floor at Nicholas's feet. "She was a whore."

Nicholas smashed the two–by–four down again a few inches from Diego's foot, forcing him to leap into the wet spot in front of the nearest open window. "You cock–sucking son of bitch. What did she do, throw you over for some other macho asshole? She ran from you all her life. What could she have possibly done to you that made you chase her all the way to Nevis just so you could kill her?"

"I didn't kill her." Rain was gushing in through the open window, soaking Diego's back and shoulders in a continual cold shower but he seemed frozen to the floor.

"You mean you didn't get your hands soiled? You had one of your buddies do the dirty work? Like your friend, Fred Martin, alias Rico, the cocaine dealer. What I want to know is, did he know that Suzanne worked for me before our coke deal or was that just a quirky accident of fate?"

"No comprendo–"

"You answer my questions, you Mexican piece of shit." Nicholas was close enough to see Diego trembling now. "What exactly was Suzanne to you? How did you find her after all these years?"

"Rico saw her. In your office. He never forgot how Suzanne ripped us off. He is the one who has never stopped searching."

Nicholas felt hot tears springing to his eyes at the realization of his own role in Suzanne's demise. Unwittingly he had trapped her neatly in his office with a ghoul from her past. He did not want Diego to see how emotional those words had made him. Angry at himself and at the whole situation, he slammed his makeshift weapon against the wall just inches from Diego's head.

"What did she ever do to you to deserve this?" he howled.

"Madre de Dios, I am telling you I didn't kill her! But whatever happened to her was her own fault. She was my brother's whore, but we all fucked her after she—"

"Liar!" This time the rusty nails stuck in the window frame and would not come loose. As Nicholas struggled to free the piece of wood, Diego was on it in a flash. His strong hands tried to wrench it from Nicholas's grasp. As the two men fought over it, the nails worked their way out of the woodwork. Without warning, Nicholas let go.

Still pulling on the water–soaked two–by–four, Diego fell backwards, propelled by the force of his own strength. The sill of the open window caught him behind his knees. His feet flew off the slippery floor and with a sudden scream, he did a backward flip out of the window and into the wailing storm. His shriek ended as abruptly as it had begun.

Nicholas peered out the window, focusing his flashlight on the ground below. Diego lay in a still heap on the wet asphalt, his neck twisted at an odd angle to his body. Nicholas sank to his knees and covered his face with his hands. It was over. He could cry now. He could do whatever he wanted.

For several minutes he sat there in a daze as horrific images of Suzanne, Diego and his own life spun in his head. A loose piece of corrugated tin flapping overhead brought him back to the reality at hand. Exhausted as he was, he had to move on. Hurricane Hugo was coming. He needed to find a more sheltered place to atone for his sins.

CHAPTER TWELVE

Several times in what seemed like a very long night, Tyler awoke and tried to get up. On each attempt, his heavy, pounding head felt as though it was in a vise and the effort of lifting it was more than it was worth. Each time he eventually slipped back into the shackles of sleep than held him prisoner in a cell of unborn nightmares.

When he finally was able to keep his eyes open and look around, he had no idea where he was. He was lying on a sagging iron bed covered with a ragged bedspread in a room with bare wood walls and a corrugated tin roof overhead. A cluttered dresser and a chair draped with clothes gave the impression of somebody's very inhabited bedroom. The steady beating of rain on the metal roof played a syncopated rhythm with the pounding of his brain.

Turning his head he saw his khaki shorts hanging from the rusting bedpost. He quickly lifted the spread to see if he really had no pants on. Had he actually been coherent enough to take off his pants before getting into this bed in a room he'd never seen before?

Nevis. He was on Nevis and Hurricane Hugo was coming. The wind rattled the louvers of the window in confirmation. He looked at his watch. Three thirty. Although the light in the room was an ominous gray, it still had to be daytime. Struggling to a sitting position, he rubbed a huge lump on the back of his head.

He remembered now. He had been following Diego and Shirella. Someone had whacked him hard on the back of his head and then he must have passed out. There was a vague recollection of something being forced into his mouth, but he wasn't sure if that wasn't just one of the nightmarish dreams that had disturbed his unconsciousness.

It had been after ten when they left Unella's. Over fifteen hours ago. He had to find out where he was. Then maybe he could remember where he was supposed to be.

He threw the covers aside and reached for his shorts. At the sound of his movement, a head poked through the door.

"He finally wakes up. I was afraid you might never."

He recognized Shirella from the night before. She wore a shabby pink bathrobe that ended above her bony knees. He pulled the bedspread back up to his waist again.

Shirella laughed. "You don't remember that I sleep in that bed next to you most of the night? You have nothing to hide from me."

Tyler's face flushed. "We didn't have sex, did we?"

She laughed again. "You were a dead man. I could not make you stand up. But we can do it now before you go."

Before he could protest she had untied the robe and slipped it off. She wore only a red lace thong underneath.

As usual when seeing another woman naked, Tyler's thoughts went immediately to Sarah. "Sarah. Damn it. The ferry. The plane. Oh, shit." His forgotten plans came rushing at him like a derailed freight train. "What time does the last ferry leave?" he shouted, ignoring Shirella's seductive approach and pulling his pants on.

"Ferry gone. No more ferry until Monday. It not run on Sundays. AND it not run during hurricane. Everything shutting down now."

171

"Damn. I can't believe this happened." He sat down on the bed again to gather his thoughts. "Where the hell's Diego, anyway?"

"Him gone, mon. He catch the ferry to Basseterre a few hours ago." She sat down next to him and put a thin hand on his leg. "It is just you and me here. My little girl is napping in the other room, but she will not wake for some time. You must stay here with me until the storm is over. I won't charge you."

Angrily he pushed her aside and stood up. "No, I've got to find Sarah. She may be waiting for me someplace. How do I get back to town from here? And where are my shoes?"

Tyler was soaked to the bone by the time he climbed the stairs to the Sea View. Sarah's note greeted him with the gaiety of an eviction notice. He stripped off his wet clothes and wrapped himself in a beach towel as the guest house shuddered and moaned in the gathering wind of the storm. Not thirty feet away the sea was becoming wild, with waves that climbed higher and higher.

Trying to steady his nerves, he reminded himself that this could be the journalistic opportunity of a lifetime, weathering out a hurricane on a tropical island and recording its aftermath. He had no choice so he might as well make the best of it.

But an old ramshackle guesthouse right on the water was definitely not the place to hole up during gale force winds and torrential downpours. He had to get to higher ground and the only place that came to mind was the Poinsettia Plantation. Those sturdy centuries–old buildings had to be safer than the Sea View as long, as he could find a way in.

Hunger overcame him as he threw his belongings helter–skelter into his suitcase. He devoured the only food he could find, which was an entire box of wheat crackers, and washed it down with a warm beer he

172

found floating in melted ice water in his cooler. Anticipating that he might have to do some walking, he abandoned the idea of bringing the cooler along.

Hopefully he could raid the refrigerators at the plantation when he got there.

His lightweight Gortex anorak did not offer much protection from the storm but it was the best he could do. At least the top half of his body would be relatively dry. Tossing his soaked leather topsiders into the suitcase, he put on a pair of colorful plastic sandals he had bought earlier that week. All the men on the island wore this flexible European–style footwear of red, green and yellow plastic; now he understood why. With a final cursory glance around the room, he was off.

It was raining harder now. As he headed for the center of town, heavy gusts of wind battered his face and assaulted his body. The storm seemed to be coming from the south and he momentarily questioned his decision to move. Although it was a mile inland from the sea, the Poinsettia was on the southern side of the island. Nevertheless, he pressed on through the empty streets.

By offering twice the normal fare, he managed to convince a taxi driver in the square to take him out towards Gingerland, the lush district on the southern slopes of Nevis.

The windshield wipers of the cab could not keep up with the head–on rain and the going was slow and precarious. In a few places swollen streams had risen almost to a level equal with the roadbed, threatening to wash out the only way back to town. The driver grumbled loudly about this possibility at each opportunity that arose.

Nearly an hour had gone by before he made the final turn onto the gravel road that led to the steep driveway of Nicholas's hotel. "You will have to make your own way from here, sir," he announced pointing an accusing finger towards the front of the car.

Tyler looked out the window and saw water pouring across a one lane wooden bridge that was between him and his destination.

"Bridge will wash away by morning," the driver declared. "Better plan to stay a few days."

For half a second Tyler reconsidered. But there was something beyond reason that was drawing him on towards the inn. He just knew he had to get there and that he would not rest until he did. He shut down the rational part of his brain and switched over to instinct.

"Thanks for your trouble, man. Good luck getting back." He slammed the car door. Slipping on his daypack and hoisting his suitcase high, he sloshed across the ankle–deep water on the bridge.

He had less than a mile to go but it was all uphill. The driveway of the Poinsettia had turned into a raging gully awash in water racing down the side of the mountain with nowhere else to go. The wind was at his back now and at times it pretended to work in his favor, hurling him forward until he tripped over a dislodged boulder in the middle of the road. The rain was a heavy curtain of water that rippled like sheets hung out to dry on a windy day. The red and green leaves of the poinsettia bushes lining the driveway floated in the run–off around his feet.

Finally the outbuildings of the hotel began to appear through the growing darkness, unidentifiable black shapes that pointed the way to the great house. Although he hated to admit it, the wind seemed worse up here. But at least there was no chance of washing out to sea.

The main building was locked and boarded up, but a swinging shutter on a window suggested a possible entry. He was surprised to find the window itself unlocked but he reasoned that if the shutters were hitched from the inside they provided an equal amount of security.

Inside at last, he breathed a sigh of relief and set down his wet baggage. Rivulets of water ran off of him and across the sloping boards of the two–hundred–year-old floor. The only light came from the unshuttered window behind him but he was able to make out that he was in the large, low–ceilinged living room. Usually airy and expansive, it was now damp and close and felt oppressive. A flick of the light switch on the wall told him instantly that the power was already off.

He found an old kerosene lamp on a mantelpiece and lit it and then another and another. The warm, golden light fought bravely to counteract the howling storm that shook the building repeatedly. Still, it seemed only about as cozy as a haunted house or Dracula's castle. Maybe after he got into some dry clothes and had something to eat, he could relax a little.

He put on his last pair of dry shorts and hunted for the kitchen. The gas stove still worked and he contented himself with a bowl of instant oatmeal covered with the local brown sugar and evaporated milk. This simple warm meal was so satisfying that he made himself another bowl. As he sat on the counter eating it, there was a terrifying crack outside. The huge building shivered and creaked as shingles and boards ripped apart above his head.

Tyler knew instantly what had happened. The enormous cottonwood tree, which had shaded the great house from the southern sun since colonial times, had blown down onto the building, smashing through to the upper floor.

With a gaping roof and open walls calling to the wind for more, the sturdy inn was no longer a fortress from the storm. The actual hurricane was not scheduled to hit until early morning which meant the worst was yet to come.

Tyler had made a grave mistake and he knew it. The only safe place in a situation like this would be underground. An image of himself and Sarah in

175

Nicholas's wine cellar drifted through his numbed brain. Had it only been yesterday they had so casually picked out a vintage Beaujolais for dinner?

The wine cellar was the answer. He could bring down some cushions and kerosene lamps and comfortably wait out the storm below ground. Holding a lamp high above his head, he hurried down the hall to the cellar door. Upstairs he could hear furniture being blown across the floors of the exposed bedrooms. Flinging open the door he started to descend the circular staircase as the cool air from below wafted up to greet him.

He had almost reached the bottom step when an unbearably bright light was abruptly shined into his face. His heart stopped beating.

"Don't come any closer. I've got a gun."

The voice was unmistakably female.

Tyler tried to shield his eyes from the light so that he could see the speaker but it was an impossible task.

"I said I've got a gun."

"Well, I don't. So why don't you put down your gun and your flashlight and let's talk for a minute."

"What are you doing here?" The voice was accusing and the light stayed where it was.

"The same thing as you, I think. Finding the safest place to wait out the hurricane. Obviously you found it first. Now if you don't mind sharing, I'm sure there's plenty of room in this wine cellar for both of us."

He started to move forward but the unmistakable click of a revolver stopped him in his tracks. He had hoped she was bluffing. "This hotel is closed down so why are you here anyway? Who are you?"

Tyler drew on all the moral strength that two bowls of instant oatmeal could provide and tried to summon up his most charming smile. "Just a journalist who missed his flight back home. Who are you?"

"I don't believe you. Where's your girlfriend?"

176

"What? Who? Sarah?" Tyler sputtered in bewilderment. "What do you know about Sarah? Where is she?"

His eyes were adjusting to the dark now and if he didn't look directly at the light, he could make out a cluster of lit candles next to an old, ticking–stripe mattress on the floor behind his assailant.

"I don't know anything about her. Or you. Or why you spent all your time on Pinney's Beach watching me."

And suddenly Tyler understood. He had not questioned the inner voice that had urged him up the mountain through the storm and now he knew why.

"I'm Tyler Mackenzie," he said in a loud clear voice. "A friend of Woody Foster's. He sent me here to find you."

"Woody sent you?"

Tyler had held his breath during the endless pause before she spoke. Now, as the arm pointing the flashlight at him lowered uncertainly, he slowly exhaled. It was too soon to relax, however. Just as he caught a glimpse of Suzanne's face, the light shot up again.

"I don't believe you. How could Woody know I was here? I haven't seen him in twenty–five years."

"But you sent him a scarf recently, didn't you? With butterflies embroidered all over it? The day that you disappeared."

"Yes. Yes, I did." The light came down more swiftly this time and Tyler tried to get a good look at Suzanne in the dim light of the cellar.

Her short, jet–black hair framed a face weary with lack of sleep and taut with stress. She was wearing blue jeans and a baggy brown sweater that obliterated whatever shape was left of her once spectacular body. She did indeed hold a small revolver in her right hand.

The worn–out deck shoes on her feet reminded Tyler that there was a good chance he was looking at a ghost.

"We saw your boat explode. We thought for sure you were dead."

Suzanne laughed mirthlessly as she flicked the switch on the flashlight. "You were supposed to think that. Woody Foster. I still can't believe it. How is old Woody?"

"Not well. He has cancer. He may die." Tyler wished he'd had a chance to rehearse for this unexpected confrontation.

"Oh, no. That's terrible. Oh, dear." Suzanne took a few steps backwards and sat down on the mattress, clasping the flashlight to her chest with a painful expression on her face.

Tyler moved towards her. "That's why we had to find you. I guess we ruined some great getaway plans, didn't we?"

"We?"

"Sarah and I."

"Who's Sarah? Woody's wife?"

"No. Woody's never been married, Suzanne." Tyler wasn't sure how far he should go with this, but he kept blundering along. "He said that no other woman ever matched up with his memories of you."

Suzanne laughed that rueful laugh again and then her eyes filled with tears. "He should see me now." She sniffed loudly and then, placing the revolver and the flashlight on the mattress beside her, she covered her face and wept in earnest.

Tyler quickly slipped the revolver into his own pocket. "I'll go get my things upstairs. I'll be right back."

By the time he returned with his suitcase and wet clothes, Suzanne was wiping her eyes and picking up some of her belongings that were spread out on the mattress. "Did you take my revolver?" she asked. "I can't seem to find it."

178

"Yes. You seemed rather suicidal." Hardly the reason and neither of them believed it.

"I'd like it back, please. I'm sure I'll be needing it more than you." She held out her hand, quietly demanding.

"And why is that?" Tyler took the hand gun out of his pocket and tried to figure out how to unload it. His only experience with firearms was via John Wayne and Clint Eastwood movies.

"I'm not even sure if it's loaded. I wasn't expecting company."

Tyler raised his eyebrows as he pulled a couple of bullets out of their chambers before handing it back to her.

"Thanks. What was that crash I heard before?"

"The big cottonwood tree in the yard blew over and came through the roof." It was cold in the cellar and Tyler, pulled a sweater from his suitcase before stashing it against the wall.

"Oh, no! How awful. The inn will be destroyed by the hurricane. I must go save a few things for Nicholas." In an instant she was up the staircase and out of view.

Tyler shook his head. He did not understand this woman's motives but he certainly had the next several hours to find out. Alone for a few moments, he took the opportunity to set up his voice–activated tape recorder which was easily hidden in the shadows of the cellar. Just in case he was not able to convince her to come back with him. At least he would be able to prove to Woody that he had found her and that she wasn't dead.

While Suzanne spent the next half hour moving paintings and pottery and hotel records to safety, Tyler spent the same time trying to create an atmosphere in the wine cellar that was cozy and conducive to talking. He brought couch cushions down and blankets and a few more lanterns. More importantly, he brought two hand–cut crystal wine glasses and a corkscrew. After all, how many people were lucky enough to wait out a hurricane with a few hundred bottles of the world's best wines?

Suzanne finally shut the cellar door for the last time, muttering to herself about the devastation on the second floor. Tyler brought her out of her reverie with an important question.

"Which do you prefer, madam, red or white?"

"What?" Suzanne looked blankly at him and then saw the two wine bottles he was exhibiting to her as though he were a waiter in a fine French restaurant. There was touch of amusement to her dry laugh this time. "Oh, but the red, of course, sir. The white cannot be properly chilled."

"An excellent choice, madam."

He knew Suzanne's eyes were carefully assessing him as he uncorked the bottle and poured the wine. He handed her one of the delicate goblets.

"To Hugo."

She shook her head. "To Woody."

"Okay, then. To Hugo and Woody."

They sipped the dry burgundy in silence for a moment. "Now explain to me how you ever found me here." Suzanne leaned back comfortably against the cushions. She was already beginning to feel more relaxed than she had in days.

"Sure, but first I want to know why you're not dead. How could you possibly know that Diego was going to blow up your boat that night?"

"Diego?" Her face suddenly paled and her eyes grew dark and suspicious. "You know Diego?"

"Well, let's say I made it my business to know him after he followed me down to Nevis." He took another swallow of wine, curious about her reaction to Diego's name.

"But then where did you get the idea that Diego was planning to blow up my boat?"

"Well, we didn't know that. We just assumed that he did because...because it was the only answer." In the

180

soft light, they peered at each other in confusion, Suzanne's brow furrowing into deep ruts as she tried to understand. A remark she had made earlier added murk to the mud in Tyler's mind. "Let's start over. Why don't you just tell me what happened."

Suzanne swallowed a mouthful of the burgundy before speaking. "I was shocked when I saw Diego in the market and knew it was just a matter of time before he and Rico caught up with me. After all these years, I could not let that happen. I didn't know why you were watching me, I thought you might be working with him. I was desperate. When I heard about Hugo on the boat radio, I realized it was my only chance. If I timed it right, with a hurricane coming, the coast guard would have more important things to do than look for a possible missing body. So I blew up the boat."

"YOU blew it up?" Tyler was astounded. "How did you manage it?"

Suzanne gave a cynical chuckle again. "Explosives 101. Ammonium nitrate and diesel fuel. Easiest bomb in the book. Part of my past that very few people know about and that I'd like to forget. 'You don't need a weatherman to know which way the wind blows.'" Tyler recognized the lyric from an old Bob Dylan song. "Guess you're too young to remember that one."

"Subterranean Homesick Blues. I'm not as young as I look. I know who the Weathermen were." He did not mention how hard it was to conceive that this middle-age woman in front of him had been part of the infamous underground anti-establishment movement of the sixties.

"Really? I'm impressed."

Tyler was uncertain if she was being sarcastic. "Well, you fooled everybody. Diego's left the island. I told him you were dead. Nicholas and Sarah think you're dead too. You did a good job. It was a perfect plan."

181

"Perfect plan. Bullshit. I don't have a boat anymore. I can't sail to South America. I'm still on the fucking run. I hid out in the jungle behind my cottage for a day until Nicholas had it boarded up. I spent last night there until I saw them leave today at noon. I'll spend a couple of nights down here and then what? You tell me." She shook her head. "No, don't say anything. Just tell me about Woody and how you found me."

Tyler refilled her glass and his own as he began his side of the story. He watched her face carefully for reactions when he talked about Woody's description of their affair and when he described Rico's abduction of Sarah and the photograph he'd found in Diego's room. Sometimes he thought she was only half–listening, lost in her own memories.

"Does Woody still have that wild curly hair?" she asked.

"He does, but it's gray now."

"Gray. It's hard to imagine. Half a lifetime has gone by. I could have had everything. I threw it all away for a tattoo on a hot afternoon in Mexico. It doesn't seem fair. Sometimes I would like a second chance."

Tyler popped the cork on another bottle of wine and filled her glass to the rim. Above their underground sanctuary, the wind blew stronger and the rain came down harder, but they were barely aware of it.

"Why are Diego and Rico out to get you?" He tried to ask the question in a non–threatening manner.

She shook her head. "I've never talked to anyone about this in twenty–five years. Why should I start now?"

"Oh, I don't know. Because this is this the first time you've ever had a hurricane party in a wine cellar on Nevis with a friend of your old friend Woody. How's that for a reason?" He grinned. "Better drink some of that wine before you spill it. Why did you run? Why not just go to the police?"

"Police. Hah. You don't understand. We're talking about a bunch of crimes committed in a third world country known for its lack of justice and understanding. A chain of unpleasant events that has kept me a prisoner of demon nightmares and memories for years."

"It might help you to get it behind you if you talk about it."

"The only thing it would help me get behind is bars."

She was a tough nut to crack and Tyler found the challenge exciting.

"All right, so forget the demons. Just tell me the good parts. Tell me how you got to Mexico in the first place and how you met Woody."

"The good parts." Suzanne snorted. "That should be a short story."

Tyler watched her in the flickering candlelight and kept his mouth shut. He hoped that he could win enough of her confidence so that he could eke the whole truth out of her.

"Well, you've got me thinking about it now. I might as well tell you the 'good parts' – it'll help pass the time."

She took several swallows of the wine and making herself comfortable, she shut her eyes. "It'll be a test. To see what positive things I can come up with from that time of my life."

"How old were you when you went to Mexico?"

"Eighteen. A child. An oversexed virgin looking for an earth–shattering relationship in a dusty seaside village called Puerto Cerrito. I was there with two high school girlfriends of mine..."

With a little prompting from Tyler, Suzanne began to spin the colorful tale of her lusty affair with Raoul in the tiny shack by the sea. At first she seemed to have a difficult time just forming the words that came out of her mouth. But after a while the images flowed rapidly and easily. When she got to the part about Woody, she

183

could not seem to speak fast enough. Tyler found it delightful to hear her describe him as a young adventurer with wild hair and a broken motorcycle who had swept her off her feet.

Then the story came to an abrupt stop.

"What happened next?" he asked.

"That's the end of the good part. Until we get to Nicholas. But that was years later."

"But who was Diego? How did he fit in?"

"Oh, he was Raoul's brother. We had a brief affair and he never forgave me for it."

"That's it? He's just a jilted lover?"

"Not exactly."

Tyler could not let the story end there. "What about Raoul? Whatever happened to him?"

"He's dead." The hollowness of Suzanne's whisper was frightening.

"I'm sorry. How did he die?"

There was no answer. The minutes ticked by. Suzanne stared at the flame of a candle, lost in memories that etched a gaunt and stricken look on her face. Tyler reached for her hand and squeezed it. When she looked up at him her eyes were full of pain.

"It doesn't leave this room."

"I promise." His tape recorder had clicked off long before.

"You'll never tell Woody."

"I swear."

"All right. Then I'll tell you. I don't know why but I guess it's time." She pulled her hand away from him and looked back at the candle, mesmerized by the flame again.

"One night after Woody had gone back to Vermont for his father's funeral, Raoul came home hopping mad. He had found out about Woody and me..."

CHAPTER THIRTEEN

"It was Diego who told him. Raoul showed up late one night with Diego, Rico and another friend named Julio. I knew they had been drinking – I could smell it on them."

Suzanne closed her eyes as the scene came back to her in all its vivid horror.

Raoul backed her up against the kitchen counter and slapped her hard across the face twice, once on each cheek so that her face flamed with color even before he attempted to humiliate her. Shouting a string of vulgar expletives at her, he took hold of the neck of her thin blouse and ripped it down the front. Before she had time to gasp, he had grabbed her by the wrists and twisted her arms behind her back, holding her against him, so her bare breasts jutted out in full of view of his leering friends.

"If you can share them with strangers, I can share them with friends," he growled. His grip tightened as she tried to twist away. "Come forward, don't be shy," he urged them. "See if you can make her nipples grow as large as they do for me."

"Raoul, no, please, I'm sorry," she begged as he shoved her towards Rico who grabbed roughly at her right breast and squeezed it hard.

"No, watch this," Raoul said. He shifted his grip and reached around her body with his left hand to pull on her left nipple with his thumb and forefinger, rubbing it back and forth until it grew dark and hard in front of their eyes. "Now suck on it, Rico."

Suzanne tried to squirm away, repulsed and frightened. "Stand still, you bitch. Maybe they'd like to stick their fingers in your cunt too." He lifted the front of her skirt so that they could see her gleaming, auburn pubic hair. "Look, Julio, she never wears any underwear so that she's ready to jump on it any time of the day or night. A true whore."

The men laughed appreciatively.

"Come on, she can probably accommodate all of us at once. She's got two tits, a cunt and an asshole." Suzanne screamed in protest and began to cry. Letting go of her wrists, Raoul pushed her back against the counter. Still holding up her skirt with one hand, Raoul unzipped his fly with the other. He was already hard and ready.

"Let's show them how you like to do it any place," he snarled. "Get up on the counter and spread your legs."

When she continued to sob and beg, he hit her again, much harder this time, before lifting her by the waist and sitting her on the wooden counter. As he forced her legs apart, she fell backwards still dizzy from the blow. One hand landed on a dish towel, the other struck the edge of a cast iron frying pan half full of refried beans.

She gripped the handle of the frying pan as Raoul began trying to shove himself inside of her. She did not think about what she was about to do. Her animal instincts for survival had taken over.

With an ear–piercing shriek, she swung the heavy pan at Raoul's head. Beans splattered around the room as the cast iron frying pan made contact with the back of his skull. His eyes met hers in a look full of hatred and painful disbelief. She swung it again, and this time it hit his neck with a loud crack. Raoul's body crumpled to the floor like an abandoned marionette.

"I don't remember much after that. Somebody went for the police, somebody held me down. Diego sat on the floor with Raoul, crying and praying. Before the police arrived they made me change my ripped shirt and tie a scarf over my head to hide my face so that I wouldn't look like I had been defending myself. But of course I didn't realize this at the time."

Stunned by the frankness of Suzanne's narrative, Tyler sat silently waiting for her to go on.

"Do you have any idea what a hell hole a Mexican jail can be?"

"Well, uh, yes, I can imagine." He was reluctant to break her narrative by starting in on his visit to Puerto Cerrito.

"For starters, nobody lets you have a phone call to your lawyer. Guilty until proven innocent is how they look at you. And if you don't have any friends or family to help you out, there's a good chance you'll starve to death if you don't rot first."

Suzanne had no idea how many days she'd spent in the filthy, rat–infested cell. Once in a while someone pushed a bowl of rotten beans and rice through the bars in the door. The first few times she tried to eat it, but had promptly thrown up. After that she had fasted.

Weak and lightheaded, she could barely sit up when the guards came to get her finally. Her knees buckled and they had to drag her out between them to the front of the Puerto Cerrito police station. She was surprised to see that it was quite dark outside and the streets were quiet and deserted. It had to be the middle of the night.

"Your friends have come for you," one of the guards sneered as they let her sink to a heap on the dusty road. "Their money talks."

Unable to comprehend what was happening to her, Suzanne looked up. Two men were leaning against a familiar looking pick–up truck, observing her with expressions of pure disgust on their faces.

"My God, she stinks! Look at her."

187

"Throw her in the back. We'll make her wash up when we get her home."

It was Diego and Rico. She could not have been more shocked if it had been President Johnson himself. What reason could they possibly have for pulling the necessary strings to get her out of jail? She decided it didn't matter as long as it brought her one step closer to getting home to the U.S.

"Shit, she's just a bag of bones," Rico commented as he tossed her unceremoniously onto some old hay in the back of the pick-up. "She's not going to be any good to us in this shape."

"Well, at least we don't have to worry about her running off." Diego laughed as he started up the truck.

Suzanne tried to understand what they were talking about but she could not think clearly. All she could manage to do was breathe the fresh air and watch the stars until the pick-up came to a halt. Struggling to a sitting position, she saw they were back at the beach shack. Her throat closed up as though strong fingers were strangling her.

"Mother of Jesus, she can't even walk. Do you think if we sit her in a washtub of water she can wash herself?"

They needn't have worried about that. She was too weak to protest when they peeled her filthy, ragged clothes off her body and put her in a galvanized tub of water with a bar of soap. The warm water seemed to renew her energy somewhat. With clean hair and a clean body, her mind became a little less foggy.

She could not understand why they were being even this nice to her, but she didn't dare ask. There had to be a reason they had obtained her release and she was sure it wasn't because they liked her. She had killed Diego's brother – what could he possibly want with her? The best thing to do was to keep her mouth shut and just go along with it for now. They were definitely up to something.

She staggered to her feet and wrapped a rough and tattered towel around her torso. Diego and Rico watched her openly from the steps of the house where they sat smoking cigarettes and talking in hushed tones. Swaying unsteadily, she made her way towards them.

"Shit. I guess we'll have to find something for her to eat. She doesn't look like she could cook anything yet."

"Yeah, well, I'll fuck her while you make her a plate of food. Then you can fuck her." Rico stood up and reached for Suzanne's arm as she started to fall backwards. With a quick jerk, he pulled the towel away to expose her nakedness. "Come on, bitch. You can pass out on the bed. All you have to do is lie on your back and spread your legs."

"Her tits don't look as big as they used to," Diego commented as Rico dragged her limp body across the room to the sagging double bed.

Suzanne knew she had no strength to fight Rico off and that the best thing to do was to be passive and get it over with. She willed her mind and heart to separate from her body, the skeletal frame which barely felt like the substantial flesh she had always called her own. Over and over again, as they took turns using her during that first terrifying night, she called upon her inner strength to rise above the physical plane.

When she was finally allowed to rest, she was left naked on the stained and wrinkled sheet, her hands tied by the wrists to the iron bed frame. Diego snored beside her; Rico slept in a hammock hung across the other side of the room. She had exchanged one hell for another. The only difference was that there was a better chance of escape from this hell.

For the first few days they let her stay in bed, eating and sleeping to regain her strength. They would not let her wear any clothes. At night they took turns having sex with her but usually just once each, not the sadistic marathon of the first night. They did not seem to notice that she never spoke or maybe they just didn't

189

care. They only tied her up when they were both asleep so that she could not run away from them.

Once her health came back to her, however, they treated her like a slave. She was allowed to wear only clothing that had been made intentionally so ragged that it could not cover her decently. Big holes were cut in the front of her blouses and her skirts were shredded to the waist. That way, if she tried to escape to town, she would be instantly noticed. She had to cook and clean for them, wash their clothes, tend the garden, haul all the water, and wait on them like a servant. Any insubordination was greeted with violent beatings and physical deprivation such as no supper and being forced to sleep on the floor or outside in the dirt with her hands and feet bound to a post.

One of them watched her at all times. If they both left the house at once, they made her strip naked and then tied her to the bed. Each night they raped her in a manner both predictable and unimaginative. After being severely beaten and then sexually abused for refusing once, Suzanne soon learned to shut herself down emotionally and physically at these times. It was always over quickly.

Unfortunately, part of the deal with the guard they had bribed, was that he also be allowed to have sex with Suzanne on his weekly night off. He was a cruel man who made Diego and Rico wait outside while he forced Suzanne to perform vulgar and humiliating acts for and with him. He would not stop until she cried out and begged him for mercy. It was the only time of the week that she spoke or cried. Afterwards she sobbed herself to sleep. Diego and Rico usually left her alone on those nights.

Because of her constant silence, Rico and Diego never included her in their conversations and sometimes rambled on, forgetting she was listening. It was during her first week with them that she overheard the reason they had liberated her from prison.

"I know she has been there. Raoul told me once she had gone with him. She was supposed to be in on it with him. She was going to do some smuggling to the States."

Rico spat on the floor. "He would have been a fool to trust her. I hope she remembers how to get there."

"We'll make her remember. And we can use her help up there during harvest time. It can be a lot of work."

"And a good fuck at the end of the day can be very relaxing." Both men laughed.

They wanted her to lead them to Raoul's marijuana patch in the mountains. It would probably be her only chance for escape. On occasions when she felt particularly desperate, she would try to devise her plan for getting away from them, but she had difficulty thinking it through. In order to deal with her current situation, she had numbed her brain so thoroughly that life was just a series of actions. Most of the time she didn't feel or think anything.

When they finally asked her if she knew the way to Raoul's plantation and she nodded her assent, they could not conceal their delight. They made their plans, buying supplies and canvas knapsacks and in the end borrowing a burro from another of Diego's brothers. It seemed that another guy was in on the deal also – an old, grizzly fellow who apparently had quite a lot of experience in harvesting and curing marijuana.

When the day came to leave, they loaded Suzanne up like a pack animal to insure that she could not easily run away from them on the trail. Just to be certain, they tied a thick rope around her waist that Diego held on the other end, making jokes about having two burros now.

When they stopped to rest at noon, Suzanne was so exhausted she could barely move. Deep red welts cut into her shoulders from the heavy pack and her midriff was chafed raw from the rough rope rubbing against it. Realizing they would make better time if she was not so loaded down, they emptied most of her pack onto the burro while she made them lunch. While they siesta–ed in their hammocks for an hour or so, Suzanne slept on a dirty blanket on the ground below them.

She did not worry about scorpions. A deadly insect bite would be an easy way out of her troubles right now.

By the time they reached their destination, two days later, Suzanne was more tired than she'd ever believed possible. Each night the three men had sat around a campfire smoking while she had collected firewood, hauled water, made supper and cleaned up afterwards. When she finally curled up on her blanket in a dreamless sleep beneath the tree to which her wrists were lashed, she was rudely awakened by Rico pulling her legs apart to satisfy his nightly animal urge. Diego didn't bother her during the journey which apparently left him exhausted each evening also. The afternoon of the third day they went slightly out of their way to a tiny mountain village that had a combination general store and bar. Each of the men had several Coronas before stumbling back to the trail to finish their journey. They promised the storekeeper they would return on Saturday night.

Finally they came to the crude shelter that Raoul had built on his last visit to house his gardening tools and supplies. Beyond the shelter was a huge sunny clearing full of eight–foot–high marijuana plants. Rico and Diego whooped for joy and smacked each other on the back.

They harvested the crop in a couple of days but the picking and drying of the leaves was a long, arduous process. Suzanne was forced to do most of this work because they found they could tie her to one of the support posts of the shelter and leave her with a pile of plants to work on and not have to keep an eye on her every minute. If she did not work fast enough, she was punished in one of their usual ways.

192

At twilight on Saturday the sky clouded over and they heard the distant sound of thunder. Working swiftly, they moved the entire crop into the shelter to keep it as dry as possible. The huge pile was impressive and Rico and Diego could not stop grinning with greed at the thought of how much money they were going to make. They decided to celebrate by going back to the little village and getting drunk with the storekeeper as promised.

Suzanne listened to them making plans as she scrubbed the dishes. Her face flushed as the topic turned to her, but she continued working as though she did not hear anything.

"What about the whore? We can't take her down there with us."

"We'll do the usual. Tie her up inside the shelter. She can sleep there until we return."

She heard the old man say he was tired and would stay at the camp, but Diego replied that they didn't trust Suzanne and would tie her up anyway.

"We ought to get rid of her soon," Rico commented in a lower tone of voice. "Her usefulness to us is nearly over."

"We can always just take her back to the jail. We could probably even get a reward out of it."

"That's true. But we may not be back to Puerto Cerrito for a very long time. Maybe never if things go well."

Suzanne was considerably shaken up after hearing this exchange. She was going to have to come up with a way to escape them soon, no matter what the risk. She was still trembling an hour later as Diego lashed her wrists together on her naked belly, bound one of her ankles to the door frame and threw her filthy clothes in a heap in the corner.

The sickly sweet smell of green marijuana was overpowering in the close humid space. Suzanne closed her eyes and tried to drift away to happier days in her

193

life. Outside she could her Diego and Rico saying their farewells to the old man, her name coming up a few times. Tonight would have been the perfect opportunity if she could have planned for it. Hopefully they would do this again soon and she would be ready.

She did not know how long she had been asleep when she felt rough hands shaking her awake. "Wake up, senorita. They said I could have my way with you tonight if I wanted to," the old man grumbled. He set a lantern down next to her head.

The smell of his unwashed body and his bad breath repulsed her and she rolled away from him.

"You are very beautiful, senorita. In another life you could be a queen." Gingerly he touched her shoulder.

Suzanne held her breath for a moment. The man had just complimented her. Maybe...it was just possible...

She cleared her throat. "Okay, senor. But first you must untie my ankle."

"You won't try to run, will you?"

"With you here? I'm not that crazy." Her mind was racing now as she watched him fumble with the knot. " You know, they never tie my hands up until they are done with me. That way I can use my hands to, you know, help you get aroused." She made a crude gesture to explain what she meant.

The old man frowned and scratched his head.

"It's true. You have seen them with me. They do not tie me up until it is time for sleep." She had always hated the thought that the old man had been watching while Diego or Rico screwed her on the dirty blanket by the campfire. But the time had come to use any resource at hand. "I wondered why they didn't offer you the chance to...to...to fuck me before."

Might as well get right down to his level. "I can see you want me bad." She nodded at the erection showing through his baggy pants. *"Why don't you undo this rope so that we can make up for lost time tonight?"*

He didn't have to be asked again. As soon he had loosened her hands, he dropped his pants to the floor. Suzanne reached up and began unbuttoning his shirt. *"Why don't we get you completely undressed so that you can really enjoy yourself?"*

He was breathing heavily now. His skinny chest, covered with a thick mat of gray hair, moved up and down rapidly. *"Lie down,"* he commanded unsteadily.

"Why don't I get on top?" she suggested gaily. *"That way you can just relax and I can do all the work."*

He groaned with anticipation as he stretched out on the straw mat she had been laying on and pulled her down on top of him. Suzanne knew she had to play along until he at least closed his eyes. She leaned forward so her breasts brushed against his face and he moaned again as he rubbed his rough beard against them, moving his mouth hungrily from one to the other. A knot was forming in the pit of Suzanne's stomach. Her right hand groped blindly for the rope; her small sigh of relief was interpreted as a sound of pleasure.

"Oh, sit on it now, senorita, please." His eyes were closed as he pushed her down in expectation.

Suzanne grabbed his hard penis with her left hand to mark the spot and carefully took aim. With all the force she possessed, she brought her knee up hard into his soft, hairy genitals.

Instantly he gagged and curled up in pain. In a flash Suzanne was on her haunches, binding the rope around his ankles as tightly as she could.

"You bitch," he gasped, still so racked with pain he was unaware of anything else. *"You'll pay for this."* He tried to stand up and howled with rage.

Shaking with fear, Suzanne looked around for something to hit him with. She saw nothing close at hand and in desperation, as he started to rise off the ground, she kicked him in the same spot again and then

195

once more. This time he turned pale and crumpled speechlessly in a faint at her feet.

She found the other rope and, jerking his arms together behind his back, hog–tied his wrists to his ankles as best as she could. He came to just as she was finishing. Twisting helplessly, he screamed with fury.

Suzanne stepped back, trembling with excitement. She had done it. All she had to do was get dressed and go. Looking around for her clothes, she saw the old man's clothing in a pile on the floor. On a sudden inspiration, she slipped into his garments instead of her own. She balled up her ragged skirt and blouse so she could toss them on the campfire; she kept the red shawl on which she had lovingly embroidered butterflies so many months ago. Rolling it up lengthwise, she tied it around her neck like a bandana. Holding the lantern high, she went out through the open doorway, headed for the campfire.

Left in darkness, the old man began rattling off a string of curses that she only half understood. The fire had died down to coals and she poked at it with a stick to get a flame going. As the end of the stick caught fire, an idea occurred to her that she could not resist.

Carrying the flaming stick like a torch, she ran back to the shelter. It caught fire in a matter of minutes, crackling and sizzling like dry tinder. Stepping inside one last time, she used the remainder of the charred wood in her hand to light her clothes before tossing them on top of the mountain of marijuana.

The old man was pleading and begging with her now at the top of his lungs. "Oh, don't worry," she said. "I don't want your blood on my hands too."

Grabbing him by the ankles, she dragged him across the dirt floor and out into the clearing, a good distance from the shed. "Breathe deeply. Maybe you'll get high." Picking up the lantern, she disappeared into the night.

"My God. What a story," Tyler shouted. The hurricane was so loud and furious now that Suzanne was leaning lean against his shoulder and speaking directly into his ear. "How quickly were you able to get out of Mexico?"

Suzanne gave her usual cynical laugh. "Oh, very quickly. It only took about a year and a half."

For three days and nights she wandered through the jungle, totally lost, heading hopelessly north. If she had not come across a small stream on the second day, she would not have made it. On the fourth morning she ran into a trail that led her to a rough track with two ruts that eventually turned into a road that led to civilization.

She had found some pesos in the pocket of the pants and a small knife. Hating to do it but knowing it was necessary, she hacked off her long auburn hair, making it as short as she could with the crude tool. As soon as she came to a town, she planned to buy a hat and a blanket she could wear as a serape so that it would hide her female shape.

The money diminished rapidly and soon she was begging for food or offering work in exchange for a meal. She soon discovered that her own disappearance was the talk of the countryside and that a reward had been posted by Rico and Diego for her capture. Despite her disguise, she took to traveling only by night, hiding out and sleeping during the day. She was soon as drawn and gaunt as when she had emerged from the horrors of her jail cell.

A few times, in desperation, she exposed the secret of her femininity at the back door of restaurants, exchanging quick impersonal sex for a meal. She never asked directions for fear of giving away her identity, she just always headed north, using the sun as her guide, knowing that eventually, one day she would hit the border and then she could go home.

Although she was no stranger to deprivation and abuse, her health began to deteriorate. Finally one evening, aching and feverish, she stumbled up to the back door of a tavern on the outskirts of a small city. A short, pleasant–looking man in a cook's apron came out to see what she wanted.

"Work for a meal–" was all she managed to croak out between thick, cracked lips before swaying sideways and bumping her head on the doorframe. Groping at the air, she slid dizzily to the floor and passed out.

When she opened her eyes, she was being carried up a staircase, held beneath the armpits and by the ankles by two dark–haired women. Her head was spinning but she thought they were dressed exactly alike, in pretty white blouses with crocheted necklines and full yellow skirts with red sashes. Unable to see clearly, she shut her eyes and let herself sink back into the sensation of floating through the air.

"He's burning with fever," she heard someone murmur as they laid her gently on a rug. "Run a cool bath while I get him out of these filthy clothes. We can scrub him up at the same time we bring his temperature down."

Suzanne tried to protest but she could make no sound come out of her swollen throat. Within in seconds she heard the woman undressing her gasp. "Luisa, come here, quickly. Look."

"My God, it is a woman! What can this mean?"

They stepped out of earshot and whispered to each other for a few minutes. Then she felt herself whisked through the air and into a bathtub full of cool water. Suzanne opened her eyes for just an instant, just to see that she really was in a white porcelain tub the way she was imagining it. Then she gave herself up to the pleasant sensation of having her body washed.

When the women finally left her, she was dressed in a clean white nightgown and tucked into a high double bed under a lacy white woven coverlet. Sinking back into the soft feather pillows, Suzanne drifted in and out of fever–ridden hallucinations, occasionally wondering if she was perhaps in heaven now. At dawn she awoke to find the two women sleeping in the big bed next to her, sharing one pillow, their arms wrapped around each other. Before she could contemplate the curiosity of this, she spun off into dark, feverish sleep again.

She lost track of how many days and nights she spent in that high white bed. During the day the women took turns caring for her, laying cool wet cloths on her forehead during the heat of the afternoon, feeding her broth once she was able to take food, helping her in and out of fresh white nightgowns. They disappeared in the evenings and did not creep back into bed until the middle of the night.

When she was finally able to sit up and converse, Suzanne learned their names were Luisa and Sophia and that they were waitresses in a very classy restaurant on the first story of the building. The building where they lived and worked was a hacienda–style hotel built around an open courtyard. It catered to tourists, most of who came on the weekends, driving down from Southern California or Arizona. Suzanne was surprised to learn she was only a hundred miles or so from the border now.

Before she was well enough to even talk to them, she had realized that Sophia and Luisa were lovers. At night when they though Suzanne was sleeping soundly just a few inches away, they would make love softly, trying to keep the sounds of their passion to a minimum. Once she got over the initial surprise of the situation, Suzanne would lie as still as possible so as not to disturb them. They were the kindest, most gentle people she had known in years and nothing they did could undermine that fact.

When she was well enough to get around in a normal fashion, Suzanne discovered she had no desire to leave the shelter of the safe haven she had found. She was content to fuss around their two rooms, cleaning and mending for them, or to sit and watch the easy-going bustle of the hotel from the privacy of their little verandah that overlooked the courtyard. Sophia and Luisa accepted her company willingly, never questioning the condition in which she had come to them or the fact that she did not want to go outside at all. They enjoyed watching her health come back and her body fill out to its natural, full self.

It was inevitable that she become lovers with them. After the sexual brutality she had experienced in the preceding year, she found the new experience of making love to a woman to be non–threatening and more satisfying than she had ever imagined possible. She looked forward to the time they spent in bed together and to waking up each dawn in a soft tangle of arms and legs.

Eventually she told them part of her story, not that she was wanted for murder, but about Rico and Diego abusing her and how she had set fire to their marijuana harvest and run for her life. They were totally sympathetic, as she had known they would be, and acted even more kindly towards her, if that was at all possible.

Occasionally they talked her into going out with them to the market or church or just for a Sunday stroll. She would only go if they helped disguise her, an activity they enjoyed thoroughly. They wound scarves around her growing hair and tied them under her chin, made her wear dark sunglasses and big fringed shawls that covered the unmistakable curves of her body. They always flanked her, arm in arm, so that nobody could approach her without confronting them as well.

Nearly a year went by in this pleasant way. Suzanne neatly pushed her past into a remote corner of her memory and did not think about her old life or who she was. Occasionally she would awaken screaming

200

from an unremembered nightmare, but Luisa and Sophia always soothed her easily back to sleep and by morning she recalled nothing.

Then, one night, as Suzanne sat quietly embroidering a blouse for Sophia, Luisa came racing unexpectedly into the room. "There's a man here asking questions about you," she whispered breathlessly. From the description she gave Suzanne, the man was obviously Rico. "He's showing your picture to people in the dining room and telling them you're wanted for murder. Whatever you do, don't leave these rooms."

When the two women returned from work a few hours later, Suzanne was still sitting in the same position in the same chair, her face a blank, frozen mask.

"He's not leaving town. Somebody tipped him off and he's certain you're here. He's staying across the road at La Riata."

Sophia knelt in front of Suzanne and took her cold hands. "Suzanne, look at me. We found you a ride out of here. Two college students from the States who were in the bar. They've been here for a couple of weeks and we think they're nice, trustworthy guys. They're leaving at dawn and they said they'd take you all the way to the border."

Suzanne's lips trembled and her eyes filled with tears. Sophia wiped the tears away with the tips of her fingers. "Ah, carita. You mustn't waste our last hours together crying."

Tyler was surprised when Suzanne stopped talking suddenly. "What's the matter? That can't possibly be the end of the story."

"Shh. Listen."

The stillness was almost deafening. "Is the hurricane over, just like that?" Tyler struggled to stand up, reeling slightly from all the wine he had consumed over the last several hours.

"My educated guess would be that we're in the eye of the storm now. Probably in a half an hour it will start up again. If you were outside you'd probably see blue sky and the sun shining." Weary from reliving her past, Suzanne made no move to rise from the mattress.

Exciting as the thought of stepping outside into the eye of a hurricane might be, Tyler was much more interested in hearing the rest of Suzanne's story. Afraid that she might fall asleep before she finished, he slid the most recently opened wine bottle out of her reach and then pressed her to continue.

"So what happened next? You rode off into the sunset with two American college boys and lived happily ever after?"

"Hardly. Things didn't really get better until I met Nicholas a year later. In the meantime, certain plans were set in motion that would change my life forever."

CHAPTER FOURTEEN

In the morning Suzanne took her seat in the back of a VW bug behind two young men introduced to her as Dan and Luther. Both of them watched her over their shoulders with increasing interest. For the first few hours she said little, listening and observing, trying to figure out what these two were all about.

Luther wore gold wire–rim glasses and his thin blond hair was pulled back in a little ponytail that just grazed his neck. Dan's carrot–red mane was parted in the middle and fell to his shoulders. He tucked it behind his ears so he could see to drive. His serious brown eyes kept looking at Suzanne in the rear view mirror and frowning. She tried not to react too violently when Luther rolled a joint and lit it up.

"Want some?" he asked in a tight voice as he held the smoke in his lungs.

Suzanne shook her head.

"You don't smoke?"

"Not any more. I had a– uh– bad experience once."

"So how long you been down here since you and your boyfriend broke up and he abandoned you?" This was the story they had been told by Sophia and Luisa as to why Suzanne had been stranded in Mexico alone. There was something in the tone of Dan's question however, that made Suzanne think he did not entirely believe the story.

"I don't know. About a month."

"And where'd you say you were from?"

She hadn't said. "Originally San Diego but a lot of places since then. You can just drop me off any place across the border and I'll hitch from there."

203

"Well, I hope you're not in a big hurry to get home." Dan took a long hit off the joint and held his breath.

"Why is that?" Her heart began to pound a little.

"Because we're not quite done our vacation yet. Thought we'd do a little camping in the desert under the stars before we cross the Rio Grande. You're welcome to come along."

"You see, really we were heading east to Laredo to cross the border there," Luther explained, "but since your friends sounded so desperate to get you home we were going to race you up to Tijuana and drop you off before heading on. But you seem much more laid back about this whole gig than we thought you'd be."

"And much better looking."

As they laughed, Suzanne saw them exchanged a glance that was full of meaning. They seemed nice enough and she really didn't know where she was heading back to. Maybe if she got to be friends with them they would take her all the way back home with them. A Midwestern college town might be the perfect place to start a new life.

With all the windows open, it was hard to hear their conversation over the sound of the Volkswagen engine. Having been up most of the night, Suzanne soon drifted off to sleep. She awoke a few hours later when they stopped at the side of the road to take a leak and switch drivers. She climbed out of the cramped back seat to stretch her hot body. Drenched with sweat, her thin white blouse stuck to her curves like wet tissue.

She pried the blouse away from her skin and fanned herself with it, trying to dry the fabric as well as the river of sweat running between her breasts. Looking up she saw Dan and Luther watching her curiously and speaking quietly to each other. She had almost forgotten what it was like to be admired by men who weren't macho beasts. A little tingle of fear mixed with excitement ran from her stomach to her groin.

"Why don't I get in back with you so we can talk?" Dan suggested when they were ready to go. Without waiting for a reply he squeezed in next to her. As soon as the engine started up again he leaned over and looked at her closely.

"You're the one in the picture, aren't you? The one the guy with the mustache was passing around last night."

The question sent a cold wave of shock over her. With visions of being turned in at the next police station, she shook her head violently.

"Look, you don't have to worry about us." He gave a dry laugh. "We'd never give you up to the pigs. We have as little to do with those motherfuckers as possible." He patted her hand reassuringly. "You stick with us. We've got all kinds of connections. We'll find you a safe set–up back in the States. We can probably even use you to help us out. We'll see."

Suzanne had no idea what he was talking about, but he seemed very sincere. But now that they knew who she was, she was going to have to be twice as careful. Better to just go along with them, no matter what it might mean. She swallowed a little as Dan's comforting pat on the hand became more like a caress.

By the time the afternoon was over, Suzanne had convinced herself that if she had to sleep with one of these guys to get back to the States safely, she could probably handle it. If she could keep from thinking about her past, she might even enjoy it.

As it turned out, she ended up sleeping with both of them. But sex had lost its meaning for her, it was merely an act to be performed, sometimes for mutual pleasure, sometimes only to please others. Indelibly scarred from her experiences, her apathy now had to be a strength rather than a hindrance in getting her to where she wanted to be.

At first she was Dan's girlfriend, and during the week they spent traveling and camping, he couldn't get

205

enough of her. One night Luther started feeling sorry for himself in a big way and when he complained to Dan that they had always shared everything before, Dan jokingly suggested to Suzanne that she help poor Luther out a little. He was surprised when she shrugged her shoulders indifferently and led Luther into the tent. For the next few days she had sex with both of them but when they got back to real life, she was just Dan's girlfriend again and Luther pretended she didn't even exist. He had other, more important, things on his mind most of the time.

The two of them shared a shabby second floor apartment that was a meeting place for a group of men and women dedicated to "the revolution" as they called it. When Dan explained Suzanne's circumstances to them, they welcomed her wholeheartedly into their midst. From what Suzanne could gather, their mission was to undermine any and all military operations that were prospering from the war in Vietnam. They had several targets in mind but so far none of them had the courage or the knowledge to build the bombs necessary to blow these places up.

Most of the time Suzanne stayed out of their meetings, still trying to keep a low profile although Dan assured her that the chances of her being extradited to Mexico for murder were slim. It distressed her that once again she was a kept woman and that she seemed to lack the ability to strike out on her own and make something of herself.

She timidly brought this idea up to Dan and Luther one night, over a dinner of take–out pizza eaten on the living room floor. For an answer, Luther tossed a book at her. "Here. You want to leave your mark on society, read this and then make something of yourself. For us."

It was a book on explosives. Mustering up all the defiance she had left in her abused ego, Suzanne decided to show them all. Within a few months she was

206

a master bomb builder; not long after that she had the perverse satisfaction of seeing the results of her handiwork when the group blew up the local Selective Service office.

"I didn't want to hurt anybody," Suzanne explained to Tyler, "but I had so much misdirected anger over the abuse I received during my time in Mexico that it gave me great satisfaction to destroy inanimate objects like buildings. You know, the way an abused child will hit a dog or another child. Of course, I wasn't seeing it through to the people whose lives were touched and sometimes ruined by these small disasters. Dan, on the other hand, pulled out of our underground after the second bombing. He had a fight with Luther and left without even saying goodbye. Luther rented his bedroom to another guy and I had no choice but to move in with Luther. I became his girlfriend by default."

Suzanne was merely another working part in Luther's underground machine. Her expertise with bombs was far more important to him than how she performed in bed or how devastatingly beautiful she looked dressed for the revolution. Her long auburn hair shined radiantly beneath her black beret, her well-defined legs were displayed in their fishnet pantyhose below her black mini–skirt, her unrestrained breasts swelled inevitably against her snug black turtleneck sweater. But behind his wire–rimmed glasses, Luther's nearsighted eyes never noticed the way other men looked at her. He didn't seem to care what she did or where she was, as long as she fulfilled her duties when the time came to blow up another piece of the government's "war machine."

In order to help with her share of household expenses, she took a job as a breakfast waitress in a diner nearby. The regular customers liked her and tipped her generously and she soon had a small nest egg of her own. She tried to dream about what she would do with her life someday, but it was still hard for her to think about being in control of her own destiny.

Without the counter–balance of Dan's political enthusiasm and anti–war principles, Luther seemed to grow colder and more calculatingly by the day. He fought continually with the other members of the group, pressuring them toward objectives that would surely jeopardize their own freedom. But after they blew up a factory that made parts for tanks and accidentally killed the night watchman on duty, Suzanne decided she'd had enough. She found herself a room in an old Victorian mansion that was now a communal household for college students, packed up her meager possessions and moved out.

That summer, for the first time in her life, she lived peacefully on her own, sleeping in a bed alone, supporting herself with her waitressing job, thinking about taking night classes and putting some direction into her existence. The big house was half–empty, most of the other occupants having gone home or away for the summer, and the students who had stayed on lived their own lives and left her alone.

Until Nicholas and Helen returned in the fall from their summer of backpacking in Europe. Suzanne had wondered who rented the big bedroom next to hers on the first floor. "Art students," had been the only reply to her inquiry and there had been much implied by those two words.

Struck by the midnight munchies, she had been rummaging in the refrigerator at two in the morning, wearing nothing but a big white T–shirt, when she heard a voice behind her exclaim, "My God, who are you? Do you live here now?"

She straightened up and looked over her shoulder. A broad–shouldered man and a petite blonde woman were staring at her. His brown hair was as long as hers was short. They both wore heavy backpacks and clothes that looked none too clean.

"Helen, look at her. What a perfect model she'll make for that Venus I want to do. Tell me that you live here and that you'll model for my sculpture."

"Nicholas, we're not even home two minutes and you're already making an asshole of yourself. Give me the key to the room. I've been up for 36 hours and I'm going to bed..."

Tyler listened intently as Suzanne recounted the same story that Nicholas had told Sarah a few weeks ago in Vermont. Surprisingly, the story did not change much; Suzanne seemed to have been as enamored of Nicholas as he had been of her. The difference was the ending. And what happened next.

It had been the beginning of what seemed like a never–ending sexual adventure. Always searching for new excitement, Nicholas never liked to do anything the same way twice, not even sex. He was constantly thinking up unbelievable and bizarre ways and places to make love. He was always amazed that Suzanne would laugh and go along with it. The only time she ever balked was when he suggested a bondage game and, surprised by her reaction, he didn't press the issue. When she awoke screaming from a violent nightmare that night, she knew he had lain awake afterwards wondering about her mysterious past.

They had sex in places Suzanne would not have believed possible – buses, coffeehouses, formal restaurants, rock concerts, at an art opening, in the snow. The kick, Nicholas told her, was in pulling it off – it didn't matter whether it was good sex or bad sex. She didn't care – it was always fun.

The fun ended abruptly one morning when Luther showed up at the diner where Suzanne still worked.

"We're in trouble," he mumbled, looking down at the cup of coffee Suzanne was pouring him.

"What do you mean, 'we'?"

"The feds are onto us. They know about me and they know about you. They're probably parked outside your house right now waiting for you to come home. They busted the apartment this morning. Luckily I wasn't there. They got Rudolph and Swenson."

Suzanne felt a sudden chill. "What do you suggest I do?"

"Leave town with me now. I'm heading for San Francisco before they catch up with me."

She glanced up at the clock behind her. "I can't go before the end of my shift. That'll look too suspicious." She pulled out a pad and pretended to be taking his order.

"What the hell, Suzanne. It's not like it's going to matter if you lose your job. You won't be coming in tomorrow anyway."

The enormity of his words reached her at last. She was going to have to walk out on her life as though it was a bad movie that she'd grown tired of watching. She was going to have to leave Nicholas without saying goodbye or explaining – it would be too dangerous to have any contact with him or to let him know what was going on. In a moment she was going to untie her apron, pick up her purse, and then trust her fate to Luther. Well, he'd rescued her once before. She'd have to let him do it again.

"I'm losing my voice and about to fall asleep," Suzanne said hoarsely. She slid down on the mattress and pulled a blanket up to her waist. All the candles had burned down except for one.

"So you moved to San Francisco with Luther."

"Not in the way you imagine it. We hitchhiked across the country, arrived in San Francisco totally broke. I dyed my hair blonde and Luther dyed his black.

210

Luther tried to get me to turn tricks to raise us a little money. In his cold heart I shouldn't have had a problem with that.

"Eventually he talked me into being a topless dancer at a sleazy nightclub. Topless – hah. I might as well have been totally naked for the little g–string I wore. But it was good money and I didn't have to fuck anybody for it. Sorry. That's how I used to think of it in those days." Her eyes were closed now.

"How did you finally get to Vermont from California?" Tyler tried to speed her along to the end. Outside the wind seemed to be finally dying down; the hurricane would be over soon.

"Vermont? We're talking light years later. Eventually the feds caught up with us, even though we were two thousand miles away. You know what gave me away – my permanent identity tag – the damned butterfly tattoo. Anyone who'd ever been to the nightclub knew I had it. They threw the book at me; they're very hard on political dissidents, want to make examples of them. Ten years in the pen – out in seven with good behavior."

"Sheesh."

"You'd think a lot of my troubles would be over. Locked up with a bunch of women. But luck is not my strong suit in this lifetime. One of the matrons had the hots for me. God, it was one of the worst experiences of my life. I was working in the prison kitchen and one of the perks was being able to eat as much as you wanted as long as no one caught on. I started putting on the pounds, trying to make myself as unattractive as possible. When a new young inmate showed up, the guard finally lost interest in me. By then I'd gained forty pounds. And that was that. I was never able to get my body back to what it had been, but by then I didn't care.

"Got moved to a minimum security prison the last few years. More like a summer camp. Got very close with a woman there – we became lovers. It was important to me because, it was the first time in my life that someone loved me for myself instead of my body."

"Except for Woody."

"Woody. Right. I guess."

"Suzanne." Tyler raised his voice slightly, afraid she'd fallen asleep.

"Mmm. What?"

"I don't know what your plans are when you leave here, but if there's any way on earth that you could possible get up to Vermont to see Woody..."

"I don't want to put him into any danger. Look what happened to you."

"Don't worry about it. Just go. It's what he wants, remember? He sent me here to find you. Please. It might help him get through this thing, and if not, it will let him die in peace."

Suzanne did not respond and Tyler thought she might have drifted off again.

"Promise me?"

"Okay, okay. I'll try. Now get some sleep, Tyler." She lifted a hand and brought it down heavily on the mattress next to her. "You never know when you'll get to sleep again."

When he awoke eight hours later, she was gone. No note, no belongings, nothing to prove she had ever been there. She had left the door at the top of the stairs open and bright sunlight streamed into the cellar, illuminating the empty wine bottles lined up in a neat row next to the mattress. It was the only evidence he had that she had been with him – he could never have drunk all that wine by himself.

He suddenly realized how incongruous it was that the sun was shining onto those bottles. The door to the wine cellar opened into a dark hall behind the kitchen. Tyler ran swiftly up the circular staircase to confirm his sinking suspicion.

The greathouse of Poinsettia Plantation was no more. Tyler stepped gingerly out onto the pile of ripped boards and broken crockery and looked around at the open spaces and blue sky where the kitchen had once been. The destruction was greater than he would have ever believed possible. Doors, bathtubs, roof beams and floor tiles vied for space on the wide green lawns. Bits of chairs and scraps of bedspreads were caught in the leafless trees on the perimeter of the property. The debris was everywhere.

Across the yard, two cottages stood intact as though the hurricane had never happened. A third was missing its roof, a fourth was flattened. The stone sugar mill was still standing as it had for the last three hundred years.

"Holy shit." Tyler sat down on the fallen trunk of the old cottonwood tree that had started the inn on its way to ruin. This was a journalistic opportunity beyond whatever wild dreams he might have had on the journey down to Nevis. It was likely that he would be stranded on this island for days now, but it hardly mattered. There would be plenty to keep him busy.

In the wake of so much devastation, the morning silence seemed deafening. He wondered where the hummingbirds had sought shelter during the storm and when they would be back. To offset his newfound concern for them, he wondered about Suzanne instead. Where had she gone? The bridge connecting the driveway to the main road had to be totally washed out.

"If I was Suzanne, how would I get out of here?" He asked the question aloud and the answer came to him as quickly as though someone had answered it.

Within the hour, he had packed up his things, and was making his way down the path behind Suzanne's cottage, through the denuded rain forest, over uprooted trees, to reach the road to town.

Getting to the main road was the easiest part of a journey that took him all day. He ended up walking the

213

entire way to Charlestown. Countless times he stopped to help small bands of villagers move trees and debris off the road. From talking to people along the way, it became apparent that Hugo had gathered strength coming across the channel of water between Montserrat and Nevis. Consequently the southern side of the island had been hit the hardest and Poinsettia Plantation had been directly in the hurricane's path.

Upon reaching Charlestown near sunset, he was more than surprised to find the Sea View still standing, virtually untouched by the storm. He could see the high water mark against the building but the old ramshackle guest house had weathered the storm remarkably well. His landlady was amazed to see him back. She handed him a candle and told him the cistern was full of water now – he could shower as long as he liked. For the first time since he arrived at the Sea View, he was thankful for the old–fashioned, gravity–fed water system that did not need an electric pump.

When he reached the top of the stairs, he discovered that most of the rooms of the decrepit inn were occupied by some very unlikely people. One of the tourist hotels by Pinney's Beach had been completely destroyed as had some expensive beach cottages farther up the west coast. These miserable refugees were waiting to get off the island as soon as possible and did not seem to be enjoying what was left of their vacations.

"Hope your expectations aren't too high," muttered a balding, overweight American who had claimed one of the two verandah chairs and was drinking rum straight from a bottle. "This place is really a dive." He lowered his voice conspiratorially. "I've bribed an airport official to get me on the first plane out of here."

Tyler laughed and shook his head as he unlocked the door to his new room. Most people didn't know adventure when it was staring them in the face. He'd be glad when they were all gone and he could have the guesthouse to himself again. In the meantime, there were stories to be written.

CHAPTER FIFTEEN

The stone pillars at the end of Nicholas's driveway signaled the end of a journey that seemed to have taken forever. With a sigh of weary relief, Sarah made the turn and the headlights illuminated the long expanse of asphalt leading up to the empty house.

Four days had passed since she had watched Tyler disappear after Diego on the dock at Nevis. After a hair–raising ferry ride, the plane ride from St. Kitts to Puerto Rico had been the most turbulent flight she had ever experienced. Nearly everyone on the plane had used their barf bag at some point and when the plane finally landed in San Juan, most faces had run the gamut from white to gray to green and back again.

It was not surprising that her connecting flight to Boston was canceled. Almost every flight was canceled. She was advised to get a hotel room away from the sea coast and wait out the hurricane. There was no possibility of getting out of San Juan until the bad weather was over.

She had let a taxi driver take her to a nearby tourist hotel and she had spent two nights there in a dark room with boarded up windows, worrying about Tyler. She managed to get a couple of stale sandwiches from the hotel restaurant and opted for a few cans of beer over the orange soda they offered. She dined and read by candlelight. But most of the time she sat huddled in bed under a blanket in the darkness, wondering if the walls would hold out and if she would survive.

It took another day of waiting in line at numerous ticket counters at the airport before she managed to book a plane out for the following day. In order to get to

Boston, she had to fly to Miami and then Washington, DC, but she was as desperate as the people in front of her and behind her were and she took what she could get.

So here she was finally, at 11:30 at night, ready to collapse into a comfortable bed for as many hours as possible. Thank goodness Nicholas had left her with the keys to his car that was parked at the airport. In the morning, after a good night's sleep, she would deal with the real issues at hand – trying to locate Tyler, and packing up in preparation to go home to West Jordan and face Woody with the sad news about Suzanne.

Grabbing her overnight bag out of the back seat, she headed for the back door of the house, stopping on the terrace by the pool to fumble for the key in her purse. She was totally unprepared for the voice that came from behind her.

"So it is only you who returns. How very, how do you say it – accommodating? – for me." A strong arm came around her waist; hard, cold metal was pressed into her side.

Sarah had heard Rico's voice in her dreams many times in the last few weeks and she recognized it immediately. Frightened and exhausted, she felt tears springing to her eyes. What could he possibly want with her now?

"What do you want?" Her words were little more than a whisper.

"You lied to me." The arm around her tightened with anger. "You said you didn't even know her and then you led my friend right to her."

Sarah gulped. She could hear the edge of hysteria in his voice – she had heard it before in people on the verge of losing control. Rather than say the wrong thing, she kept quiet and waited, trembling, for him to go on.

"Twenty–five years I have waited for my revenge. Twenty–five years. It was almost in my hand and then,

217

ping, it is gone. You stole my pleasure and now you will pay."

"I–I have no idea what you're talking about." He was squeezing her diaphragm so hard that she could not take a deep breath.

He swung her around suddenly and struck her across the face with the back of his hand. "Embustera! Liar! Diego called me before the hurricane. I was hoping he would say, 'Come. I have her at last.' But, no. He told me you and your boyfriend had blown Suzanne and her boat to tiny pieces."

"What? Us? That's ridiculous!" Sarah began to lift her hand to her smarting cheek but Rico knocked her arm aside and grabbed her by the wrist. He twisted it painfully behind her back.

"I told you what I would do to you if you talked about me to anybody else. First you lie to me, then you betray my trust, then you destroy the person I have searched for most of my life. I wanted to make her pay for what she did, before I killed her slowly and watched her die. Well, senorita, you can pay instead."

Sarah was truly frightened now. Somehow she had to get away from this madman and get help. She tried to squirm free of his grasp but he pressed the gun into her ribs again, hard enough to make her wince.

"Nicholas is coming soon," she lied frantically. "He's with Tyler in Tyler's car. They stopped for gas and should be here any minute."

Rico barked a harsh laugh in her ear. "Tyler? That is your boyfriend? He is not coming. Diego took care of him on that island. I know he was not on the plane with you. Which means you are lying to me again, you whore!" With a swift motion, he flung her down onto the harsh flagstones of the terrace and put his knee on her chest.

What he was suggesting was too horrifying to be true. The thought filled Sarah with such fierce rage that she wanted to tear his eyes out. But as the dampness of the wet ground seeped through her sweater, the reality of her situation sunk in. She was miles from the nearest neighbor, alone at midnight, outside a house that had been unoccupied for a week and a half. The chances of anyone coming to her rescue were slim. If she was going to save herself from this demon, she would have to use her brains against his brawn.

She willed her body to go limp and submissive and realized that she was still clenching the key to the house in her left hand. As Rico struck her again, she tried to envision herself unlocking the door and walking inside, leading him some place she could entrap him. But her head reeled from the blow and she could not think straight.

"Take your pants off."

He was ready to rape her right here on the hard slate walkway.

"Why don't we go inside and use a bed instead?" she heard herself saying.

He seemed slightly unnerved by her suggestion. He had probably expected her to scream and kick in protest. A cold drizzle had begun to fall, making the idea seem good even to him.

"Okay. But no tricks." He pulled her roughly to her feet and held her tightly against him as they moved towards the door. "Less chance of somebody hearing your screams from inside."

Her hand was shaking so hard she could barely insert the key in the lock. As they stepped inside, the lights of the burglar alarm pad gleamed dimly in the darkness. Her numbed brain could not remember the code numbers she was supposed to key in to shut it off.

"Turn that thing off now." Rico shoved her toward the lighted alarm.

She hesitated for a fraction of a second. He probably was expecting a blaring siren to go off momentarily. When Nicholas had his security system installed, he had known there would be little use for a burglar alarm of that sort out here in the country. Instead, if the number was keyed incorrectly or not keyed at all, the police station in Emporia was electronically alerted. If you did not call them within a couple of minutes to let them know you had made an error, they automatically responded.

Trying not to appear reckless, Sarah punched in the first number that came to mind – her home telephone number in West Jordan.

In the semi–darkness, Rico forced her down the steps into the living room. There were only three steps and on the last one, Sarah purposely lost her footing, sending both of them sprawling awkwardly onto the parquet wood floor. Rico involuntarily relaxed his grip on her and she seized the opportunity she had been hoping for.

Leaping to the top of the stairs, she ran down the dark downstairs hallway. Her main advantage was that she knew the house and he did not. He was only a few steps behind when she opened the door on her left and slammed it closed after her. She barely had time to lock it before Rico was pounding on the other side.

Gasping for breath, she realized she was in the hot tub room. Above and below the huge glass window in one wall were narrow windows that cranked out, but they were only about a foot wide and not big enough to slip through. Rico was pounding on the door behind her back, cursing at her in Spanish. In the distance she heard the telephone ringing.

The telephone? It was probably the police, trying to avoid a trip out here in the middle of the night. As the message machine picked up the call, Rico stopped banging momentarily to listen. Sarah prayed that they would not leave some kind of message that would tip him off.

She groped for the light switch on the wall, flooding the room with light. The canvas cover was still on the sunken cedar tub. She lifted a corner of it to see if there was still water in it. A little scummy and unheated, but yes, there was still water.

By the time Rico began smashing at the door with some hard object, she was running around the room, unscrewing the light bulbs from the wall sconces. When the door swung in on sagging hinges, she was standing on the bench that ran along the opposite side of the hot tub, up to her knees in water. The room was dark again and the dim light from the hallway cast misleading shadows across the tile floor.

Rico stepped into the room, automatically reaching for the light switch. "Cuno!" He swore at her as he stood in the doorway letting his eyes adjust to the darkness.

Sarah did not want him to be able to see well. She coughed discreetly to let him know where she was.

Rico ran towards her with a cry of rage that became a strangled gasp as he slid wildly on the slippery tiles that Sarah had hastily wet down. In the second before he fell blindly into four feet of water, Sarah heard his hand gun hit the floor. Instantly Sarah hit the button her finger had been resting on. The water began to churn and bubble, like a great murky, cauldron. Totally disoriented, Rico began to scream with panic. As he floundered around in the bubbling water, swearing at the top of his lungs over the noise, Sarah slipped easily out of the tub and moved carefully to where she heard the gun fall.

Her heart pounded harder as her fingers closed around the metal, still slick from the sweat of Rico's palms. Just to let him know she had it, she aimed for the ceiling and pulled the trigger. At the sound of the gunshot echoing through the room, Rico stopped his pointless flailing and turned in her direction. The square of light from the doorway illuminated Sarah's defiant stance and also showed him the edge of the tub.

"Give me the gun." He tried to sound tough as he hauled himself out of the water.

221

"Don't come near me or I swear to God, I'll shoot you." Sarah felt ridiculous uttering words that she'd heard in dozens of bad cop movies, but she meant what she said. Tyler had always told her that the reason he would not become a professional private investigator was that he didn't believe in guns. Tyler... remembering what Rico had said about Tyler spurred her angrily on.

Rico snarled a laugh and took a step toward her. Sarah stood her ground, holding the gun in front of her with both hands, her finger on the trigger.

"I mean it," she warned.

"And I don't believe you." He took another step and reached out for the gun.

At the last second, she pointed the barrel down slightly before she pulled the trigger. Rico howled in pain and disbelief as he saw the blood spurting from his right leg. He swung out at her as he went down on his left knee but she stepped back a few feet still holding the gun on him. He was a perverted son of a bitch and she didn't feel at all guilty for having shot him.

"Now stay where you are or I'll shoot you in the other leg as well," she commanded. The sound of footsteps at the other end of the hall told her the police had arrived at last.

"Down here!" she shouted. "Hurry!"

She looked down at the open wound on Rico's leg oozing blood through his ripped pants onto the floor. Without warning her stomach heaved. As the police came into the room, they found her holding the gun high above her head while she threw up all over Rico.

It was late morning by the time she finally sat down with a cup of coffee and played the messages on Nicholas's answering machine. Sleep had been out of the question when she returned from the police station at dawn. She wanted desperately to share the previous night's events with someone who cared and she was out of her mind with worry about Tyler.

Her heart leaped at the sound of his voice on the answering machine. "I know it seems impossible that I should get through to you but the telephone system here is fiber optics buried underground and an emergency operating system was easy to set up. There probably won't be electricity for months however. There are a line of people behind me so I better get to the point. First of all, Nicholas, I hope you're sitting down because your plantation is gone. Flattened. Second of all, Sarah, don't say anything to Woody about Suzanne until I come back and talk to you. I'm afraid to say any more on tape. I'll be back as soon as I can. Don't worry about me, this is journalist's heaven. I'm collecting some great material for stories – I only wish my camera hadn't been stolen. Love you."

By the time she had listened to his message a second time, she had calmed down enough to be angry with him. He probably wasn't even trying to get off the island! "Journalist's heaven!" she grumbled. A moment before she'd been near tears thinking he was dead. Wasn't it just like Tyler to pull a stunt like this? Despite his promises, he'd never change.

She could barely sit still to run through the rest of the tape. The last message was from Nicholas. The time was less than an hour before. "Sarah? I hope you're there. I'm booked on a plane out of New York this afternoon and should get into Burlington around 5:30. Hope you can meet me with the car. Thanks. Later."

Well, there went her plans for going home tonight. If she went to sleep now, she might catch a few hours of sleep before she had to drive back to the airport again.

Before she lay down, she decided to give Woody a call, just to let him know she was back. His cousin Frances answered the phone. "He's just fallen asleep," she informed Sarah in hushed tones. "We just got back from a treatment at the hospital and he doesn't feel very well. Probably it'd be best to wait a day or two before you come by."

Ever since she had left West Jordan a month ago, Sarah had had a recurring sense that she was walking on a suspension bridge over a dangerously steep canyon. As she made her unsteady way across the rickety, swaying bridge, the far bank never seemed to grow any closer. She seemed to be stuck in the middle with the eerie sensation that no matter how fast she walked she would never reach the safety of the other side. Much as she wanted it to remain unchanged, her life would never be the same as it was again.

She stood in Woody's living room feeling like a nervous schoolgirl on a blind date. She did not know what to expect – how Woody would look, how he would react and whether he was ready to accept the news she had to tell him. After a long discussion with Nicholas (which included the description of the demise of Diego), she had decided it was unfair to withhold the story from him until Tyler decided he was ready to come home from Nevis.

True, there were some discrepancies now. They decided that Tyler had probably figured out who the true perpetrator of the crime against Suzanne was and that was what he wanted to tell them. But at this point, they felt it wouldn't matter to Woody how she had died. Sarah just knew she would not be able to lie to him when the subject came up.

"Anybody home?" She knocked on the open bedroom door before poking her head inside.

"Hey! Sarah! Come in!" Woody was lying on top of the bed covers, propped up on a pile of pillows and watching TV. She was relieved to see he was not a pale invalid in pajamas and bathrobe, as she had imagined him. He was certainly thinner than he'd ever been. His baggy jeans and flannel shirt hung loosely on his frame. A few wisps of gray hair had sneaked out of the large red bandana that was tied around his head.

"I know I look bizarre," he immediately apologized and tapped his bandana before she even had a chance to speak, "but my hair is starting to fall out from the chemo and I look even worse without this."

"Woody, you look great. You can't imagine what I was expecting." She kissed him on the cheek and then sat gingerly on the foot of the bed, leaning back against one of the bedposts of the old four poster. "So you must be doing pretty well."

After searching for a few seconds for the remote control, he clicked off the TV. "Sarah, I don't know how to thank you and Tyler." Woody's eyes filled with tears suddenly and he turned his face away from her, pretending to look out the window.

"What?" Sarah was alarmed and confused by his expression. She leaned forward. "What are you talking about?"

"She was here yesterday. Stayed all afternoon."

"Who was here?" Sarah began to worry that Woody was not doing as well as she thought.

He laughed in disbelief as though she were joking with him. "Suzanne, of course."

"Suzanne? Your Suzanne?" The medication must be affecting his imagination, she thought. He must not be able to separate his dreams from his reality. Not knowing how to react, she went along with him. "Really? Is that right?"

Her words lacked just enough conviction that he turned to stare at her. His blank, puzzled look suddenly cleared and he laughed again. "You don't know, do you? I forgot, you weren't there. It was only Tyler who was with her."

"Woody, what are you talking about?"

"During the hurricane. Suzanne and Tyler spent the hurricane together in the wine cellar of your friend's plantation. He convinced her it was okay to come here and visit me."

"But– but– we saw her boat blow up! There was no way she could have survived!" The words were out before Sarah could contain them. She clapped a horrified hand to her mouth.

But Woody only gave a beatific smile. "That's what she intended you to think. She wasn't on the boat. She blew it up herself."

Sarah was still afraid this was some kind of trick on Tyler's part to make Woody happy. "Are you sure it was her?"

"What – do you think just because she cut her hair and dyed it black I wouldn't know her? Sure, we're both middle–aged now – she's put on some weight, I've taken some off. She's had a hard life; she spared me most of the grisly details. But it was a dream come true, having her finally sitting right here in my own bed with me in Vermont, talking like two old people who've spent their whole life together." The smile faded suddenly. "But we haven't and she's gone again."

Sarah wasn't so sure Woody hadn't been dreaming. "How did she manage to get here so fast? From what I heard it was still nearly impossible to get off of Nevis a few days ago."

"She got a ride in an empty relief supplies helicopter headed back to Miami. Don't ask me how she pulled it off. She's pretty amazing."

"But she didn't stay?"

"No, she's still on the run. Says a couple of those Mexicans from all those years ago are still after her for something that happened back in the sixties. She was afraid it would be too easy for them to find her here and she didn't want me to get involved. Says they might even remember me."

Sarah nodded. "Diego and Rico...shit. I can't believe this. Did she tell you where she was going?"

"Diego...is that one of the Mexicans?...I remember a Diego. He was the brother of the guy Suzanne lived with. A jealous son of a bitch. Always had the hots for her..."

"Woody! Did she give you an address where you can reach her?"

"Well..." His hesitation indicated he'd obviously been sworn to secrecy. "What difference does it make? She's afraid to come back yet."

"Shit. I'll tell you what difference it makes. Diego is dead and Rico is in jail. AND he thinks Suzanne is dead. They can't hurt her anymore. She can do whatever she wants! And so can you!" Any joy Sarah felt at the moment was angrily overshadowed by the unfairness of it all.

Woody looked bewildered and exhausted. He sank back on the pillows and closed his eyes. His hands searched in the rumpled bed covers again. "She said she was headed for Montreal. It's not that far away. She promised to call me in a few weeks when she was more settled." His voice was little more than a whisper now. "I told her everything would be okay. Oh, Sarah, if I hadn't been sick I wouldn't have let her get away from me again..."

She saw that he had found what he was searching for in the sheets. The old faded, embroidered shawl was wrapped tightly around his hand, his fingers stroking the tattered fringe.

Sarah placed her own hand on top of his. "Don't worry, Woody. We found her once, didn't we? Well, we can find her again. I'll make that hurricane–chasing boyfriend of mine come back from Nevis and we'll go up to Montreal. As aggravating as he is, he's pretty good at what he does."

Woody did not open his eyes but she saw a trace of a smile playing on his lips again. "And what exactly does that mean, Sarah?"

"Everything you're thinking and more." She did not have to force the laughter that bubbled up inside of her. "So when are we opening the inn again, Woody?"

"When are you opening the inn is the question. I think you're going to have to run the operation from now on, Sarah. The doctor's suggesting I take things easy for a while. You'll have to hire a cook and a bartender or two. But I'm sure you can manage it."

Sarah had only been joking and was not ready for Woody's answer. Earlier that day, Nicholas had tried to convince her to stay on at Newfield's and work for him. She had turned down his offer without any idea of what the future might hold instead. "You're kidding me, aren't you?"

"Not in the least. I'm having my lawyer draw up some business partnership papers. Now, really, Sarah, think about it. Who else would I want to run the inn? Now, get out of here. I'm nauseous and I want to sleep." He sat up to give her a kiss on the cheek. "Hey what happened to your face? How'd you get these black and blue marks?"

"Oh, I fell down on Nicholas's flagstone terrace one night in the dark." It was almost the truth. "Hey, Tyler hasn't called here, has he?"

"Not that I know of. Why?"

"Nothing. I was just wondering." She started for the door.

"Listen, Sarah. Thanks for everything, but I don't want you and Tyler to go after Suzanne this time. She'll call me when she's ready – she knows where I am now. Besides, I need some time to get my health back."

Sarah opened her mouth to reply and then quickly shut it. Woody was right. It was time to just let things be. She was anxious to get home to her own little cottage and have her life return to normal.

Cousin Frances's bulk filled the doorway suddenly. "Sarah, you have a call from overseas. Someone named Tyler."

"Now how could he have known you were here?"

228

Sarah laughed. "Woody, get real. We're talking about Tyler. I'll take it in the other room, Frances." And she went out the bedroom door to answer the phone.

ABOUT THE AUTHOR

A lifelong lover of travel, mysteries and creative expression, Marilinne Cooper has always enjoyed the escapist pleasure of combining her passions in a good story. She lives in the White Mountains of New Hampshire and is also a freelance copywriting professional. To learn more, visit marilinnecooper.com.

ALSO BY MARILINNE COOPER

available at amazon.com

Night Heron
Butterfly Tattoo
Blue Moon
Double Phoenix
Dead Reckoning

Jamaican Draw

34606079R00130

Made in the USA
Middletown, DE
28 August 2016